Flirting
Under
a Full
Moon

ASHLYN CHASE

sourcebooks
casablanca

Published by Sourcebooks Casablanca, an imprint of Sourcebooks, Inc.
P.O. Box 4410, Naperville, Illinois 60567-4410
(630) 961-3900
Fax: (630) 961-2168
www.sourcebooks.com

Printed and bound in Canada
WC 10 9 8 7 6 5 4 3 2 1

To my friends and fans on AshlynsNewBestFriends Yahoo! group and to my street team. You really are the best buds an insecure author could have. According to you, I'm always right. And even when I'm wrong, I'm still funny and adorable. You keep me off ledges; I love you all more than you know.

Chapter 1

OVER THE DIN OF CLINKING ICE AND LIVELY CON-versation, the entire bar heard waitress Brandee Hanson wail, "Dumped in a text message? *Really?*"

Suddenly the place quieted. Heat crept up her neck, and she dropped her BlackBerry into her apron pocket. She was about to slink off to the ladies' room when Sadie Maven, the owner's eccentric aunt, waved her over to the booth she regularly occupied.

"Have a seat, dear. Let me do a quick reading for you—on the house." Sadie was already shuffling her tarot cards.

Brandee slumped onto the opposite bench and set down her tray.

"I had a premonition about you just now." Sadie winked. "It might make you feel better."

Brandee sighed. "I'm all for feeling better. Just don't talk about my love life. I've sworn off men."

"Since when?"

"Since just now."

Sadie spread the cards across the table. "Pick one."

Brandee pulled one card from the middle and turned it over. On it was a picture of a couple entwined in a passionate embrace, and the text beneath proclaimed: *The Lovers*.

"Ah. I was right. You'll meet your true love soon. In fact, he could be the next man to walk through that door."

Psychic Sadie nodded toward Boston Uncommon's Charles Street entrance.

Brandee gazed at the door expectantly. It swung open and a tall, blond, broad-shouldered hunk of a man breezed in.

Oh no. It couldn't be. "One-Night Nick? Are you kidding me?" She burst out laughing.

Sadie shrugged one shoulder. "You never know…"

Brandee picked up her tray and returned to work, still chuckling and shaking her head.

"What put that smile on your face, beautiful? Besides seeing me, of course." Nick Wolfensen grabbed a stool and sat on it backward. Even with the stool's height, his big feet hit the floor. His powerful thighs bulged under his blue jeans. That wasn't the only bulge she thought she saw.

Brandee knew her regulars and Nick was a good tipper. She'd play nice, even though Sadie's omen sat uncomfortably in the back of her mind. "Just something Sadie said. I think I've served her one too many White Russians."

"Well, you haven't served me at all, girl. I'm parched."

"What can I get you?"

"Whatever Sam Adams you have on tap."

"Coming right up."

Usually Angie would get Nick's beer, but the bartender looked engrossed in a conversation. Brandee lifted the part of the bar that flipped up and strode in. "It must be your evening off. You're not in uniform, and you're ordering a brew."

Nick frowned. "Yeah, kind of."

His set jaw and the twitch in his cheek told her she shouldn't pursue the subject. She simply grabbed a frosted mug and held it at an angle under the tap like

Angie had shown her. It created less froth and made room for more beer.

When she set it in front of him, his cocky smile returned. "Ah, you're a good girl. I'd sing 'Brandy' but you've probably heard it a few thousand times."

"Yeah, thanks for not doing that." Brandee played the song in her head, and when the words pointed out what a good wife she would be, she scurried away, mumbling, "Well, I gotta get back to work."

She grabbed a clean rag and wiped down a table that didn't need it. Over her shoulder she caught Nick unabashedly admiring her rear end. She quickly moved on to another empty table and made sure she was facing him. As soon as she bent over to reach the surface, her V-neck dipped. Now he was gazing at her cleavage like he might drool. She bolted upright.

Oh, my Fruity Pebbles. Why can't he turn around?

Nick rose, left his beer on the bar, and strolled over to her. He leaned down so he could whisper in her ear. "When, Brandee?"

She tried to look casual. "When what?"

"When are you going to let me show you the time of your life?"

She smiled, thinking what that might entail, but quickly schooled her expression. "I'm not that kind of girl."

He tried to look innocent, but she knew it was an act. Players like Nick scared her. Not that it stopped her from fantasizing about him. Handsome, charming, intelligent, and dangerous. Whether she had just been dumped or not, he wasn't the kind of guy she needed right now—or maybe ever.

Nick backed up a step. "What are you talking about?"

Brandee rested a hand on her hip and tried to look uncompromising. "I know your reputation. They don't call you 'One-Night Nick' for nothing."

"At least I'm honest about it. I never lead girls on by saying, 'I'll call you,' then leave them to wonder why I didn't. A lot of guys do. I treat a woman to an awesome night she'll never forget. I'm just not interested in getting tied down right now."

She lowered her voice. "Look, I'm not saying I want to get married either. But casual sex isn't my style."

He feigned shock, then boomed in his baritone, "Who said anything about sex? Of course if that's what *you* want, I'd be happy to oblige."

"Oh, my Playboy penthouse... Lower your voice, dammit." She glanced around, but people seemed to have lost interest in her. They continued their own conversations or preoccupation with the football game. *Thank you, Tom Brady*.

"What's your penthouse got to do with anything?"

She chuckled. "I don't live in a penthouse. I live over the bar. That's just something I do when I'm shocked. Instead of saying, "Oh my God—I substitute some other word or words for God."

"Are you religious? Don't want to take the Lord's name in vain or something?"

"Heck no. It's just way overused. I don't want to wear it out." She faced Sadie, who she knew took an interest in all the waitresses' love lives. Sadie shuffled her tarot cards with a knowing smile on her face.

He chuckled. "I'm not going to lie to you, Brandee. I think you're sexy as hell, and redheads are my weakness, but if you can't allow yourself a night of fun without some damn commitment..."

She sighed. "It's not like that."

"Then what is it?"

She couldn't put her feelings into words. Sure she'd like to have a good time, but was one night worth the trouble and expense of getting a full body wax and a mani-pedi and buying a new outfit? She needed her tips to pay for her photography supplies. A night with the handsome cop would probably steal her breath away, but she didn't want to risk losing her heart too.

He waved and walked away. "Forget it."

By the time he had retaken his stool and started watching the game, Brandee regretted her hesitancy. Damn it all, Nick was hot. His blond hair was growing out just enough to curl around his ears, and his sapphire blue eyes were impossible to ignore. A suspect wouldn't stand a chance against that intense stare. Hell. *She* didn't stand a chance when he looked at her with those gorgeous eyes.

Still, "No casual sex, no matter how tempting the guy might be" was a good policy. She *did* want to fall in love and get married some day. Even a protected one-night stand could result in a life-altering "accident." And if that happened, it would *not* be with a playboy like Nick Wolfensen.

A man who only dated to have a night of fun with a different woman each time must be extremely superficial. How satisfying could that be? What would make someone do that? Had he been hurt so badly he didn't want to risk it again? She couldn't think of any other reason.

Sadie caught her attention and held up her empty glass, calling for another.

Oh my pickled herring…that woman can put them away. But her nephew owned the bar and he'd told the staff to keep her happy. Not only did Anthony seem genuinely fond of his aunt, but she was good for business. To sit at her booth and have a tarot card reading, the patron had to meet the one-drink minimum.

When Brandee delivered Sadie's fourth White Russian, the fortune-teller said, "You know, my Dmitri was like that once."

"Like what?"

She smirked. "You should know better than to feign innocence with a psychic."

Brandee rolled her eyes. "Fine. So, you had a commitment-phobic boyfriend."

Sadie shuffled the cards again. "It wasn't that as much as he wanted to be free when the right woman came along. He really didn't like the idea of hurting anyone." She flipped over a card. "I think your Nick is doing the same thing."

"First of all, he's not *my* Nick."

Sadie pushed the card across the table toward her. "If you say so."

Brandee glanced at the card, then stared more closely. It was the same one. A man and a woman entwined in a passionate embrace. The Lovers.

Oh, my heartbreak...I'm toast.

"What's got your jockstrap in a twist?" Konrad asked.

Nick sat across from his twin brother, with a big mahogany desk between them. "It's nothing." He reached out and ran his hand over the polished surface, glancing at the gleaming brass plate that read Dean Konrad Wolfensen. "Jeez, I can't visit you without feeling like I've been sent to the principal's office."

Konrad laughed. "Maybe you were there too many times when we were kids. What's going on?"

"I quit."

Konrad's jaw dropped. "The force?"

"Yeah, what else do I have to quit?"

"Why?"

Nick fidgeted in his seat. He couldn't very well say his brother's high-profile court case had damaged his credibility, could he? Just because they looked exactly alike and Konrad had incurred public wrath and humiliation, Nick couldn't be absolutely sure that was the only reason his honor had been questioned—more than once—even though he had done nothing to deserve it. He hated the idea that it might be his brother's fault.

"I was butting heads with some of the guys."

"What about?"

Nick shrugged. "Nothing in particular. John Q. Public has been pissing me off too."

"Are you sleeping?"

"Not well."

"You look like you've lost weight."

Nick glanced down at his baggy Dockers. "Yeah, maybe a little."

"Sorry, Bro. I hate to say it, but it sounds like symptoms of depression."

Nick laughed. "Me? What do I have to be depressed about?"

Konrad gave him a sympathetic smile. "You just stood up for me as my best man. Maybe without realizing it…"

"You think I'm jealous? Of you?" Nick was about to

let out another bellowing laugh, but he thought better
of it. He didn't want to insult his brother—or his new
sister-in-law. Roz was a great girl and Konrad had found
his true mate. Marriage was right for him. Nick didn't
want to settle for less than that, and he didn't have to.
He just had to be patient—correction—*more* patient, but
it better not take much longer. At one hundred and one
years old, Nick's secret wish was to find the *right* one
without being attached to the wrong one.

"So tell me about quitting the force after nine years.
It can't be over a few personality clashes."

Nick shifted uncomfortably. "What are you, my
shrink now?"

"No, of course not, but you called and said you
wanted to see me."

"I was bored."

Konrad leaned back in his big, oak armchair. "You
were bored? You interrupted my workday because you
were bored?"

"Hey, sorry I bothered you." Nick rose, ready to
walk out.

"Stop. I didn't mean to run you off. You're here now,
and I'm sure you weren't in the neighborhood. Newton
isn't exactly around the corner."

"Nah, you're right. I should let you get back to work."

"Not if you need me. Look, I know you're not telling
me everything. What's going on?"

Nick let out a long sigh. Konrad was right. There
was more to it than just quitting his job. His lifestyle
didn't hold the same glamour it once had, but he didn't
dare voice that thought. Everyone was quick to tell him
he needed to find a nice girl and settle down. Better to

blame his boredom on job dissatisfaction. "I need to work for myself. I'm tired of taking orders, but I don't want to give them either."

"Then you're kind of fucked."

"Not necessarily. I thought of a way to work for myself without taking on a bunch of pesky employees. I'm getting my PI license."

"Private investigator?"

"No, public idiot. Of course private investigator. I'd be perfect for it. With my experience as a cop, I know the law—and how to get around it. As a paranormal PI, I can corner a niche market. There aren't any others in Boston."

"I don't know," Konrad said. "Public idiot sounds a lot more fun."

Nick snorted. "Well, I've made up my mind. I'm going to be a paranormal PI. There's only one thing left to do. I need three upstanding citizens to vouch for me."

"So that's why you're here?"

"That and to see my brother and his lovely wife."

"Stay for dinner. I'll give Roz a call." Konrad picked up the phone.

"If it's no trouble. Since she's an attorney, I was hoping to ask her to be one of my three upstanding citizens."

"I'm sure she'd be honored."

"I'll get out of your hair and see who might be hanging around the teachers' lounge. Is it okay if I stop back later to see what she says about dinner?"

"Why don't you wait a minute? Then you won't have to interrupt me twice."

After a brief conversation, Konrad ended the call with a whispered endearment. He grinned and hung up.

A pang of envy took Nick by surprise. *Damn it,*

maybe he and everyone else is right. All I need is the right girl...wherever she is. So why is it taking so long?

"Roz said she'll thaw another steak. Not to worry. You're always welcome."

"Thanks. Well, I'll let you get back to work. What time should I show up at your apartment?"

"Six would be good."

"I'll be there. Meanwhile, I'll see if I can find two more upstanding citizens who will vouch for me."

Konrad rose. "What about me?"

Good God. How can I turn down my brother's generous offer without offending the hell out of him? My identical twin brother, who got busted for the biggest art heist in history, won't go a long way toward credibility. Even though he was proven innocent, people will believe what they want to believe.

"I think you're too close. I mean, really...it's like getting your mom to say what a good boy you are."

"Yeah. I can see that. Well, good luck finding any of the fifty pack members who love you to attest to your character."

Nick smiled. *Yeah, there are advantages to being in good stead with one's werewolf pack—at last. I'm glad I wasn't the only one who believed in my brother's innocence.*

Chapter 2

"ONE-NIGHT NICK? WAS SADIE SOBER?" BRANDEE'S bartender-roommate stretched the kinks out of her shoulders after a long shift.

"I think so. I can usually tell when Sadie's had enough." Brandee dropped onto the soft sectional in their living room, removed her shoes, and massaged her aching feet.

"Do you think she was dealing from the bottom of the deck?"

"Nope. She was shuffling the cards as she always does."

It was nice of Angie to attempt to discredit the psychic to make Brandee feel better, but Sadie was never wrong. *Never*.

"Did she come right out and say it was a prediction?"

"Kinda, sorta, not really."

"What exactly did she say?"

"Something about having a premonition that I'd be meeting Mr. Right soon. Then she said the next man through the door could be the love of my life...and Nick walked in."

"She said 'could.' That means she *could be* wrong."

"Have you ever known Sadie to be wrong? I think she just says 'could' because she doesn't want to imply a person has no free will. Maybe she's afraid of being wrong if a person is determined to prove her wrong."

Angie gave her a sympathetic look. "Maybe. Or

maybe there really aren't any guarantees. I know she's constantly been right before, but there's always a first time to mess up, right?"

"Let's hope so. I need my heart broken like a nunnery needs a condom dispenser." Brandee rested her elbows on her knees and dropped her head in her hands. "I thought maybe the jerk-face who dumped me was my ticket out of Boringsville."

Angie scrutinized her. "What do you mean?"

"You know. Living above the place I work. Struggling to make ends meet and hopefully save a little money for a rainy day. Hell, I thought I might even be able to afford my dream of owning a gallery if he and I…" She let out a long sigh. "Forget it."

"You're kidding. You really expect some guy to swoop in and rescue you from a life you don't like?"

"No! Oh, my female gigolo…no." Brandee shook her head emphatically. "It's just damn hard to make it as an artist and support myself at the same time."

"Did you think he was Mr. Right?"

She shrugged. "Mr. Possible, maybe." *Time to change the subject*. "By the way, as soon as you're ready for bed, can I commandeer the bathroom for the rest of the night?"

"Oh, crap. Did you forget you're lactose intolerant again?"

Brandee snorted. "No. Do you hear me burping up a lung? And for your information, I don't *forget* my condition. I just forget to take my medication with me sometimes and then can't resist a special treat.

"I want to set up a temporary darkroom in the bathroom. I *have* to begin selling my work, not just to get a few dollars ahead, but also to build a name for myself."

"I get that. So what do you have to do to sell your photographs?"

"Create a look or product no one else has. Make my name synonymous with that product. Capitalize on opportunities for publicity, and make everyone who can afford my work want to collect it."

"That's all, huh?" Angie gave her a sympathetic look. "I'll get you a glass of wine."

"I'll get it. You do that all day."

Angie was already walking toward the kitchen. "It's how I show I care."

Brandee chuckled. "It's how you support yourself. Besides, I know you care. Otherwise I wouldn't have told you what I'm going through."

"Yes you would," Angie called from the next room. The refrigerator door opened and clunked shut. A few moments later she strolled back into the living room, holding two glasses of white wine. "You tell me everything."

"Do you ever get tired of it?"

"Tired of what? Your train wreck of a life?"

"Not just mine. Lots of people tell you more than you want to hear. It looked as if someone was talking your ear off when I was getting Nick his beer."

"Nah. That was just a tourist wanting recommendations for cheap hotels. Like fifty bucks a night."

Angie handed her a glass of Chardonnay, and Brandee took a welcome sip. "Fifty dollars? In this city?"

"Yeah, that's a hoot, huh? I tried to recommend the hostel I'd heard about, but they weren't interested."

Brandee leaned back against the loose pillows. "So, getting back to me…if you were in my knockoff shoes, would you accept a date with Nick Wolfensen?"

"Not unless he changed his policy."

"That's what I was thinking. But how do you tell a guy to completely change his lifestyle?"

"Just come right out and say it. Someone needs to." Angie sipped her wine.

"I guess so. I've got nothing to lose if there's nothing to gain."

Angie scratched her head. "I think that made sense."

Brandee thumped her feet onto the coffee table and crossed them at the ankles. "Okay, I'll confront him."

"Good. Do it where I can watch."

"Pervert."

—◌◌◌—

"Nick, I know this is your first case, but we're desperate. The mayor's stepdaughter has been kidnapped."

"Desperate?" *That's hardly a vote of confidence.* "If you're so desperate, why use a brand-new PI? There are plenty of options for a kidnapping case." *Nick wanted the job, but his cop instincts told him something didn't sound right.* Captain Hunter had arranged this meeting fifteen minutes ago. They met at Boston Uncommon but left the bar immediately so they could talk in private.

"There are paranormal circumstances, and we don't have time for lengthy explanations."

"I see. What are these 'circumstances'?"

"She's a fire mage."

Nick's eyebrows shot up. "Shit." He stopped at a bench and glanced around. No one was within earshot, so he and Hunter sat down. "Do you think the kidnappers know this?"

"Don't know. No ransom demands have been made. There's been no contact at all."

"Any witnesses?"

"A neighbor thought she heard something like a muffled yelp of surprise, but when she looked out her window she didn't see anything."

"Where were her parents?"

"The mayor was at City Hall and her mother was in the house. She didn't think she needed to supervise a twelve-year-old in her own backyard. Now she's sick with guilt."

Nick felt for the poor woman. The best way to help her was to find her daughter. "So they may have kidnapped her for her power." Nick rubbed his chin. "The criminal who's not looking for money is usually looking for some kind of power."

"It gets worse. The girl doesn't know what she can do yet. A female fire mage won't realize her power until the first solar eclipse after she hits puberty. Her mother kept putting off telling her."

"Shit. She's untrained and unprepared. Her parents must be frantic."

"To put it mildly." The captain rested his hand on Nick's shoulder. "This case could make or break your career. I wouldn't blame you if you decline, but I hope you won't. I think you're our only hope."

How could he refuse? Not only would he feel responsible if anything happened to the girl, but she could burn the city to the ground if the kidnappers couldn't teach her how to control the power she didn't even know she had—the power to set fires with no more than a thought.

"I'll do my best."

The captain let out a long breath, as if he'd been

holding it for a while. "You'd better do better than your best. The next solar eclipse is in nine days."

———————

"Sadie, I need your psychic services." Nick slid into the booth opposite the woman who was becoming famous for her gift. Anthony's aunt was certainly good for business. The bar had never been this busy in the afternoon.

"You know the drill," she answered matter-of-factly.

"Yeah, yeah. The one-drink minimum."

He held up his finger to catch Wendy's eye. He'd have preferred Brandee to wait on him, but he didn't see her.

Wendy strode right over. "What can I get you?"

"What are you drinking, Sadie?" Nick asked.

"Aren't you having anything?" Sadie seemed surprised. Maybe she wasn't all that psychic after all.

"No. I need to be sharp."

"White Russians are my favorite."

"One White Russian for the lady and a glass of water for me, please."

"Sure 'nuff," Wendy said. She practically skipped away and threaded through the Friday afternoon crowd.

"So, what did you need my services for?" Sadie asked.

"A case."

"I wonder if congratulations are in order first. Either you've been promoted to detective or you have a brand-new job altogether."

"The latter. I'm a PI now."

"Wonderful. Police work is dangerous, and you'll have a family counting on you…someday."

He chuckled. "You're not going to hijack this

conversation, are you? Because I didn't come here to ask about my love life. I know that's your specialty, but…"

"Not at all. Just stating a fact. Besides, you're better than a beat cop."

"Thanks, I think. What's wrong with being a friendly, neighborhood police officer?"

"It's the uniform. It's like wearing a target on your chest. As I said, you need to watch out for your safety."

The word "target" hit him like a shock wave. *Is that some kind of prediction?* A moment later, he decided, *nah*, it couldn't be. After all, she was talking about the uniform. He'd left the force and wasn't going back.

"Okay. Message delivered. Back to business, then." Wendy interrupted just long enough to deliver Sadie's drink, then flitted away. She'd forgotten Nick's water, but he really didn't care.

As soon as she was out of earshot, Nick continued. "It's my first case. What I tell you has to remain confidential. Can you do that?"

"I keep all of my readings confidential."

"I don't need a reading, just your vibes or premonitions or something. You're supposed to be psychic with or without the cards. Right?"

Sadie's lip curled up on one side, and she began shuffling the cards anyway. "Go on."

"The mayor's little girl has been kidnapped. There's no ransom demand—so it seems as if they have another purpose."

"I hate to say it, but there are a lot of things they could want with a public figure's daughter. Blackmail, maybe?"

"I doubt it. The mayor's afraid to involve the police. He's worried he'll never see Katie again if this goes public. He's still hoping some sort of demand will follow, but none has."

Mayor Bennett had let his good friend the police chief know about the situation, as well as the delicacy with which it had to be handled. It turned out to be the right call. Chief Stone spoke to Captain Hunter, and Hunter spoke to Nick. But they'd let him know that if he screwed up, they'd never use his services again. Neither would anyone else.

Nick tapped his foot in frustration. *How much does Sadie know about the paranormal side of Boston?*

"I know there are many paranormal factions in this city," she said, as if she'd heard his thought clearly. "If neither ransom nor blackmail are involved, I get the feeling this girl might be gifted in some way and her captors want to exploit her gift for their own purposes."

Nick straightened. "Bingo. That's what I was thinking. What else can you tell me?"

"What else can *you* tell *me*?" she parroted.

Nick shifted uncomfortably. Still, this was important enough to take a chance on Sadie's discretion. "The little girl is a fire mage. She has no idea what's about to happen to her. Her mother never told her about their inherited curse, much less taught her how to control it. Now that she's entered puberty, her power will be triggered on the next solar eclipse — eight days from now."

Sadie nodded. She spread the cards across the table. "Pick seven."

Nick huffed. "I don't think those cards can pinpoint her location."

"Is that what you wanted?"

"I had hoped you could sense her, but if not…" He started to get up.

Sadie reached over and covered his hand. "Don't leave. If you have something that belongs to her, I might be able to help you."

"Okay, good." Nick got comfortable again and pulled a small plastic bag out of his pocket. "This is her hair. Can you get anything from that?"

Sadie took the bag and opened it.

She didn't ask how or why he had the girl's hair. Maybe she already knew. As a wolf, Nick could sniff out any victim. A reminder of her scent would help if he didn't locate her quickly. There was another reason to have a hair sample…one he didn't want to think about. So when he'd seen the girl's hairbrush in her bedroom, he'd snagged a few.

———〜———

Brandee trotted down the stairs from her apartment over the bar to start her shift. As she breezed in, she noticed Nick leaning over the table toward Sadie. They were talking in hushed tones.

That's weird. Nick never consults Sadie. He doesn't seem like the type.

But there he was. Sadie had spread the cards out and he was turning over a few of them. Brandee wondered what would change a skeptic's mind and make him want to… *Oh dear.* She knew Sadie took an interest in the employees' love lives, but so far she hadn't bothered the regular patrons.

On the other hand, Brandee hadn't seen him in his uniform for quite some time. Today he was wearing a black polo shirt and jeans. *I hope he hasn't been laid off.* People who didn't believe in psychics sometimes got desperate enough to try anything if they were in trouble.

Brandee might not want to date him—correction, she *totally* wanted to date him, but she didn't want to be discarded after only one night. She'd been dumped in every possible way, including via text message. There was no reason to encourage a guy whose mantra was "Love 'em and leave 'em."

Even so, she considered him a friend, like many of the regulars. How could she find out what had happened without putting Sadie in the middle?

No one sat near Sadie's booth that she could wait on, but—*ah-ha*—the next booth over needed to be cleaned up. Brandee grabbed an empty tray and a damp cloth, then casually made her way to the empty booth.

Nick's back was to Brandee as he said, "Is that all you can tell me, Sadie? She's in the theater district? Nothing more?"

Sadie glanced at Brandee, who quickly went to work wiping the table.

"I'm surprised I could tell you that much. The cards aren't really designed to pinpoint locations. Is there any other information you can give me that might spark some of my purely psychic senses?"

"She's twelve."

Twelve? Dear Lord, I hope Sadie isn't talking about his future wife.

Nick continued talking. "And as you could see already, her distinguishing characteristic is white hair."

"White? I thought it was platinum blond."

"No. She was born with no pigment in her hair at all.

The pieces you saw were broken off. It's long. Halfway down her back."

Brandee couldn't believe what she was hearing. He was describing her little cousin Katie. The daughter of Boston's new mayor and Brandee's new step-uncle. But why?

"How long has it been since her kidnapping?" Sadie asked.

Brandee snapped upright. "She's been *kidnapped*?"

Nick craned his neck to look behind him. "How much did you hear?"

Brandee rounded on him. "Enough to know you're describing my cousin Katie. What's happened to her?"

"I'm not at liberty—"

She tossed the rag on the other table and crossed her arms. "I'm not going anywhere until you answer my question."

Nick patted the seat. "You'd better sit down."

Brandee slid in beside him. He smelled good. A faint hint of spice tantalized her.

"I'm working as a private investigator now, Brandee. I've been hired to find a missing girl. What's your cousin's last name?"

"St. George."

"Whew. Wrong kid. Your cousin's in the clear."

"Wait. She was adopted by her stepdad. I forgot about that. Her name was probably changed to his—Bennett?"

Nick blew out a slow breath. "I'm sorry. Kate Bennett *is* the little girl I'm looking for."

Brandee's jaw dropped and she couldn't speak for a moment. Nick placed his big hand on her shoulder and massaged it. "Are you okay?"

"Yeah, I'm...I'm just a little shocked. How can I help?"

"What can you tell me about her?"

"Probably nothing more than her parents could. We're not that close. I mean, the family gets together at my grand-parents' home every Christmas Eve, but she's so much younger than I am. I mostly say 'Hi, Katie. How's school?' She says, 'Fine,' and then I go off to talk to the adults."

Guilt washed over her. *What a horrible person I am. If Nick brings her home safely, I'll play with her, braid her hair, take her places. All the things I should have been doing before this.*

Nick didn't look as if he judged her for it. He just waited, maybe hoping she'd recall something that could help.

"She's in seventh grade at Cambridge Academy, and she plays soccer."

"Yes, I've talked to most of the teachers, her coach, the parents who drive her to and from practices, and her teammates."

"Then you probably know more about her than I do." Brandee dropped her gaze to her lap. "I wish there was more I could tell you."

He placed a gentle hand on her thigh. A warm tingle rushed through her.

"Me too. But don't worry. I'll do everything in my power to find her."

His determined gaze spoke as strongly as his voice did. Brandee was sure he wouldn't leave a stone unturned.

"Please let me help. There must be something I can do."

He offered her a sympathetic smile. "If you think of anything else..." He pulled a card out of his pocket and handed it to her.

The card read, *Wolfensen Investigations, Licensed*

Private Investigators, and then the address of an office and a telephone number. Nowhere did it mention he was a cop.

"Is this what you're doing now—full time?"

"Yup."

She was hoping he'd explain his career change, but he didn't offer any more information than that.

"You know, I'm a photographer by training, and I just waitress to pay the bills. I could help you take pictures…"

"Of what?"

"I don't know. Evidence?"

He chuckled. "I think I'd be better off taking my own pictures right away rather than calling you to come and do it if I find something."

Duh. "Then let me come with you. I can't just sit back and do nothing."

"Yes, you can. An investigation like this could be dangerous."

"So it's okay for you to risk your safety when you don't even know her, but not for me? She's *my* cousin."

"Yes, and you're *my* waitress. Who'll get me a beer if something happens to you?" He flashed his charming smile.

She knew he was trying to lighten the mood, but it didn't work. She felt impotent and angry. Impotent because there was nothing she could do and angry because of her impotence. But then the major emotion surfaced: fear. Katie was a sweet kid who wouldn't put up a struggle. Brandee had to hope that temperament would keep her cousin alive long enough for Nick to find her. She didn't want to think about any other possibility.

"Find her, Nick. I don't care what you have to do. Just find her."

"I intend to, sweetheart."

Chapter 3

THE THEATER DISTRICT WASN'T MUCH TO GO ON, but it would help. Nick had tried using his human senses and was no closer to finding Katie than he had been an hour ago. Meanwhile, night had fallen, so under the cover of darkness he could shift and use his wolf senses. He'd try to stay out of sight, but even if someone spotted him, most Bostonians didn't know a wolf from a German shepherd.

Finding a private spot in an alley behind a Dumpster, he stripped naked. It didn't matter if an onlooker thought he was a wolf or a dog. Either one wearing clothes would kind of stick out. He concentrated on his wolf form and began the painful process of shifting. He steeled himself not to groan or growl as he went through it. During a full moon, a werewolf had no choice and would shift regardless. He didn't relish the idea of going through it more often, but when his alternate form provided a distinct advantage, he'd use it.

As soon as the transformation was complete, he relaxed into his new form. He heard a click. He thought he'd heard a series of clicks before, but he was too preoccupied with the shift to concentrate on anything else.

He whipped his head in the direction of the sound and saw a woman in gray sweats up on the hill and several yards away. A hoodie almost hid Brandee's beautiful red hair, but a few strands blew in the cool breeze. She must have followed him with her camera.

Damn it. Did she see me shift?

From the scent of fear rolling off her and her muttered "Oh, my wendigo…" he'd say she had.

He caught another scent at almost the same time—the one he was looking for. *Katie!*

Now he had a major dilemma. Should he shift back and try to sweet-talk the camera away from Brandee? Undoubtedly, she must have thought she was losing her mind. Or should he just concentrate on the little girl's scent and take the chance that Brandee would never divulge the secret existence of paranormals. But what would she do with the damning evidence?

Shit, shit, shit. The number one rule of any pack was to protect the pack. It was crucial to never reveal their alternate forms to humanity. And that didn't just pertain to werewolves. *Any* paranormal who exposed their existence endangered them all.

And she had proof!

He had completely blown it. Unless he could reach her quickly, he could forget about his PI job. He'd be in a government lab before he could say, "There are no such things as werewolves."

He dashed behind a fence that hid him from her view and shifted back as quickly as he could. Now he had to get to her before she disappeared but with the added problem of being stark naked.

He caught sight of her fleeing and called, "Brandee! Wait up." He had to dash to the spot where he'd left his clothes, snatch them up, then charge after her. "Brandee, stop!" She was getting away. There was no time to get dressed. He had to chase her down with his clothes in his fist, covering his junk.

~~~

Brandee made it as far as the Boston Common before Nick grabbed her arm and brought her to an awkward, flailing halt. Her shoulder hurt as if it had been wrenched out of its socket. At least she still had a good hold on her camera.

"Let me go, you freak!"

His grip on her arm dug in painfully, and the adrenaline rush made her quiver all over, like she'd swallowed a vibrator. Even so, she couldn't help but notice his virile body. The part she most wanted to see was covered by his fistful of clothing.

"Will you promise not to run if I let go?"

"Will you promise to get dressed if I promise not to run?"

He had the audacity to laugh but agreed. As soon as he let go, she turned her back so he could put on his clothes in relative privacy. Considering that a dozen gaping mouths were riveted in their direction, privacy wasn't really possible.

"Okay, you can turn around now," Nick said, as he zipped his jeans.

Brandee had no idea what to say. Should she confront him on what she thought she saw? If her eyes were playing tricks on her, would he think she was nuts? And speaking of nuts, why was he naked if he hadn't just been a huge dog?

She clapped a hand against her forehead. "Ow. My aching head."

A movement from behind a tree caught her eye. She looked past Nick and saw creepy Mr. Balog watching them. Her upstairs neighbor seemed to enjoy spying on the patrons and employees of the bar. She might have a problem with Nick at the moment, but that didn't mean she wanted him to get arrested.

"Nick," she whispered. "Balog's behind you. He probably thinks you're a rapist."

"Shit." He swiveled enough to spot the man lurking.

Mr. Balog disappeared behind the tree again.

Nick said loud enough for the eavesdropper to hear, "I'm sorry, baby. I didn't mean to upset you. Let's kiss and make up."

Before she could do more than open her mouth to protest, his lips descended on hers in a passionate, overwhelming, drugging kiss. His tongue found hers and they entwined in a warm swirling dance. Her body melded to his as if they were two halves of a locket that fit together perfectly. Flutters of pleasure rippled from her head to her toes.

She didn't know if the kiss lasted for minutes, hours, or days. The world fell away and the only things that remained were Nick and her liquid insides.

When they finally pulled apart, his blue eyes stared down at her, appearing as shocked as she felt.

~~~

Balog rode the elevator to the top floor of the innocuous-looking office building. He had to report what he saw to the Council right away.

When he arrived at Supernatural Headquarters and the elevator doors whooshed open, bright sunlight met him. He'd never get used to that. It was pitch black outside, but looking out of the invisible glass dome over the entire top floor, he saw puffy clouds and sunshine as bright as noon.

And they say "Don't mess with Mother Nature." As soon as that thought traveled through his brain, the entity herself marched over to him.

"Balog. What's wrong?"

"What makes you think something's wrong? Couldn't I just be here for a visit?"

She crossed her arms and frowned. "You'd better not be. You know how I feel about socializing with people."

"I'm not most people."

"You sure as hell aren't. You're one of the weirdest humans I've ever met."

Balog sighed. He'd never get used to Mother Nature being a trash-talker. He had originally pictured her as a sweet, winsome, young woman with flowers in her hair. Instead he had been introduced to a middle-aged, foul-mouthed cynic who was just as apt to wear weeds as flowers along with her flowing white robe and flip-flops.

"So, skip the niceties. What did you see, Balog?"

"A werewolf revealed himself to a human."

Mother Nature balled her fists and yelled, "What the frack? Was it an accident? Never mind. Doesn't matter. Someone's in deep shit. Which werewolf?"

"Nicholas Wolfensen."

One of the other Council members, sitting with four white-robed males at a round table, interrupted their poker game to add his two cents. "That wasn't very bright of him."

Mother Nature whirled on him. "No shit, Olympian Obvious."

Balog let out another long-suffering sigh. "Wait. It gets worse."

"Crap. Well, give it to me straight. You know how I hate sugarcoating."

"Yes, ma'am. His shift was caught on camera."

Mother Nature's jaw dropped. Apparently she didn't

have any words foul enough for the situation. Eventually, she looked up at the sky and bellowed something that sounded like, "Gaaaaah!"

Playing cards flew everywhere. As they fluttered to the floor, Mother Nature bowed over at the waist, as if she'd been punched in the gut.

Balog took a deep breath and hoped for the best. "What would you like me to do?"

"You?" She straightened up, clasped her hands behind her back, and began to pace. "You can do your usual nothing. I'll take care of this myself. Better yet, I'll create a diversion and you can play fetch."

"Wow." Nick gathered Brandee in his arms and held her against his pounding chest. His inner wolf had awakened when he kissed her. His nerves tingled and he had an incredible urge to howl. It was as if something clicked as it fell into place and the sensation had brought not only a feeling of *belonging*, but also relief.

She tucked her head beneath his chin, and he stroked her back. An overwhelming urge to protect her overcame him. He had never felt this strongly about shielding a woman before. Apparently, Brandee wasn't just any woman. He tried to let go and couldn't.

What was happening? Women didn't affect him this way. Why did he want to envelop her in his arms and never let go? It was almost as if an invisible force demanded he shelter her. Take care of her.

"Yeah, wow is right," she said. "I-I've never…"

"Me neither." He leaned back and tipped up her chin so he could look in her eyes. "You know what I said before?"

She shook her head. "About what?"

"You know...about my not dating any woman more than one time."

Her soft expression suddenly hardened. "Oh yeah. *That*."

"Well, forget it. It doesn't pertain to you."

Her mouth opened but no words came out, so he took advantage of the moment and leaned down to kiss her again.

Suddenly a fierce wind blew up from nowhere. Brandee's long auburn hair whipped his neck and face.

"Holy..." Nick braced his feet against the raging wind and grasped his girl, squeezing her tight.

"Nick, what's happening?" Brandee had to shout to be heard over the wind.

"Don't know. Freak storm. Microburst maybe. Come on." He took her hand, and as he was dragging her to the safety of a huge tree to block the wind and debris, her camera flew off her shoulder.

"Nick! My camera!"

Squinting against the dirt swirling around them, he could barely see it. The camera quickly tumbled out of view altogether. "We'll get it later. Just hold on to me."

Brandee did as he asked, clinging to his shirt with all her might. He had to be careful not to use all of his werewolf strength, or he could crush her.

At last the wind died down. They were covered with dirt and Brandee's hair was a mess, but other than that, they were fine.

Nick let out a long breath of relief.

"Oh, my freak of nature... What was that?" she asked.

"Might have been a tornado."

Brandee laughed. "We don't have tornadoes in New England."

"Sure we do. They're not usually as bad as the ones that rip through Tornado Alley in the Midwest, but we've had a few."

"Seriously?"

"I answered a call a few years ago that sounded like vandalism, but it turned out to be a tornado that had tossed some lawn furniture through an elderly couple's window."

"Damn," she breathed. "I felt my feet lifting off the ground at one point. You probably saved me from Oz, or at least flying away like my camera. Speaking of which…" She swiveled one way, then the other. "I don't see it."

"Last I saw, it was traveling that way." He pointed to Tremont Street.

A refrigeration truck rumbled across the pavement along with any number of cars and taxis. The streetlamps provided enough light to scan the area. Nothing resembling a camera could be seen.

"Oh, no. I'm afraid my camera must have been run over by now."

"I'm sorry, babe. I'll get you another one."

She stared up at him, surprised.

Nick smirked. "What? You thought I'd be an asshole once you got to know me?"

She laughed. "No, but I wouldn't expect you to buy me a new camera. It wasn't your fault I lost it. Heck, you kept *me* from being blown away. I didn't think you…" She seemed lost for words.

"What? Cared?"

"Not exactly. I—uh…" Brandee hesitated.

"You, uh, what?"

"I don't know if I can trust you to mean what you say."

"About what?"

"That one-night thing."

He stared into her eyes with an intensity that indicated he meant business. "You can trust me."

"I should have my head examined, but for some crazy reason, I believe you."

———

"Good work, Balog." Mother Nature liberated the camera from Mr. Balog's tight grasp.

"Is there anything else I can do?" *Thank God she seems to have calmed down. The last thing I want to do is get into trouble with the head of the Supernatural Council.*

"Not right now. At some point I may need to have a little talk with Mr. Wolfensen. In the meantime, keep an eye on him and make sure he doesn't have any more stupid slipups."

"I will," Mr. Balog promised.

"How's Anthony doing, by the way?"

"The owner of Boston Uncommon? He seems all right. I know you were against the whole idea of the bar, but it certainly makes it easier for us to keep an eye on the paranormals if they all congregate in one place. It's kind of amazing to see a werewolf, a vampire, and other supes become friends."

Her imperfect eyebrows arched. "Are you saying I may have been wrong?"

"No! Not at all. You're *never* wrong. It's just that I couldn't very well talk him out of opening a bar for paranormals when I'm not supposed to know paranormals exist."

"Yes, I can see that I assigned you a difficult task. But the fact remains. You failed to keep the city safe."

"If I may be so bold, maybe not. So far Anthony's theory seems to be paying off. Hostilities between different paranormal factions seem to be easing as they get to know each other as, well, fellow misfits."

Mother Nature crossed her arms. "Is that so?"

"Isn't that *good* news?"

She huffed. "I suppose. But let's not forget. I don't make mistakes, so calling them misfits is a trifle disrespectful."

Balog clasped his hands and looked at the floor. "I apologize."

Mother Nature shrugged. "I'm glad that they're behaving themselves, but it's kind of boring for the other Council members, as you can see." She gestured over her shoulder with her thumb.

All the white-robed Greek gods playing poker seemed perfectly content to Balog.

"I mean *I* can always entertain myself," she continued. "An earthquake here, a tornado there. I enjoyed the heck out of Hurricane Bob." She chuckled. "Just enough to make everyone scramble—but not enough to do a lot of damage. Perfect."

While she was in a good mood, he thought he might as well chat up the Council's chairwoman. He'd like to test Anthony's theory and see if getting to know each other better would improve their relationship. "Can you control the intensity of storms?"

Mother Nature grimaced. "Uh…not always. Sometimes I get a little storm going, and then it takes on a life of its own. *Oopsy*."

"So Katrina? The Japanese earthquakes and tsunami? Those were mistakes?"

Her lips narrowed into a hard line. "Oh, hell. Let's change the subject."

"What? Why?"

"When, where, how? You're getting a little too inquisitive, Balog. Why don't you stick to what you're good at?"

"Subterfuge?"

"Sure. If that's what you like to call it. Now get back out there and keep tabs on my paranormals."

"Yes, ma'am. Um, there's one more thing."

Mother Nature pinched the bridge of her nose and spoke in a bored monotone. "What is it?"

"I—uh…"

"Spit it out."

"I wondered if you might make good on your promise. You said if I did a good job…"

"Ha. As if I'd release you and your family just when it's paying off. Think again, Einstein."

Chapter 4

"YOU NEED TO STAY OUT OF THIS, BRANDEE. I won't risk your safety." Nick stood with his feet firmly planted shoulder-width apart and his hands on his hips. This was his "and that's final" posture. Hopefully she'd understand body language since his verbal skills weren't convincing her.

"But I can be helpful. I know I can."

"Maybe some other time, but not with this case." Nick needed his wolf senses, and Brandee couldn't witness him shifting again. It was just luck that she'd lost her camera.

He'd managed to convince her she had seen an actual dog, and, no, he wasn't leaving a lover when her husband showed up—he would never get involved with a married woman. Grasping at straws, he said he was naked to crawl through a tight basement window—that he was about to grease up his body but dropped the baby oil in his rush to keep her safe. It was far-fetched, but she seemed to reluctantly believe him...at least she let it drop.

Nick had finally made it to Brandee's apartment an hour after the fiasco, figuring Brandee would be back home by then. She was, and he wanted her to stay there. He had hidden a change of clothes and a gun behind the same Dumpster where he'd shifted before. This time he wouldn't take any chances and wouldn't be followed.

When all seemed quiet, he went to an old church in Copley Square. It had a round turret atop a curved flight of stairs with waist-high solid walls but no doors to seal it off from the riffraff below. There were so few places that lent themselves to a safe shift. He folded his clothes and left them in the corner. As soon as his transformation was complete, he eased out, sniffed the air, and decided no one was close by.

He ran less than a mile to reach the theater district. He sniffed through the alley he'd visited before. Katie's scent had faded, but he was still able to pick up faint remnants. He narrowed it down to the back entrance of a building that housed a comedy club. Ironic, since this situation was anything but funny.

Getting in required him to shift back to his human form. Nick hid behind the Dumpster where he'd left some clothes earlier. He dropped onto his hands and knees and concentrated on his human form. His body stretched in some places and shrank in others. He gritted his teeth until it was over. At last, he dressed and tucked the weapon into his waistband behind his back. He left the safety on, because he really didn't want to add another sphincter back there.

As he stepped out from behind the Dumpster, he came face to face with none other than the persistent cocktail waitress.

Brandee crossed her arms. "I knew it."

At first Nick was shocked. *She knows I'm a werewolf? And she isn't scared to death?*

"I knew you'd be back. Where's your dog? I thought I saw him a few minutes ago."

Apparently she thought he had been hiding behind the Dumpster all along—and had a dog.

"That's not my dog. And I don't know where he went. He must live around here."

"So have you figured out where my cousin is yet?"

"I think so, but what I don't need right now is your interference."

"Interference?" she shouted. "I'm here to help. I can be your lookout."

A light went on in the basement of the building Nick had wanted to check out further. "Shhh…for God's sake, be quiet. I don't need a lookout. I need you to be safe."

"I'm perfectly safe. I'm with you," she whispered loudly. "I know you won't let anything happen to me."

The basement light went out and he breathed a sigh of relief. Whomever they'd awakened must have decided to go back to bed.

"Don't you understand, Brandee? If I'm distracted or preoccupied with protecting you, I could miss something important."

"Or I might see something that you miss."

Suddenly an outside light clicked on and the door swung open. A heavyset guy with a long, gray ponytail stepped out. He had one hand behind his back.

"What can I do for you, folks?"

"Nothing," Nick said. "We were just out for a walk and had a disagreement. I'm sorry if we woke you."

"You were out for a walk in a dead-end alley?" He pulled out a gun and aimed it at Brandee. "Step inside. Both of you."

Two other guys appeared behind the first one. Both were armed, and they were big. Wrestler big. One was dark-haired, broad, and muscular with a pockmarked face. The other was younger, maybe late teens or early twenties, and could have been good-looking if not for the red veins in his haunted eyes and a scar from his ear to his Adam's apple.

Crap. Nick held up his hands. "Look, this is just a little misunderstanding. Don't do anything rash." He glanced over at Brandee. Her eyes were wide and she trembled. "Don't aim that thing at her. Just let us be on our way."

"I don't think so," the guy with the gun said. He stepped into the alley and waved the gun toward the door. "Inside. *Now.*"

"You need some help, boss?" one of the goons asked. "We can pick 'em up and carry 'em inside for ya."

"Look, just let her go," Nick demanded. "I'll come quietly."

The guy laughed and said, "Yeah, right. She'll go straight to the police."

"I won't. I promise," Brandee said, barely above a whisper.

The boss spoke without taking his eyes off Nick. "Oh, well, if you promise..." He rolled his eyes. "Bring her inside, Mr. B. And Mr. M., frisk this guy."

Nick had to make a decision and make it fast. With his superior strength, he could overpower any one of these guys individually, but not all three of them. And one of them had a weapon trained on Brandee. He couldn't take a chance with her life. He'd just have to go along and hope they'd make a mistake he could take advantage of. Eventually they were bound to let down their guard.

After Nick was frisked and relieved of his gun, the two hostages were brought inside. Mr. M., as he was called, dead-bolted the door behind them.

Mr. B. asked, "What do we do with 'em, boss?"

"Put them downstairs with the other one. Tie them up. Shoot the girl if this guy makes any move to save her. If either of them make any noise, duct-tape their mouths shut."

"Sure thing." He pointed his weapon at Nick. "Move."

"Move where?"

"Oh, yeah. You don't know where the cellar is. Follow me."

The boss let off a sound of disgust. "Mr. M., go with them. I don't trust this guy."

Nick wasn't sure if the boss was referring to him or to his own guy. Fortunately Mr. B. didn't seem like the sharpest knife in the drawer.

"C'mon," Mr. B. said, as he strode toward a door Nick assumed led to the basement.

Mr. M. poked him in the back with his gun and snarled, "Move."

Brandee hoped they weren't being taken to an old, dank cellar with a dirt floor and cobwebs. She pictured a single, dangling lightbulb, which would cast frightening shadows.

At least if they found Katie alive down there, this wouldn't be a total disaster. The boss had said, "Put them with the other one."

Mr. B. slid off a simple chain-type lock and opened

the door. He flicked a switch, and light revealed a wooden staircase.

Dear God, if you exist, please get us out of this alive. I'll go to church. I'll work in a soup kitchen. I'll do every good deed I can as long as we make it out of here safely.

At the bottom of the steps, the basement didn't appear as bad as she had thought it would be. Sure, it was basic and looked like it was used for storage. It had a linoleum floor, wood-paneled walls, and fluorescent lights. Must have been finished in the sixties or seventies.

A rustle in the corner alerted her. Long, white hair draped over one end of a sleeping bag.

Katie!

The young girl rolled over and opened her eyes. "Brandee?"

"Oh, thank goodness you're alive." She rushed over to her niece. "Did they hurt you, honey?"

Katie sat up and shook her head. "No. But they won't let me go home. They won't even let me call Mom."

Brandee kneeled and grasped her cousin, giving her a hug she hoped would be reassuring. Since Mr. M. still had his gun aimed at her, she didn't know how much comfort she could offer.

Mr. B. retrieved some rope and asked, "You know her?"

Brandee didn't want to give them any more information than necessary, so she just ignored him.

Mr. M. answered him. "Obviously. Lady, your re-union is touching and all, but it's over. Go sit against that post." He jerked his head toward a lally column. "And you..." he said to Nick, "sit next to the other pole."

Nick did as he was asked.

"Hands clasped behind the pole," Mr. M. barked.

Mr. B. immediately lashed Nick's wrists together and then tied them to the support column.

Brandee's heart sank. *This is all my fault. Why the hell didn't I listen to him when he told me to be quiet?*

She hesitated to leave her cousin's side. "Are they feeding you, sweetheart?"

"Yeah. Cheese and crackers."

Crap. With my lactose intolerance, I'll be less than the perfect hostage. Although with all the burping and farting, they might just let me go.

Then Mr. M. yelled, "Move."

Brandee scrambled to the column she had been directed to and sat facing Katie.

"Aw, keeping an eye on your little friend, huh?" Mr. B. said. "I don't think so. Face the other way."

Brandee glared at him and summoned every ounce of courage she had. "No. She needs to see a friendly face. She's just a little girl."

She could tell from Mr. B.'s angry expression he was about to give her a hard time, until Mr. M. interjected, "Who cares which way she faces? Just tie her up."

Mr. B. shot a look of resentment at Mr. M. and muttered, "Whatever."

He jerked Brandee's hands together. As he wound the rope around her wrists, she was afraid he was cutting off the circulation.

"Ow! Hey, that's too tight. My hands are tingling already."

Mr. M. came over and inspected his cohort's work. "Ease up a bit. Her skin is turning purple."

Mr. B. let go of her and shot to his feet. "If you don't like the job I'm doing, *you* tie her up."

Brandee tried to wriggle out of the ropes while they were arguing. Nick saw what she was doing and gave her a quick head shake. *Is he telling me not to take advantage of the momentary distraction?*

She quickly thought it through. *Two big guys with guns would overpower me in a second—or worse. I could be pistol-whipped or shot.* She sighed and stopped struggling.

At least they hadn't made any move to take advantage of her sexually, and it looked like they had left Katie alone. She hoped beyond hope that Nick had a plan. The certainty on his face suggested he did.

Finally, Mr. B. rebound her wrists. She figured he knotted it a second or third time, because Mr. M. eventually said, "All right already. She's secure. Now let's tell the boss they're not going anywhere and see what else he wants us to do."

The two of them tromped up the stairs and closed the door behind them. A faint clacking sound meant they'd slid the chain lock in place.

"Nick, what do we do now?" Brandee whispered frantically.

"We wait. When they let down their guard and make a mistake I can exploit, I'll tell you what to do."

"Oh, my legal beagle… That's it? That's your big plan?"

"Who said I had a big plan? I didn't ask them to drag us inside."

Brandee hung her head. "I shouldn't have followed you. This is my fault."

"No argument there."

She glared at him. Then an idea came to her. "Maybe

in a few minutes I can ask to go to the bathroom. They'll have to untie me for that, right?"

"Don't count on it."

"They let me go to the bathroom when I needed to," Katie said.

"That's probably because you weren't giving them any trouble. And that was smart of you, by the way."

Katie smiled.

"It's worth a try, though, don't you think?" Brandee pleaded.

"What are you going to do if they say yes and untie you?"

"I don't know yet."

Nick rolled his eyes. "I think your plan needs a little work."

"Well, it's better than yours."

Katie wriggled out of her sleeping bag. "Don't fight. I'll untie you."

Brandee grinned. It seemed as if Nick was right and they'd made the mistake he was hoping for.

"Do you think you can, honey?" he asked.

"I can try. But if they catch me, they'll be mad."

"We won't let them catch you. Untie me first," Nick said. "If you hear the door open, just run back to your sleeping bag and pretend you're asleep. I'll say I slipped out of the ropes myself."

"Okay."

Katie kneeled behind Nick and tried to undo the knot. After several attempts she sat back on her heels and sniffed. "I can't get it. It's too tight."

"That's okay, honey. I think you loosened it."

Brandee's heart melted a little bit. Nick could have

gotten frustrated or angry, but instead he took Katie's
feelings into account.

Katie sighed. "Let me try yours, Brandee."

She walked around behind her cousin and said, "Oh,
no. There's a whole bunch of knots here. I'll try anyway."

"Thanks, sweetie, but I think I'm pretty much stuck."
What else could she say? If Katie couldn't untie one
knot, there was little chance of her freeing her from "a
bunch" of them. *Why, oh why did I open my big mouth
and anger Mr. Whatever-letter-he-was?*

Katie pried and grunted. She had to give her little
cousin credit for trying.

Suddenly the door at the top of the stairs rattled and
Katie ran back to her sleeping bag. She was scooting
down into it when footsteps sounded on the stairs. She
managed to lay her head on the pillow and close her eyes
before Mr. B., the younger guy with the scar, saw her.

Fortunately, he was alone. He dragged a folding chair
from the corner to approximately ten feet in front of the
bound adults and opened it. Then he took the gun from
his waistband and sat down. "I'm here to guard you. No
talking. Those are the boss's orders."

*Probably so he won't fall for my asking to go to the
bathroom or some other escape plan.*

Nick just nodded and remained calm. If he could stay
cool, she could too.

Chapter 5

"HELLO, AUNT SADIE. HOW'S EVERY LITTLE THING?" Anthony kissed his "aunt" on top of her gray head.

Sadie smiled up at her "nephew," a vampire who masqueraded as an ordinary bar owner. He was actually more than three hundred years old and her seventh great-uncle. "I'm worried about Brandee."

"Really? Why?"

"She worked the earlier shift, but an old friend from art school was supposed to meet her here tonight. Brandee never showed and Angie can't get hold of her."

"Maybe she just forgot and went out. She could have left her cell   "

"No. It's more than that. I sensed a portent of danger earlier. Now I'm sure it's connected to Brandee. I really think she's in trouble."

Sadie's psychic gift was so accurate that he didn't dare ignore it. "How can I help if no one knows where she is?"

"Maybe you can enlist the talents of some of your regulars." She glanced over at the bar. "I'm sure they'd lend you their tracking skills if you asked them."

Anthony scoped out the bar and saw them sitting at one end. Ex-military helicopter pilot Kurt Morgan was a wizard. Tory Montana was a shapeshifting coyote. Perhaps with one in the air and the other on the ground they could find Brandee. "Thanks, Sadie. Are you sure you have no idea where she might be?"

"Just one. Last night I was helping Nick Wolfensen find a kidnapping victim. I told him to look in the theater district. Brandee overheard and wanted to go with him. Apparently she's related to the victim."

"Nick let a waitress accompany him on a kidnapping case? That seems bizarre. Why would Nick take a mere human into a dangerous situation?"

"I don't think he did. At least he didn't mean to. I got the definite feeling Brandee wasn't about to take no for an answer."

"Maybe I can find her on my own. The fewer people who know, the better."

Anthony sensed someone approaching. A quick look over his shoulder revealed Ruxandra striding toward them. "Speaking of not taking no for an answer..."

Sadie whispered, "Oh no. She still won't leave you alone?"

"She'll have to—eventually."

Ruxandra stopped a few feet away and planted her hands on her hips. "I know you're talking about me."

"We weren't until you came over here," Anthony said.

Sadie returned to shuffling her tarot cards. Anthony suspected it was a nervous habit, and he knew his ex-girlfriend made Sadie nervous.

"Not only that, but I know you were talking about one of the waitresses before that. It was the little harlot Brandee, wasn't it?"

Don't rise to the bait. "I have things to do. Important things. Please leave us."

Ruxandra focused her glare on Sadie. "Oh, you'd like that, wouldn't you? I suppose you're trying to fix up your nephew just like you play matchmaker with everyone else."

Sadie took a deep breath. "I was doing nothing of the kind. Now, if you'd like a reading, I can give you one in a few minutes."

"Ha. I make my own future."

Anthony took Ruxandra's elbow and escorted her away from Sadie's booth. "Don't cause a scene." When they got farther away, he whispered to her, "You know Sadie's readings bring in a lot of business. I won't have you undermining her." *Or scaring her to death.*

"Fine. I'll leave then."

Finally. Anthony schooled his features so he wouldn't look too relieved. "Very well. Have a nice evening, Ruxandra."

She headed toward the back door. Anthony wondered why she'd want to go out the alley way, but at the moment he didn't much care. As long as she was gone.

Mr. B. was doing that nodding off and snapping to semi-consciousness thing that Nick hoped meant he was about to fall sound asleep. Little Katie's breaths were lifting and lowering her sleeping bag in long, slow motions, so she seemed to be sleeping too. Now if he could just be sure Brandee was out, he could shift. His smaller paws would slip out of the ropes, but his wolf body would hurt like hell bound in his present position.

Nick really didn't have any better options. Even if he broke a shoulder, he'd heal quickly. He glanced over at Brandee. Her head lolled to one side. She *could be* asleep. Mr. B. started snoring and Brandee didn't seem to notice.

It's now or never.

Nick gritted his teeth and steeled himself for the inevitable pain of a shift. He concentrated mainly on his wrists. The minute he was able to slip his bonds, he'd do so and hope for the best.

His muscles began to change and pop. The sound of his bones grinding could have awakened Mr. B., but he continued to snore. Nick breathed his way through the sharp pain and continued.

A gasp came from his right. He had no choice but to complete his shift. If Brandee or Katie had seen him, at least they hadn't screamed.

At last his left paw slipped from the ropes and he was able to spin toward the pole, yanking his right paw out. He lay on the floor for a few moments, panting and waiting for the pain to ease.

When he raised his furry head, he saw Brandee staring at him—her eyes so wide he could see white all around the irises. He couldn't blame her. He bet it wasn't every day she saw a wolf in people's clothing. *Shit*.

~~~

"Angie!"

Anthony had to raise his voice to be heard over the din of the crowd. She held up one finger. "Be right there." On her way to see what he wanted, she dropped off the bottle of Corona Tory had been patiently waiting for and gave him a smile.

She ignored a customer who called to her as she walked by because Anthony was drumming his fingers on the edge of the bar. "Hi, boss. What's up?"

"Have you heard from Brandee yet?"

"No. I've left three messages."

"Is she apt to ignore her messages for a while?"

"No. In fact her phone beeps every five minutes if she misses a call."

"How long has it been since your last call?"

"Hours. This isn't like her. I'm really, really worried."

Anthony raked his fingers through his hair. "I'm going to look for her. Any idea where she might go?"

Ruxandra strode in from the back hall and slammed her fist on the bar between them. "I knew it!"

Angie just about jumped out of her skin. Everyone sitting around the bar halted their conversations and stared in Ruxandra's direction. The owner's psychotic ex-girlfriend was about as subtle as a brick through a window.

"I knew you were having an affair with that redheaded slut."

Thank God I'm a blond. Angie backed away slowly, leaving Anthony to deal with something that obviously didn't involve her.

"Ruxandra. Lower your voice." Anthony's lips thinned, and for once, he looked like he wasn't going to mollify her.

"Why? So people won't know you're a lying, cheating dog?"

"I don't have time for this." Anthony strode out the front door.

"Come back here!" After waiting several moments, Ruxandra must have realized Anthony had ignored her and was gone. She shrieked, picked up a stool, and smashed it over the bar. Angie squealed and ducked behind the cash register. She couldn't see what was happening, but she heard several more loud crashes and curses. Not all of them from Hurricane Ruxandra.

When items stopped flying and smashing, Angie peeked over the register. Ex-NFL player Tory and Kurt, an ex-marine, had Ruxandra firmly in their grasps.

"Put me down, you Moorish, boorish bastards!"

Kurt jerked his head toward the back door and Tory nodded in silent agreement. Ruxandra screamed and struggled, but she was no match for the two strong, black men. They lifted her off the ground and carried her wriggling body to the back.

Tory called over his shoulder, "Angie, honey. Would you kindly get the door? We have our hands full."

She was starting toward them when Ruxandra threatened, "If she comes near me, I'll break free *just* to gouge her eyes out!"

Angie halted, unsure what to do.

"I've got it," Kurt said. He squeezed Ruxandra's arm with one big hand and opened the door with the other. Together the men tossed her into the alley and slammed the door shut. Tory twisted the dead bolt but continued to hold on to the handle while it shook. Ruxandra sputtered curses from the other side until, at last, she seemed finished with her tirade.

"One of us better stand guard here for a little while," Kurt said.

Tory nodded. "I'll hang out by the front door—just in case."

Angie reached for the wall telephone and said in a shaky voice, "I'll call the cops."

Tory vaulted over the bar so fast she didn't see him coming. He gently pried her fingers off the receiver and replaced it back in its cradle. "No need to do that, Angie. She's gone, and we'll keep an eye on the place.

If Anthony wants to report it later, he can. I doubt he will, though. Blue lights outside are bad for business, you know?"

"So is Ruxandra."

"Anthony will know how to deal with her better than the cops."

Angie took a deep breath and let it out, willing her calm to return. "Yes. I guess you're right."

"That's a girl. Don't worry. We won't let anything happen to you." He smiled in that soft way that meant he was genuinely fond of her.

Angie relaxed a little more. "I believe you."

Oh, my Little Red Riding Hood… What just happened?

Nick had turned into a large dog. Or a wolf. Or some version of both…or neither.

Brandee's head began to spin. She suddenly realized she had taken in a huge gasp of breath but hadn't let it out. *Breathe, Brandee, breathe!*

The doglike creature was free and looking up at her with soulful eyes.

What now? Should she try to get Lassie to untie her? Could he? She could barely wrap her head around whatever kind of trick this was.

The only thing she knew *not* to do was make any noise. Mr. B. snorted a little like he might wake up, then smacked his lips and returned to snoring.

The dog—wolf, whatever he was—struggled to his paws and watched the snoring man for a moment. Then he glanced back toward Brandee and Katie. He seemed as confused about what to do as she did.

Is this some kind of magic gone wrong? Is he cursed?

At last he seemed to make some kind of decision. He crept over to Mr. B. and gently worked the gun out of the man's loose grasp. She held her breath, hoping Mr. B. wouldn't wake up and shoot the dog.

As soon as the dog had the gun in his mouth, he trotted over to Brandee and hid behind her. She heard a couple of metallic clicks as if he'd laid the gun on the floor. Then the same noises that woke her came from behind her—popping and grinding.

She wished she knew what the hell was going on, but as long as Mr. B. slept, she wasn't going to say a word. She was just happy he no longer had a weapon he could put his hands on. Speaking of hands, she felt warm fingers on the back of her neck and Nick's voice whispering in her ear. "Stay quiet, sweetheart. I'll have you out of here in no time."

She nodded and waited anxiously while he worked on the knots binding her to the pole. Before long, she could move again. She pulled her arms forward and the ropes fell away. She wanted to jump to her feet and throw her arms around his neck, but any sudden movement or noise could wake Mr. B.

She rose slowly and tiptoed over to Katie while rubbing her tingling arms. Nick held the gun trained on Mr. B. while Brandee woke Katie with a gentle wiggle to her arm. When the girl opened her eyes, Brandee held a finger to her lips and whispered, "Shhh…" She unzipped the sleeping bag as slowly and quietly as she could, then peeled back the top layer.

Mr. B. snorted and adjusted in the chair.

They waited an anxious second, and when he returned

to his rhythmic snoring, Katie crept out and stood on her bare feet. Brandee wondered if her cousin should take the time to put on her sneakers but decided against it. She just picked them up and gave them to Katie to hold. Then she looked to Nick and he tipped his head toward the staircase.

The girls glanced at Mr. B. while silently padding their way over to the stairs.

Nick followed behind them. He stopped Brandee with a hand on her arm and whispered, "Wait for me at the top."

She nodded and stepped in front of Katie. If the little girl had an adult on either side, hopefully, she'd be safe.

The three of them crept silently up the stairs. Nick maneuvered around them as soon as they reached the top step. "Stay behind me until you see an opportunity to get outside, then take it."

They both nodded. Brandee held her breath, wondering what he had planned.

He threw his whole weight against the door. His body smashed clear through and broke the lock. He shook off the door and checked behind him. Brandee suddenly realized he was using himself as a shield to get them to the outer door.

"Hey!" Mr. M. charged out from the office with a gun. Mr. B. had awakened and was swearing as he dashed up the stairs.

"Run, girls," Nick yelled.

She grabbed Katie's hand and rushed toward the outside door. A shot rang out and then another. Someone swore loudly, but she didn't stop to see who it was. She yanked open the door and ran out of their prison, holding Katie's hand.

Brandee didn't stop running until they reached the end of the block and rounded the corner. She leaned over, panting, and her hair covered her face. "Call the police," she yelled to no one in particular. Then she bumped into a tall, dark, solid body.

Looking up, she saw her boss. "Anthony?"

He braced her with his hands against her arms. "What happened?"

"Nick needs help." She pointed to the alley.

"Stay here," he ordered.

When Anthony rushed down the alley, she called out to stop him. All she wanted him to do was call the cops, not go running into gunfire.

"Oh, my stupid bravery!"

A young couple neared them, took one look, and began to cross the street.

"Wait. We need your help. If you have a cell phone, call 911." The couple just rushed off faster. "Please!"

—◦◦◦—

Nick had managed to disarm Mr. M. without getting shot, but now he was wrestling both thugs for the gun. He shoved Mr. B. against the wall, hoping to knock him out, but that only happened in the movies. Mr. B. got right back up and jumped on Nick's back as Nick fought with Mr. M. He landed a good blow to Mr. M.'s chin and stunned him for a moment. Just long enough to flip Mr. B. off his back.

A good right hook to Mr. B.'s diaphragm knocked the wind out of him and temporarily stopped him from getting back up. Nick saw an opening and kicked, aiming for Mr. M.'s knee. The guy cried out and crumpled to the floor.

Anthony rushed through the back door at that moment and took in the scene. "Looks like you've got things well in hand."

Mr. B. jumped up and said, "That's a little premature, asshole." He rushed Anthony, but before Mr. B. could land a blow, Anthony stepped aside and the criminal ran right past him and bounced off the wall.

"Let me," Nick said. He grabbed Mr. B. by the hair and slammed his head against the wall again. This time Mr. B. slid down the wall into an unconscious heap. "He won't give us any trouble for a while."

Nick was panting, heavily. "Are the girls safe?"

"Yeah, they're at the end of the block. I told them to wait for me there. Why don't you step outside and catch your breath," Anthony suggested.

"First, I'd like to know who hired these guys and why. I have the feeling someone else was having them do his dirty work. Someone who knew about the little girl's ability."

"I'll mesmerize them and see what I can find out. I'll meet you and the girls as soon as I clean up in here." He gazed at the two goons. "I've been a little hungry lately."

Nick chuckled. "Be my guest. These are Misters B. and M. Don't be surprised if they taste like shit."

With that, Nick stumbled out into the alley and enjoyed the sound of Mr. M. begging for his miserable life. Anthony probably wouldn't kill them. He'd just weaken and glamour them so they wouldn't remember being bitten and, hopefully, wouldn't remember kidnapping anyone. Nick just hoped Anthony would get more information from them before he was through. Nick might have saved Katie, for now, but to keep her safe, he had to find whoever was behind this.

Chapter 6

NICK DIDN'T SEE THE GIRLS AND HAD A SICK FEELING they were calling the cops. He had no control over which cops would show up. If one of his fellow werewolves answered the call, he'd be able to explain the situation, but if not...

He charged out into the street where a drunk was stumbling along. "Two girls. Where are they?" Nick asked, winded.

The guy slurred, "Whaz in it fer me?"

"How about, I let you live."

Anthony exited the building and quickly strode to Nick, who was sniffing the air to catch the girls' scents. Just as he locked on a direction, Anthony joined him. Nick pointed toward a nightclub. "That way."

Nick could run faster than a normal human, but the vampire ran so fast he seemed to disappear. The drunk gasped and said, "I gotta quit drinkin'."

By the time Nick caught up, Anthony was already escorting the girls out of the nearby nightclub. He had interrupted them just as Brandee was about to call the cops on a borrowed phone.

"But we *have to* call the police," Brandee said. "Oh, my obstruction of justice. There are kidnappers, and Katie's parents need to be notified, and—"

Nick strode over to her, cupped her face, and focused her attention directly on him. "I was hired to keep the police out of this, Brandee. She'll get home much faster if I take her myself."

"But—but, the kidnappers! What about them?"

"They've been dealt with," Anthony interjected.

"How?"

Nick and Anthony stared at each other. At last Nick answered. "I knocked them both out. Anthony tied them up. Later we'll make an anonymous phone call to the police."

She seemed mollified.

Anthony said, "Now, let's get you home. Your roommate is worried sick about you."

"She must be. Angie and I always tell each other if we're spending the night somewhere else. Hell, we tell each other *everything*."

Nick pulled Anthony aside and whispered so softly that only a vamp could hear him. "I hate to ask, but can you glamour her? She saw me shift. She thought I was a dog, but can you erase her memory of seeing an animal at all?"

Anthony nodded.

"Thanks. One less mess to contend with. I really care about her and I wish I could tell her more, but the code…"

"I understand," Anthony said. "And I have more to tell you later."

"Brandee, go with Anthony. Let Angie see that you're all right so she can get some sleep. I'll come over to your place later and check on you."

"But…what if I'm asleep too?"

Nick set his hands on his hips. "Are you really apt to go right to sleep after all this? It'll take me fifteen minutes to take Katie home and get to your place." He frowned, almost daring her to defy him.

She sighed. "You're right. Just let me say good night to Katie."

He nodded and stepped away so she and her cousin could hold each other for a moment. When Brandee let go of Katie, she said, "As soon as you're safe and things are back to normal, we'll have a girls' day out. Shopping. A movie. Whatever you want. Okay?"

Katie grinned and nodded. "Okay."

Brandee ruffled the white hair on her cousin's head. "See you soon, kiddo. You were very brave back there."

"You were too."

With that, Katie took Nick's outstretched hand and he escorted her to a taxicab.

Anthony let Brandee watch until they pulled away. As soon as she turned to look at him, he snared her gaze. Her jaw went slack and he knew he had her.

"You saw nothing unusual tonight. You were not kidnapped or tied up. You did not see a wolf or a dog anywhere. All you remember is having a wonderful night out with Nick."

Brandee nodded, and reiterated, "...a wonderful night out with Nick."

"Very good. Now I'm taking you home, because Nick got called away on business. But he said he'd come over to your place later."

"Okay. Why?"

"He cares about you very much."

Brandee nodded, smiling. "And I care about him."

Back in her apartment, Brandee rubbed her wrists and wondered why they were sore. She didn't want to turn on a light, however, because that might wake Angie.

She tiptoed to her bedroom, but before she got there, Angie's bedroom door flew open and her roommate stood there in her flannel pajamas with a baseball bat cocked and ready to swing. As soon as she saw Brandee, she dropped the bat and rushed to hug her roommate.

"Brandee! Oh my God, I thought you had been kidnapped, raped, and left for dead."

"Jeez, Ange. Get a grip. I'm fine."

Angie took a step back. Her mouth hung open. "Excuse me, did you just say, 'Get a grip?' Because if you did—and I'm fairly sure you didn't—our friendship is in trouble."

Brandee reared back, surprised by this crazy lady who had taken over her friend's body. "Okay…I guess I didn't say that. What's wrong? Why are you so jumpy?"

"Are you kidding me? You were MIA for hours. You didn't answer your phone. Didn't leave a note. What the hell?"

"Oh." Brandee wondered how in the world time had gotten away from her like that. Was one night with Nick Wolfensen that mind-blowing that she didn't remember most of it?

"'Oh'? That's all you have to say for yourself? Just 'Oh'?"

Angie's tone irritated her. She'd be worried about a missing roomie too, but did Angie have to sound like her mother? That's why Brandee moved out on her own in the first place. Ever since her dad left, she'd had a *smother*.

"Look, Ange. I know this is going to sound strange, but I don't remember being gone that long. All I remember is being with Nick and having the time of my life."

Angie crossed her arms. "Nick. You went out with *One-Night Nick*, and you expect me to believe you had so much fun you didn't realize a whole afternoon, evening, and half the night had gone by? You didn't hear your phone ring or the beeps that signaled missed messages? What did you do?"

"Good question. What *did* we do?" *Oh, my first date jitters…what did we do?*

Angie's eyes narrowed. "Did that bastard drug you?"

"Of course not!" Brandee was becoming more concerned by the minute, but she didn't want to worry her poor roommate any more than she already was. "I don't remember having anything to eat or drink. In fact, I'm starving."

"Well, I'm relieved. I didn't *really* think he drugged you. That doesn't sound like the Nick we know. So why didn't you answer your phone?"

Brandee glanced around the apartment and looked for her purse. "I must have left my phone here."

Now that Angie was up, Brandee switched on the living room light and saw her purse where she usually left it. She wandered over to it and pulled out her cell phone. "Looks like it's out of juice."

Angie rolled her eyes. "Well, when you charge it, you can delete my half a dozen messages. Each one is more hysterical than the last."

Why did I leave without my purse? How did I get in? Every answered question brought up another one. Maybe her camera would fill in some of the blanks. She remembered taking her camera with her. *But why?*

She opened the closet where she kept her photography equipment. Everything was there except her 35 mm Nikon.

"Where's my camera? I remember taking it with me…" A partial memory returned. "Oh! I know what happened now."

Angie had followed her into the living room and looked more concerned than ever. "What? I'm dying to hear this."

"Nick was holding me. There was a tornado or a microburst. Anyway, my camera flew off my shoulder. If not for Nick, I'd have been sucked up into the wind too. He grabbed me and pulled me over next to a tree for shelter. I must have bumped my head."

She glanced at her wrists. That must have been what happened to them. He'd grabbed onto her so tightly! Now they were sore. But she only remembered him grabbing one of her wrists. Why were they both sore?

Angie's tented eyebrows said she was having a hard time with the explanation.

"You hit your head on a tree during a tornado on Boston Common? Did you see any Munchkins? Wicked witches?"

Brandee laughed. "Very funny. No trips to Oz for me. Nick will be coming over later. He can tell me what happened."

"Nick's coming here?"

"Yeah." Brandee *did* remember one thing. That kiss. She touched her lips and smiled.

"Oh, no. You aren't falling for Nick Wolfensen, are you?"

Brandee sighed. "You don't understand. We kissed.

It was the most incredible, mind-altering, toe-curling kiss of my entire life…and his. He told me his one-night rule didn't apply to me. I think he was just as affected by the kiss as I was."

"Oh. My. God. I don't believe this."

Brandee giggled. "Oh, my lucky day… That's the one thing I *do* believe. Like you, I was completely skeptical, but he convinced me beyond the shadow of any doubt. He really cares about me, Ange."

Angie snorted. "Yeah, right. I'll believe it when I see it."

At that moment, there was a knock at their door. "What the…who's coming here at this time of night?"

Brandee strode to the door. "I told you, Nick said he'd be coming by later. He got called away and asked Anthony to see me safely home."

That answered another question. How she'd managed to get in if she'd left her purse behind. Anthony owned the building, so of course he had a key.

She peered through the peephole and her heart leaped when she saw Nick. She quickly finger-combed her hair and opened the door.

Nick took one long stride into the apartment, grasped her in his arms, and kissed her thoroughly. His kiss had a frenzied quality to it—as if he hadn't seen her for weeks, or like they'd just been through some kind of life-altering event. Hmmm… Was he *that* worried about her after the tornado incident?

Angie cleared her throat and the couple parted, but neither of them looked away. He gazed at her with so much longing. If Brandee didn't know better, she'd say he wanted to make love to her right then and there.

"I don't believe this," Angie muttered.

Nick finally turned toward Angie but kept a possessive arm around Brandee's waist.

"Look, I know with my past it might be hard to believe, but I'm crazy about this girl." He gave Brandee a
side squeeze that made her giggle.

Angie tossed her hands in the air. "Now I've heard
everything."

"Not everything," Brandee amended. "Nick, I don't
remember anything since hitting my head on that tree. I'm
afraid to say you'll have to fill me in on most of our date."

He nodded. "Ah, yes. The tornado. You probably remember me telling you I'd buy you a new camera, right?"

"Oh, yeah. I do now. But you don't have to do that. I
should probably do everything with my digital camera
now. Film is sort of old school."

"But I thought you were a purist," Angie interrupted.
"You said you liked the control you had with the different lenses and film speeds. You enjoyed using different
tricks in the darkroom too."

Brandee shrugged. "Yeah, I guess there are a few
things I can do manually that I can't do on the computer,
but not much."

"I'll get you a new old camera," Nick said. "I insist."

Angie yawned. "Look, you guys can work that out
without me. I'm beat. I'll see you in the morning, Bran.
G'night, Nick."

Angie waved and went back to bed.

That left Brandee with Nick, not quite knowing what
to do. She was exhausted, but it was too soon to invite
him to her bedroom. Thankfully, he spoke first.

"Well, I just wanted to check to be sure you got
home okay, sweetheart. If you want, I'll go and let

you get your beauty sleep...not that you need it."
He grinned.

Every one of his killer grins and corny lines affected her the same way. They gave her hope and made her nervous at the same time. *I hope he really has changed. If he left me now, I'd be so disappointed.*

"Don't go. We need to talk."

Nick took a deep breath. "Okay." He had come up with a scenario in case she wanted to know what happened. *Of course she'd want to know what happened.* Hopefully after the meager explanation he'd come up with, he could distract her—somehow.

She led him to the couch and they sat side by side. "So, Nick. I'm really confused. How did we spend our evening and why can't I remember?"

"We were walking through the Common, and I'd planned to take you to the Ritz for a drink before we decided where to go for dinner. That's when the tornado touched down." *Thank goodness for weird weather right when I needed an excuse for weirder things.*

"And you're saying I forgot everything that happened after that?"

He shrugged. "I guess so. You were knocked out so I carried you to my apartment. When you came to, you seemed kind of out of it."

"Is that when you asked Anthony to take me home?"

"I waited until you seemed physically stable, but I got called away. I thought you'd be more comfortable in your own bed."

"So you didn't take advantage of me?"

His eyebrows shot up. "Of course not. What kind of guy do you think I am?"

She shrugged. "I don't know. I mean, I've known you for about a year—ever since I started working at the bar. You seem like a good guy, but I don't really know anything about you."

This was the distraction he had been looking for. "Ask me anything. I'm an open book."

"Okay. Why did you quit being a cop?"

As uncomfortable a subject as it was, he'd prefer talking about that to talking about what happened that night.

"I have an identical twin. He was in trouble with the law more than once and was eventually tried in a high-profile case. People saw his face on TV and plastered all over the newspapers last year. Plenty of people mistook me for my brother, and even my fellow cops thought I must have had something to do with it."

"I don't pay attention to the news, I'm afraid. It's all bad anyway. So what was he accused of?"

"Remember the Isabella Stewart Gardener Museum heist?"

"Oh, my Rembrandt. That's terrible. I love art and art museums. It broke my heart to see the empty frames where priceless paintings used to be."

"My brother was the last person who'd do something like that, but he was set up. The fact that the robbers wore Boston Police uniforms to get past the security guards convinced the rumor mill I had something to do with it. I wasn't even a cop at the time."

"Then how could they blame you?"

"The public didn't know how long I had been a cop.

And even if they did, people believe what they want to believe."

"That sucks." Her hand flew to cover her mouth. "I'm sorry. I mean, that's really awful."

He chuckled. "I like how you try to avoid offensive language, but why around me? I've certainly heard worse."

She blushed. "When I was in art school, my mouth was pretty filthy. I realized how bad I sounded after hearing myself on a friend's answering machine. 'Trailer trash' was the term that sprang to mind. I attracted the wrong kind of guys back then. Eventually, I figured out why."

He put his arm around her shoulder. "I know my reputation isn't stellar, but I promise I'll be good to you."

He leaned in for a kiss, and she met his lips eagerly. Her lips parted and their tongues sought each other out, swirling together as if this dance was second nature. Fire sprung up between them and he clutched her close.

Desire hit him in the gut…and lower. This wasn't the normal horniness of a man attracted to a hot woman. An overwhelming desire to take her and mark her, then and there, pounded through his veins.

If he didn't stop soon, he might not be able to. He broke the kiss and found himself panting hard. "Brandee, I'd better go."

"Is everything all right?"

He took a moment to compose himself. "Everything is too right. If I don't leave now, I'm afraid I'll pressure you to go too far too fast."

She nodded as if she understood. "Yeah. And then I'll never get any sleep."

―――⌁―――

"Kidnapped! What do you mean I was kidnapped?" Brandee couldn't believe what her aunt was telling her. She pulled the phone away from her ear and stared at it as if she could see if it was lying.

"Katie said you were with her. And that you were tied up."

Oh, my rubber ducky. "Why would she say that?"

"I-I don't know why she'd make that up. I just called to thank you. She said you kept her calm and helped her escape. Well, you and Mr. Wolfensen."

"Nick was there?"

"Yes, we hired him. But why were you with him? That's what I can't understand."

Brandee was speechless. She had been out with Nick on a date last night. A terrific date from what she could recall—but that's about all she remembered. Since when did kidnapping count as a great date?

"Aunt Dee, I'll have to call you back."

"Of course, dear. But, before you go, is there anything we can do?" The worry in her aunt's voice came through.

"No, I'll be okay. I just need to talk to someone." *Someone who apparently lied to me about what happened last night.*

"Yes, I should say so."

Brandee realized how that sounded. *Great, now she thinks I'm nuts.*

"Love you, bye." She shouldn't have hurried her aunt off the phone like that, but she really didn't want to hear any more about her "lost night" until she spoke to Nick. *He'd better not try to lie to me, either.*

On the off chance he was downstairs in the bar already, she decided to go in a bit early. She could always say she was making up for being late more often than not. Claudia, the daytime manager might faint, but Wendy would appreciate a hand if it was busy. It was a beautiful September day, and tourists would be getting thirsty.

Thank goodness Angie had the day off and was gone before Brandee woke up. She didn't need to answer any more of her roommate's questions until she got more answers herself.

Chapter 7

NICK WAITED, SHIFTING FROM FOOT TO FOOT OUT-side the bar. He didn't need an audience when he saw Brandee. He knew there was a good chance she'd want to fill in more of the blanks from their so-called date.

The morning news had paused between their stories of assaults and accidents to report a short-lived tornado hitting the Boston Common. Because there had been no damage, the event was ignored by the newspapers. He had hoped for an article he could show Brandee, but alas, it wouldn't be that easy.

Regardless, the idea that she had hit her head and had temporary amnesia served his purpose well. He'd said he took her to his place to let her lie down and rest. She wouldn't remember where he lived or what the place looked like. He could joke with her and say thank goodness she didn't remember it, because his apartment was a mess.

Suddenly the woman in question appeared before him.

"Just the man I wanted to see." Her expression was unreadable.

"Good. I wanted to see you too, sweetheart. How are you feeling today?"

"Just fine except for my wrists, which is strange. They're a little bruised, but you'd think my head would hurt if I bumped it."

"Uh, yeah. You got lucky, I guess." He patted her on the head. "You must have a hard noggin'."

She eyed him suspiciously. "What really happened, Nick?"

Uh-oh. "What do you mean? Oh, I guess you want to know what happened after that."

"Sure. Go ahead. Give me the details, and don't you dare lie. I'll know if you do."

Sweat broke out on Nick's brow. She was probably bluffing. She couldn't know if he was lying or not. "We were strolling across the Common, discussing, you know, life and stuff. We never made it for drinks or dinner. The tornado struck and you must have bumped your head. You seemed disoriented. That in itself was frightening. I took you to my place to recover from your scare."

Yeah, that sounds reasonable. Maybe she'll think she blocked it out of her memory due to the traumatic nature of the incident, and that would explain why her head doesn't hurt.

"Oh, so you live in a basement? And instead of letting me lie down, you tied me to a pole?"

"Uh…" *Shit. Who told her?* The one loose end he hadn't tied up completely was Katie. He'd hinted that she might want to spare her parents the details, but the girl must have told them what happened anyway. *Of course she'd cave when her parents asked her to tell them everything. Why would she listen to some guy she didn't know over her parents?*

Anthony didn't erase Katie's memory, only Brandee's. *Why, oh why didn't I think that through?* Perhaps Anthony could have mesmerized both girls at once. Nick had just assumed his vampire friend couldn't.

He had to change the subject. He grabbed Brandee and kissed her for all he was worth. At first she stiffened, but shortly after that she relaxed and molded her body to his.

Suddenly she pulled away and shoved his chest. "Don't try to distract me."

"I'm not. I just missed you, baby. That's all."

"Look, I'm not satisfied with your answers and don't call me 'baby.' I'm an adult."

"But I did miss you. That's the God's honest truth."

"Maybe so, but I was talking about last night. Something happened that I can't remember. I don't know why I can't remember it, but if I find out you drugged me—"

"Jesus!" He couldn't have her thinking that. He had to make her believe something else. *Anything* else. "No, Brandee. No way would I do that to you. I'd never do that to any woman. How can you even think that?"

She opened her mouth to speak but he laid a finger against her lips. "I'll tell you exactly what happened. I just didn't want to frighten you—again. You were so scared...It was a blessing when you blocked it out."

She crossed her arms. "So, you're saying I was so afraid I blacked out?"

"No. Not exactly. Sometimes traumatic situations are so overwhelming, the mind just does the victim a favor and temporary amnesia is the result."

He could almost see the wheels turning in her mind. At least she was considering the idea.

"I'm not a delicate, fragile flower, Nick. What was so traumatic I couldn't handle it?"

Actually, he *did* think of her as delicate. Physically, anyway. Mentally, she seemed rock solid. That might not be handy in this case, but he liked a woman he didn't have to treat with extreme caution. He'd known a few unstable babes in his long time on earth.

The amnesia story might be difficult, but he had to make it fly. "You were held at gunpoint, sweetheart. In fact, that's the only reason I didn't try to escape until the guy guarding us fell asleep. They said they'd kill you if I moved a muscle. I'm sure they meant it. You probably believed you were looking at your imminent death." That was all true, so he hoped his delivery was persuasive.

Brandee didn't appear convinced, but it was all he had. He knew better than to talk too much. That's how criminals got caught in lies.

He took her in his arms again and rubbed her back in slow circles. "I'm so sorry that happened, sweetheart. I owe you a real date."

"No, you owe me a real explanation." She pulled away. "Why did my aunt say we were with Katie?"

"Because we were. That's how we wound up in that situation. I was hired to find your cousin, and you followed me."

She leaned back and looked up at him. "What happened to my camera?"

"That was the tornado. Did you see the story on the news this morning?"

"No, I didn't."

"Maybe they have it online. Check it out."

"I'll have to do that later. I have to get to work now."

"What time do you get off work? I'll come by and take you camera shopping."

"I don't think I'm up to it tonight, Nick. I'll see you." She started to walk away, but he caught her arm.

"Don't I get a kiss?"

She stared at him as if she wasn't sure she could trust him. He knew better than to push it. She might go back to the idea of being drugged and forced to do something against her will.

Finally she tipped up her face for a kiss and he gave her a relieved peck on the lips.

Whew. "I'll call you tonight. What time do you go to bed?"

She shrugged. "Depends."

"On what?"

"On whether or not I get kidnapped, I guess."

———

"Nicholas Wolfensen?"

Nick stopped walking and turned around, surprised to see Mr. Balog's son.

"Yeah?"

"You have been summoned to appear before the Supernatural Council."

The back of his neck prickled. Nick had heard of it but wasn't sure the Council really existed. No one he knew had ever met the mysterious society of elders — or whatever they were.

"I was just heading home. Why don't you give me a way to get in touch with them, and I'll make an appointment."

"That's not how it works. You're to come with me right away."

What the hell? Nick stretched himself to his full six feet, three inches, at which point he towered over the young man. "And what if I don't want to?"

Young Balog pulled a pouch from his inner jacket

pocket and opened it. He shook out some kind of powder and tossed it up in the air. It shimmered and spread, covering both of them. Before Nick knew what was happening, he was somewhere else—standing under some kind of glass bubble or dome.

"Thank you, Balog," said a stern-looking, middle-aged woman in a flowing white robe. "You may go now."

Adolf bowed and strode to an elevator. He punched the down button and waited. Nick gazed at his surroundings. All around the round room, people in white robes strolled and chatted with each other. The only one who seemed interested in him was the woman.

"Wolfensen. Do you know who I am?"

"No, I can't say that I do."

"My name is Gaia, but you might know me by my other name, Mother Nature. I'd welcome you, but you're not actually welcome. I don't invite anyone here unless they're doing my bidding or I'm pissed at them. Guess which situation you're in."

"Uh..."

"You're a real conversationalist, aren't you?"

Nick scratched his chin. "Look. I'm not sure how I got here or why you want to speak with me, but I don't want to assume anything either. Is this the Supernatural Council?"

"And what if it wasn't? You'd have just tipped off a mortal that such a thing exists—if I was mortal. That's why you're here, big mouth."

"I've never told anyone about the Council."

"And you won't if you know what's good for you. However, I understand you allowed yourself to be photographed during a shapeshifting occurrence."

"It was an accident. I didn't *allow*—"

"Silence," she bellowed. The others in the room paused and listened. "There is no excuse for this kind of breach. Now, how far has this mess spread, and what do you intend to do about it?"

"It's been contained. My vampire friend glamoured the mortal."

"Anthony did this?"

"Yes." Nick hoped he wasn't getting Anthony in trouble.

"At least you asked someone who you could trust," Gaia said. "What if you had to go to one of the less friendly vampires? Someone who would just love to expose your kind?"

"I-I wouldn't have."

"So, what would you have done had Anthony not been there to bail you out?"

"I know a couple other vampires I could ask."

"Do you, now? So, I guess that makes it all right. You have a couple of backup vampires in case you screw up."

"Well, I guess so…" A bead of sweat trickled down his spine.

"Wrong!" she yelled. "That's the wrong answer, dipshit."

"What's the right answer?"

"The only answer is this: if you ever expose the existence of paranormal beings again, I'll send you to Mount Vesuvius and go all Pompeii on your ass. You get me?"

Nick's mouth went dry. "Yes, ma'am."

"Don't call me 'ma'am'! You can call me Mother Nature, Gaia, or Goddess. Got it?"

"Got it."

"Good. Now get out." She pointed toward the elevators.

"But I don't know where I am or where to go."

She jammed her hands on her hips and leaned toward him. "Oh, I'll tell you where to go if you stand here much longer, believe me."

One of the white-robed men hurried over and grabbed him by the arm. "I'll show him out, Gaia."

She spun on her heel and marched off toward the small forest in the corner.

The elder, or whatever he was, ushered Nick to the elevator and pushed the down button. While they were waiting, Nick figured he'd use his one and only chance to ask a question or two.

"So, the Council members...who are you exactly?"

The white-robed man looked at him with a pitying expression. Nick imagined him thinking something like: "You poor, dumb earthling," but instead the man answered in a voice that seemed sincere.

"We're the Gods And Immortals Association. Thus the initials, GAIA." He leaned in and whispered, "It's just like her to name the whole shebang after herself."

"I heard that," a female voice called out.

The white-robed gentleman rolled his eyes. Nick decided to press his limited opportunity and ask another question.

"Are there any other females on the Council? If so, where are they?"

"There are other female immortals, all working for the greater good. Some are goddesses and some are mere muses, but they don't hang out here very often." He whispered behind his hand conspiratorially, "Gaia likes to be the center of attention, so she stays here most of the time and delegates all the tasks she doesn't want to do."

"Apollo!" Mother Nature's voice bellowed.

Nick gasped. "*The* Apollo?"

At that moment, the elevator doors whooshed open and the god shoved Nick inside. There were no buttons to push for a particular floor and no need for any. The doors slammed shut and the elevator dropped like a rock. Just when Nick was afraid he was about to hit the ground, it slowed to a stop. He felt as if he had left his stomach a few stories up.

The doors opened on a familiar lobby. Nick stepped out and noticed the directory on one wall. He scanned it, not knowing what he'd find there. It seemed innocent enough. The building was made up mostly of law offices. Nowhere did it say "GAIA." or anything that could be construed that way. He went back to the elevator he had just exited and saw a whole panel of buttons to push for the different floors.

Whoa, that wasn't there a minute ago. "I must be losing my mind," Nick muttered to himself.

He thought he heard a feminine laugh.

Brandee was just walking past the bar's large window when it shattered. Someone screamed, so she dropped her tray and hit the deck.

"What was that?" Wendy yelled.

Malcolm, the bartender who alternated with Angie, shouted, "Holy shit, is that a harpoon?"

Brandee took in the scene directly opposite the window. A long, rusted metal rod with a sharp barb at the end was sticking out of the wooden edge of the bar. People were rushing out the door faster than you could shout, "Danger, Will Robinson."

She gathered her wits and picked up her tray, replacing the unbroken shot glasses and two glass beer mugs while avoiding the shards from the window all around her. It was too dark outside to see who was there.

Anthony came running out of his office. "What the hell happened?" He rounded the corner of the bar and gripped Brandee around her waist. Quicker than she thought possible, he lifted her off the ground and rushed her to the opposite side of the bar.

"Stay down," he ordered. Then Anthony dashed out the front door, bellowing, "Ruxandra!"

His ex-girlfriend did that? Oh, my boiled bunny!

Wendy hurried over to where Brandee crouched. "Are you okay?"

"Yeah, I'm fine. Did Ruxandra actually throw that harpoon through our front window?"

"Probably. I think she was aiming for you. She's wicked jealous."

Brandee gasped. "Aiming for me? Why?"

Kurt stood at the end of the bar. "Sorry, sweet cheeks. Wendy's right. Ruxandra is jealous of you. You should have seen how she trashed the place last night."

"Last night? But I wasn't even here."

"Yeah, when Anthony went looking for you, that's when she decided you were too important to him and she went ballistic." He glanced around the bar. "I'm amazed it was all cleaned up and ready to go tonight."

"He must have a kick-ass cleaning crew. I had no idea the place was wrecked last night."

Kurt leaned on the bar. "It was messed up. She tossed chairs, broke bottles, and really busted up the place. I hate to say it, but if you're smart, you'll find another job."

"And you'll have to find another place to live," Wendy added. "I'm sure she knows about the apartment over the bar.

"Why would she target *me?* I haven't flirted or even looked twice at Anthony."

Sadie moseyed over. "Don't you dare quit or move because of Ruxandra. You haven't done anything wrong. She just needs someone to blame for the breakup, even though she's the one who drove Anthony away."

"And she picked me? Faaan-tastic."

Sadie extended her hand. "You're safe. You can stand up now."

"I don't know. Someone should probably call the police first."

"Anthony wouldn't want that." Sadie began wandering away, then turned and said, "Brandee, dear. Would you get me another White Russian, please?"

I could use one myself. Brandee let out a long breath, then peeked over the top of the bar. Other than the smashed window and lack of customers, everything looked fairly normal. Malcolm was already sweeping up the broken glass.

"I'll get that, Malcolm," Brandee said. "Sadie wants another drink."

"She can wait. You need to stay away from the windows." Malcolm emptied the dustpan into the trash.

Nick burst through the front door. "Brandee. Are you all right?"

"Yes, I'm fine." Her voice quivered.

He dropped his bag on the bar, reached her in two long strides, then pulled her into a strong embrace. "What the hell happened here?"

Kurt rested his elbow on the bar casually. "Hurricane Ruxandra struck again."

"Anthony ought to press charges this time. I know he doesn't want to..." Nick yanked the harpoon out of the wooden bar and tossed it in the trash bucket. "But it would be for everyone's safety, including Ruxandra's. If anything happens to my girlfriend, Anthony's psycho bitch won't make it to jail in one piece."

Kurt raised his eyebrows. "Your girlfriend? What's this? Have you turned over a new leaf?"

Nick placed a kiss on Brandee's head. "Yeah. What of it?"

He declared us a couple in public! Maybe I can trust him... If he'll just tell me the truth from now on.

Kurt held up both hands. "I wasn't challenging you. I just didn't think I'd see the day."

"Well, now you have."

"Brandee, are you really willing to take a chance on this lug?"

She gazed up at Nick and smiled. "Yeah. He's worth it."

Anthony opened the front door and dragged Ruxandra inside. He aimed a stern glare at her. "Apologize."

"I will not apologize to that little whore." Ruxandra was wearing an all-black catsuit as if she had planned on breaking and entering, rather than just breaking.

Nick reached her in less than a second and grabbed her by the throat. "You'd better not be talking about Brandee that way."

Nick's jaw twitched and his arm quivered. His eyes flashed with a dangerous intensity she'd never seen before.

Anthony crossed his arms. "I told you. Nick and

Brandee are together. She's not my mistress. I think you owe her an apology."

"Ugh. Can't. Breathe."

Nick let go of her and she rubbed her throat. After a brief hesitation and another dark glare from Anthony, she crossed her arms and tipped her nose in the air. "Fine. I apologize."

Brandee bit her lip. Her voice quivered when she said, "Your apology is accepted."

"Frankly, I don't give a rat's ass if you accept my apology or not. Just stay away from my Anthony." She pointed a long red fingernail at the rest of the staff. "That goes for all of you."

Anthony sighed. "I don't date my employees—but more importantly, Ruxandra, I'm not dating you, either. You're unstable, erratic, and I can't trust you to conduct yourself in a civilized manner. This is my business you're disrupting. If you care about me, you have an odd way of showing it."

Ruxandra balled her fists and stomped her foot. "We've been together for a cent—for a long, long time. How dare you talk to me that way in front of your peons!"

Anthony grabbed her by the back of her stiff collar. He opened the door and tossed his troublesome ex-girlfriend out, then slammed it behind her. Facing the staff he said, "For the record, I've never called any of you 'peons.' I value your hard work and loyalty. In light of the situation, I'll offer a thousand-dollar retention bonus to anyone who stays for the next six months."

Wendy spoke up. "I can really use the money, but do you think Ruxandra will move on soon—or ever?"

Anthony covered his eyes with one big, pale hand. "I truly hope so."

-----~-----

Nick insisted on staying the rest of the evening so he could walk Brandee right to her door. No way was he going to allow anything to happen to his mate, if Brandee was the one…and he had an inexplicable feeling that she was. His overwhelming need to keep her in his sight, making sure she was safe, trumped anything he'd ever experienced. He would take a bullet for his partner or his brother, but he'd throw himself in front of a freight train for Brandee.

He had waited too long to find her, and he was anxious to secure her commitment. For that to happen he'd have to prove himself trustworthy. He knew she still had questions, so he expected to walk a fine line between telling the truth and withholding bits of information.

Maybe if he brought it up instead of waiting for her to do it, he'd look as if he wasn't hiding a big, fat secret. Anything was worth a try.

As they ascended the steps to the second floor apartment, Nick asked, "So, have any of your memories returned yet?"

Brandee frowned and shook her head. "No. It's weird. It's as if it didn't even happen."

Whew. Thank you, Anthony. "That's a blessing, right?"

She shrugged. "I guess so."

Pausing in front of her door, she fished out her key.

"Here. Let me get that for you." Nick hoped some old-fashioned good manners would help his cause.

Brandee's eyebrows lifted, but she handed him her key. He transferred the plastic bag to the other hand and opened the door, but he didn't make a move to follow her in. He hoped she'd invite him. When all she did was hold out her hand for her key, he said, "Can I come in for a few minutes? I have a surprise for you."

"Really?" She smiled and glanced at the bag in his left hand. "Sure. Come in."

"It looks like you trust me again."

"I-I want to. We have some things to work out, but I know you mean well. I don't think you'd hurt me, at least not on purpose."

"I'd *never* hurt you, Brandee."

He strolled to her sectional sofa and sat on the lounger. She took the seat beside him. He had hoped she'd share the spot right next to him, so he could pull her down and invite her to stretch out beside him. Suddenly just thinking about lying down with Brandee in his arms was doing something to his self-control. He had to hold it together. She'd just barely let him in the door. He could blow it if he came on too strong now.

Nick was relatively sure it was too soon for her, but he was certainly feeling it. A bead of sweat broke out on his brow. He *had to* rein in his behavior. The urge to mate had never been this incredibly strong. Just because he was ready to rip off her little black apron and everything else she was wearing didn't mean she was up for it. He was afraid his hands would shake if he reached for her right now. *Damn, it's hard to wait, but I'd scare her to death if I let my inner wolf rule me now.*

Without any preliminaries, he handed her the bag.

Brandee grinned and peeked inside. She gasped and pulled out the old-school Nikon he had tracked down.

"You didn't." She turned the camera over in her hands, admiring its different features.

"I did."

Her smile suddenly faded and she tried to hand it back. "I can't accept this. It's much too expensive a gift, and I know you just changed jobs…"

He pushed the camera back toward her. "It wasn't that expensive. It was refurbished. With everything going digital, it was the only one I could find that used thirty-five millimeter film."

"Are you sure? Because this is a beauty."

"I'm sure. I hope you'll think of me whenever you use it." He smiled.

"I think of you a lot already." She leaned forward, set the camera on the coffee table, then moved over and gave him a quick peck. "Nick Wolfensen, you're full of surprises."

He smoothed her hair down her back. "Nice ones, I hope."

"Definitely." She leaned in and kissed him again, only this time it wasn't a peck. She opened her mouth, inviting him to deepen the kiss if he wanted to. His tongue met hers and stroked. He pulled her closer and had to discipline himself not to squeeze her too hard.

I can't wait any longer.

He jumped up, grasping her around the waist, and she squealed as he lifted her off the floor. When he transferred her to the lounger, she giggled. Using that as his go-ahead signal, he lowered her until she was lying down, and then he aligned his body alongside, facing her.

Lying next to each other felt so right. Just like he'd pictured it in his fantasies—even though his daydreams involved a lot less clothing.

"Nick, did you give me the camera just to get into my pants?"

He feigned shock. "Hell, no. Of course if you want me to, I won't fight about it."

Laughing, she poked him in the ribs. "No, I didn't think you would."

He reached over and cupped the back of her head, then drew her close and kissed her tenderly. The kiss continued and deepened. Nick rolled her on top of him so he could access all of her. He slid his palm over the dip in her lower back, waiting to see if she'd stop him.

When he reached her ass cheek and gave it a squeeze, her response was to push her bum farther into his hand, then thrust her pelvis forward and wiggle against his erection. Triumphant, he broke the kiss just long enough to whisper, "You've already seen me naked. I'd love to get some of these clothes off." He tugged her top button free. "After all, it's only fair."

She laughed. "That's right. I still can't believe you were going to grease yourself up to fit through a basement window." Becoming a bit more somber, she asked, "Was it the place where Katie was being held?"

"Yes." *Uh-oh.* "But, getting back to the subject at hand…" He popped another button on her white blouse. Then another and another. Soon he had the whole shirt unbuttoned, so he peeled it back.

His breath caught. Even covered in the white lace bra, her breasts looked like they would provide a generous handful. He cupped the one closest to him and tested its weight. "You're absolutely beautiful." Then he leaned over and took the nipple into his mouth, lace and all. He sucked while she moaned softly.

Chapter 8

BRANDEE WASN'T SURE WHAT TO DO. HOW FAR should she let Nick go? An expensive gift didn't mean anything—not really. She didn't ask him to buy it. Could she be sure he wasn't just trying to get into her pants?

Then again, did it matter? She wanted him as badly as he wanted her. Angie was off visiting her sister, so Brandee had the apartment to herself. Her roomie wasn't planning to return until the next day. This would be the perfect time *if* it was going to happen.

Wait! The conversation. We haven't had the conversation yet.

Brandee grasped Nick's jaw and broke the luscious suction he was lavishing on her breast. "Nick?"

He groaned.

"I—we…"

He looked into her eyes and smiled sadly. She was afraid she'd see anger or frustration there. Instead, he looked resigned—prepared to accept whatever she doled out. He probably thought she wanted to slow down. It made her admire him even more.

She smiled and splayed her fingers through his blond hair. "Do you have condoms with you?"

His eyes suddenly went from sad to hopeful. "I have one in my wallet."

In a way, one was better than a whole box. It meant

he was prepared for a moment like this but not expecting it. "I'm on the pill."

He grinned. "I've been tested for HIV and Hep C, but only because, as a cop, I came in contact with a junkie's blood. The test was negative. I'm clean."

"But what about all those one-night stands?"

"There weren't as many as you think. And I never went without protection."

"Oh. Whew." She worried her lip, wondering what to say next. He took the decision away when he stood and held his hand out to her.

I guess we're going to the bedroom. She rose and put her hand in his.

On the way to the hall, he gave her apron string a yank and the apron fell off. "Oops."

"Yeah, that was real accidental." She rolled her eyes.

He flashed his killer grin her way. "Which room is yours?"

"The door on the right."

He turned the knob and let her go in first. Relieved she had made her bed that morning, she did a quick inventory of the rest of the room. Clothes in hamper. Check. Carpet vacuumed. Check. Dusted headboard? Ugh. She always forgot to dust, and the dark wood showed every speck.

He didn't seem to notice or care. He set her down in the middle of the bed and removed her unbuttoned shirt. He reached for the button at the top of her black slacks, but she batted his hand away. "No fair. Your turn."

He grinned, then quickly pulled the polo shirt over his head and flung it to the floor. His chest was ripped—totally muscled, still slightly tanned even though summer had ended, and with a smattering of golden chest hair in the shape of a V, he looked like a mighty Viking.

"Now it's your turn again," he said.

Why on earth was she worried about a little dust? There was only one thing on Nick Wolfensen's mind, and it was pretty easy to tell what that was. His hungry stare left no doubt.

She unbuttoned her skirt and opened the zipper. She wished she had a tan, but her fair skin with light reddish-brown freckles was all she had to offer.

Apparently she was taking too long, because as soon as she had wriggled the waistband over her hips, he grasped the fabric and pulled off her skirt the rest of the way.

"You're beautiful, Brandee."

Nick had probably wanted to seduce her for months. She was glad she made him wait until he promised to stick around. He unfastened his own jeans and stepped out of them. From the impressive bulge under his boxer briefs, she knew she was in for a hell of a ride. He didn't reveal all the goods, though. He crawled in beside her on the bed and gave her a long, languorous kiss.

Their hands traveled all over each other. Caressing, fondling, learning each other's shapes and texture. The warmth of his flesh seeped into her, and she heated quickly.

Their movements became more frantic. He reached behind her and popped her bra clasp. Brandee wrestled off the item as if it were a straitjacket. She divested him of his underwear and took a moment to appreciate what she found. If a man's cock could be beautiful, then his was gorgeous. Erect and proud with an impressive length and girth.

He tugged off her panties, and finally, they lay skin to skin. Face to face. Nick found Brandee's hand and brought it to his lips. He kissed her fingers as he gazed into her eyes.

"I know it's soon, but I want you to know a woman's never made me feel like this. I think I'm falling for you."

His admission stunned her. Sure, her feelings for him had been steadily deepening, but she hadn't thought they would be reciprocated that quickly. She thought she'd have to keep her secret under wraps for a while until he caught up. That was usually how it went with men, right?

He stroked her cheek. "You don't have to say anything. I can see I surprised you."

"No, it's not that…it's just that…well, yeah. It's that. I'm surprised." She grinned. "Pleasantly, though."

He smiled and kissed her again.

"What is it you like about me?" she asked.

"Everything." He gave her a peck on her pert nose.

"Everything? You don't know everything about me yet. I could be hiding some horrible secret."

"Are you?"

"No."

"Then why question how I feel?"

"It's just that we haven't been together that long."

He took a deep breath. "I'm a man of few words, but let me try. There's a lot I like about you. I like your easy smile. That tells me you're a happy person." He gave her a kiss on the corner of her mouth. "I like how you make up your own expressions. That tells me you're creative." He kissed her forehead.

"I like your grace and how you can stand up for

yourself without losing it. That tells me you're secure."
He kissed her throat. "I like how you're not afraid of
people who are a little different. That tells me you have
an open mind." He kissed her nose. "But mostly, I like
how happy I feel when I'm with you." He kissed her
mouth and didn't pull away until she kissed him back.

The kiss deepened. Their tongues met and swirled.
He cupped her breast and stroked her nipple with his
thumb. Glorious sensations spread from her breast to her
womb and radiated out.

Before long, she was on fire and the only thing she
craved was Nick between her damp thighs, pounding
into her.

"Oh, God. I need you." She hadn't meant to say that.
It sounded so—needy. *Ick.*

Apparently he didn't mind. He whispered, "You have
me." Then he rolled her onto her back and positioned
himself between her legs.

Kneeling, he ran his hands up and down her thighs.
"You're so beautiful."

Before she could think of anything else to say, he
lifted her legs over his shoulders and kissed the inside
of one thigh, then the other. His kisses came closer and
closer to her apex. "Nick…"

He inhaled and something like a growl emanated from
his throat. His tongue lapped her in long, slow strokes.

She gasped.

Incredible sensations overwhelmed her and spread
throughout her body. His tongue rasped back and forth
against her clit at warp speed. All she could do was
grip the sheets and hang on. Wave after wave of luscious pleasure rolled over her until it all spiraled and

the tension seemed unbearable. At last, it broke and she came apart, screaming his name.

Nick held on fast and continued his wicked onslaught to her senses until her legs were quivering and she had to beg him to stop. She felt a sob in the back of her throat but held it in.

When she could finally speak again, she rasped, "Holy moly…" and panted heavily. "I've never felt… anything like that."

He brushed her damp hair away from her forehead. "It's all for you, sweetheart—for as long as you can stand it."

"I can't stand at all. I'm sure of that. I wouldn't even try."

He chuckled.

Even though she deliberately misinterpreted what he meant by "stand," he didn't correct her. That was something her ex-boyfriend did that drove her nuts. Just to have the freedom to say whatever nonsense she wanted to say was a relief. As soon as she had semi-recovered, she asked, "Aren't you going in for the kill?"

He raised his eyebrows. "That's an interesting way to put it—but no. I'm not."

Brandee couldn't believe her ears. She rolled up onto her elbow, facing him. "What? Why not?"

"Only one condom, remember? I'd rather make it last as long as possible."

Does that mean he intends to go for another round? Or two? Or three? "Nick, I don't think I can handle much more."

"I'll give you time to rest. Hey, how about if you

show me how your new camera works? Maybe I can take some pictures of you all mussed and glowing."

She laughed. "Yeah, like I'd let you do that."

"Why not? You don't have to be nude or anything. Only you and I will know why you have that Mona Lisa smile on your face." He waggled his eyebrows.

"Why don't I take a few pictures of you instead?"

He ran a hand over her backside. The warmth felt good. Her slight sheen of sweat was beginning to cool her off.

"I'd have no problem with it, except that my new job means I should keep as low a profile as possible."

"Oh well. It would have been a nice idea. Maybe on my next day off we can take some pictures of the city."

"You have a car, right? Maybe we could get out of the city altogether. We could go to Cape Cod…"

"My car is apt to break down before we hit the southeast expressway. There's plenty to take pictures of around this area, though. All the gorgeous architecture, for instance."

"Are you into architecture?"

"Not per se. I just admire anything well crafted." She looked him up and down. "You, for instance."

He let out a loud bark of a laugh. "Smooth."

"I learned it from the master."

"Oh, now you're calling me master? I like the sound of that."

She shoved his shoulder. "As if…"

She was enjoying their banter but continued to feel unsure about leaving him unsatisfied. He rolled up onto the edge of the bed and pulled on his boxer briefs. "Do you have anything to eat? I'm starved."

"Not a lot. I mostly eat salads. Do you like salad?" She rolled out of bed and padded over to her closet for her robe.

"Ugh, you're not a vegetarian, are you?"

"No, but what if I was?" She fastened her robe and strolled over to him. "I hear it's a very healthy way to live."

"Darling, that's a deal-breaker."

Her jaw dropped. "Seriously?"

He laughed and pulled her into his embrace. "No, I was kidding. We'd just have to eat out a lot. I'm a big-time carnivore. I could order a steak and you could order a salad."

She ran her fingers through his hair. "I don't *only* eat salads, you know."

"So you'd go to a steakhouse with me?"

She wrapped her arms around his trim waist. "Of course…as long as you're paying."

He laughed. "Don't worry. I know you need your waitressing tips. Besides, I'd never let a woman pay. What kind of cheapskate would I be if I did that?"

She chuckled. "I need my tips all right. I'm trying to make a career in photography, and it takes time and money to get established. It's a very competitive field, but I have my heart set on it."

"I know."

"Is that why you've always been a generous tipper?"

"Well, that and I kind of had a crush on the pretty red-haired cocktail waitress."

"Ah, I see. Well, for that I'll find some eggs or something."

—∞—

"Ruxandra, you destroyed my bar and tried to skewer one of my waitresses. Why should I take you back?" Anthony demanded.

Ruxandra squirmed on the bench next to him. They sat under one of the old trees in the Public Garden. She was still wearing her catsuit, which Anthony had to admit was kind of turning him on. The lamplight glimmered off her light blond hair, almost making her look like the innocent he'd first met and fallen in love *with*.

He knew better now. He thought he had saved her from the clutches of the evil Marquis de Sade. It wasn't until months later he learned she'd gone to the nobleman's castle willingly. After the marquis had left her for dead, Anthony turned her to save her.

Her head was bowed and her fingers laced in her lap. She couldn't have looked more contrite. Maybe he could suggest an acting career in New York or Hollywood and get her out of his hair that way.

"We had something special." She looked up at him, and red tears shimmered in the corners of her eyes.

"Don't cry." He took a deep breath and tried to steel his resolve. "Look, I'm here, aren't I? You said you wanted to talk. So, talk."

"I love you, Anthony. I've always loved you." She shifted so she faced him squarely. "Three hundred years ago when I was just a simple farm girl turned by an evil vampire to be his sex slave, you freed me from that awful castle. You showed me the world and all I had been missing. You opened my eyes."

"And now that you know what's out there, why don't you pursue something that interests you?"

"Because *you* interest me. You're all I want. Besides,

when we're together, we can feed off each other and skip that nasty butcher-shop crap you insist vampires drink if they don't have a thrall."

"It doesn't sound like you share my values. You certainly don't respect my property or my business or what I'm trying to accomplish, creating a safe place for paranormals to congregate."

"Oh, piddly poo. Yes I do."

He frowned. *You have a strange way of showing it.*

She crossed her arms and stuck out her lower lip. Her pout used to wrap him around her little finger. No more. He wouldn't fall for it again. He knew there *had* to be more to a good relationship than lust. He'd witnessed it in other couples, so why couldn't he find that? Oh, yeah. A jealous ex-lover named Ruxandra kept getting in the way.

He rose. "Well, if that's all you have to say…"

She sprang to her feet and grasped his wrists. "No. There's more. Much more. Please hear me out."

"This better not take all night. I have a bar to repair." Her eyes begged him to listen. He sighed. "Fine. Get on with it."

She sat and tried to pull him down onto the bench beside her. She wasn't strong enough to make him, but he doubted she'd let go or finish their conversation unless he sat down. So he did.

"I'm sorry. More than anything, that's what I wanted to say. I was just so jealous when it looked like you cared more about one of your waitresses than me."

"Am I supposed to read your mind?"

"Some vampires can read each other's minds. Why can't we?"

He shrugged. He suspected he knew the answer but wasn't about to tell her while she was in this agitated state. Legend had it when a vampire found his "beloved" they could communicate telepathically. Anthony was relieved the two of them didn't meet the criterion.

"Ruxandra. We had fun. In the beginning, we had a lot of fun. But things haven't been fun for a long time."

"That's what you want? Fun? I can be fun."

I doubt it. It's a good thing they couldn't read each other's thoughts. Some of the things that ran through his brain would enrage Ruxandra—even more. Then she was speaking again and he had to drag his mind back.

"Honey, lover...can we try again? Just one more time." She ran a seductive finger up his suit jacket sleeve. "I promise I'll be good."

Despite everything, it was a tempting offer. She was right about one thing. Feeding from each other was beyond compare, especially when they combined it with uninhibited, wild, cathartic sex. It had been the best thing about their relationship. But was that enough?

Her eyes widened as if she couldn't believe he was actually considering it. He could barely believe it himself. Still, to save his business and protect his employees, it might be worth a shot. It would be a temporary fix at best, but right now a truce sounded good.

"*If* I give you another chance, and I'm not saying I will, how can I know you'll keep your promise?"

"What promise? The one to be good?"

"The detailed one you're going to make, *if* I take you back."

She gasped. "You will? I mean, you might? I'll

promise you anything. And I'll mean it. I'll write it in blood, or whatever you want."

"I'm not worried that you'll agree to my conditions. I need to *know* you'll honor any pact we make."

She crossed her heart. "I will. I swear."

He hesitated. There really was no guarantee, but if he made her think her behavior going forward made a difference, perhaps he could make the necessary repairs and keep his bar open. "In that case, I'll consider it. That's not a yes or no, you understand. It all depends on you and your future behavior."

"Of course. I'll do whatever it takes to earn back your trust. You'll see."

"In that case, I'll mull it over and get back to you." *I must be out of my mind.*

Chapter 9

BRANDEE HAD WHIPPED UP SOME SCRAMBLED EGGS, but the whole time, Nick was nibbling on her ear and making suggestive remarks. He wanted to get her back into bed in the worst way, but he'd had to fight his animalistic nature and force himself out of bed so he didn't just flip her over and take her savagely.

He should have known one condom wouldn't do it when the two of them finally gave in to their desire. It was more than just physical need. Nick suspected it was love. He thought about her all the time. He wanted to make her happy, and it killed him to think of ever losing her. If he was right—if she was his mate—it was a love that would never end.

He didn't want to scare her, so he had employed every measure of self-control he could think of to hold his animal nature in check. He mentally recited baseball statistics, counted to one thousand backward, and repeated the police officer oath of honor one hundred times. Too bad there wasn't a boyfriend oath of honor. That's what he really needed right now.

"Thanks for the early breakfast, sweetheart."

"It was no trouble. I'm glad you told me you were hungry."

"I'm still hungry, but not for food."

Her eyes lit up. "You mean you're fortified enough for round two?"

"Oh, yeah." He picked her up and carried her over his shoulder to the bedroom while she laughed and grasped him around his torso.

As soon as he set her on her feet, he peeled off her robe and let it slip to the floor. "Damn, you're incredible."

She blushed. Redheads were prone to it, but she seemed to redden every time he gave her a compliment.

"So are you." She dropped to her knees, carefully pulled his underwear out and over his erect cock, then yanked down his boxer briefs.

He stepped out of them, lifted her, and tossed her onto the bed. She squealed and laughed as she bounced on the mattress.

He caught himself grinning. He hadn't smiled like this in ages. He could only hope she had let go of those gaps in her memory from the night of their abduction.

He lay down beside her and took in her scent. Musk and some flowery fragrance. The beast in him wanted to pounce, nip, and nuzzle. Maybe someday.

She licked her lips. A quick, nervous movement that caused his cock to swell even more in anticipation. His gaze slipped down her body. She had perfect breasts. Not too large or too small. Just right for his hands and mouth. Her waist was trim and her hips full, giving her beautiful curves. She took his breath away.

She reached out and stroked his jaw. "It used to make me mad that you were so unbelievably gorgeous."

Surprised, he muttered, "Huh?"

"I didn't want to fall for you. I thought you were one of those guys who considered himself God's gift to women. I never imagined you'd be so…different."

"I'm actually sort of on the shy side. I may have over-compensated a bit."

She laughed. "A bit?"

"Those days are over, Brandee." His gaze dropped to her lips. Full. Soft. *So kissable*. He leaned over and pressed his mouth to hers. His tongue slid past her lips and swept inside.

She let out a little moan and met his tongue.

He kissed her like he had a right to plunder her mouth. She wrapped her arms around his shoulders and hung on, as if for dear life.

Her mouth was locked to his. *So hot*.

His hands slid over her curves, cupping her breasts and teasing her nipples. *Touching her soft skin feels so good. So unbelievably good*. And all the while, he kept kissing her, stroking her with his tongue, seducing her.

He cupped her ass and dragged her against his arousal so she could see what she did to him. Her hips rocked against him.

He tore his lips from hers and groaned. Then he nibbled the column of her neck. "You taste so good."

"So do you," she whispered. He caught a glimpse of her bedroom eyes. "I want to taste you—everywhere."

Whoa. Did she mean *that?* He wouldn't be able to control himself if she so much as licked him down there. He didn't dare lose it. He already felt the instinct to mark her tugging at his heart, and his canine teeth ached to come out.

"Not today, sweetheart. There's plenty of time for that. Right now I'm holding on by a thread. I want our first time together to be, well, *together*."

"But it's your turn."

"I'm not keeping score, and I don't want you to, either." He moved down slightly and sucked her nipple into his mouth.

She arched and moaned. She was so responsive. So sensitive. He could make love to her for days, but he didn't want to wear her out. He had to remind himself that she didn't have the same stamina he did.

Her soft body pressed against him. Her musky scent surrounded his nose, and his cock stiffened painfully.

"I want you," she whispered.

He didn't say a word. He couldn't. He simply grabbed the condom from her nightstand and ripped open the packet.

"Here, let me." Brandee reached for the condom.

If she stroked him before rolling it on, he'd come all over her. "I've got it," he said, almost shaking as he covered himself.

Brandee blinked her gorgeous blue eyes and stared.

"Lie back."

She did as he asked and spread her legs wide.

He took a deep breath and forced himself to go slow. He kneeled and positioned himself at her opening. He wanted to slam into her body and just take her. Instead he entered a couple of inches and paused. "Are you all right, sweetheart?"

"I'm fine."

He pushed in another inch.

"Nick, you don't have to treat me like I'm made of glass."

If only she knew. He wanted her so badly his body ached. He kissed her, drinking in her sweetness as he pushed in farther. At last he was fully seated.

With effort, Nick pulled his mouth from hers and began the age-old rhythm of lovemaking. She met his thrusts with her own. They stared into each other's eyes as they mated for the first time.

"God, that feels so good," she said, breathlessly.

Her hot channel felt so right around him. He thrust a little harder. A little faster. *So close…* He gritted his teeth and managed to hold himself back.

She was moaning and he knew she was close. He ground against her, hoping to drive her over the edge with him.

At last, she shuddered and cried out—then screamed. Her inner muscles squeezed his cock and he exploded. His climax ripped through him hard and fast. He could have sworn he saw stars—or fireworks. He rode the wave of pleasure to the very last aftershock.

"My God," he croaked.

Eyes closed, Brandee was panting hard.

"Are you all right, sweetheart?" he asked.

She opened her eyes and smiled. "I've never been better."

They were still basking in the afterglow when someone knocked on the apartment door.

Oh, no. My screams must have alarmed the Balogs. Brandee rolled out of bed and grabbed her robe off the floor. Nick snatched up his clothes and strode to the bathroom.

The knocking grew louder and more insistent.

"Just a minute," she called out.

When she finally threw open the door, Mrs. Balog stood there wearing a robe, slippers, curlers, and a nasty frown.

"Mrs. Balog, what can I do for you?"

"You can make less noise," she said crossly. "I couldn't hear my TV show over the screaming."

"Oh, I'm sorry." *Nice of you to be worried about me.*

Nick, now dressed, rounded the corner. "Is everything all right out here?"

Mrs. Balog sniffed the air and muttered something under her breath.

Brandee rested a hand on her hip. "I said I was sorry. Besides, you folks aren't exactly quiet, either. I hear all kinds of weird noises coming from upstairs."

Mrs. Balog bit her lip.

"Like?" Nick asked.

"Like moaning and howling," Brandee said.

Nick seemed startled. "Howling? Mrs. Balog, is it the kind of howling that comes from a human, or…"

Mrs. Balog muttered something in another language and fled up the stairs.

"That was weird," Brandee said as she closed the door. "What do you supposed she said?"

"I don't know."

Brandee had the feeling he wasn't telling her everything—again.

"What is it, Nick? What's bothering you?"

"Tell me exactly what the noises upstairs sound like."

"Like I said. Howling. Sometimes moaning and banging. Sometimes growling. Sometimes grunting. But it's an old building. Angie and I figured part of the noise was the wind, and part was the old furnace or air in the pipes. Why? What are you thinking?"

He hesitated.

"What aren't you telling me, Nick? I thought I could trust you to tell me the truth from now on."

He placed his hands on her shoulders. "Nothing. It's nothing. I just wondered if they had an illegal animal up there or something. I just want to be sure you're safe."

"You're not going to turn into one of those overprotective boyfriends, are you? Because I've been taking care of myself for quite a while. I don't need a hovering—"

"Look. I need to be sure you and Angie are safe here. I know how dangerous this city can be. Remember, I was a cop for a long time. You'd be surprised about the kind of so-called pets some crackpots keep in their apartments. If anything happened to you…"

She sighed and flopped down on her sofa. "Okay. I get it. I know the Balogs are strange, but I doubt they have tigers or wolves up there." She laughed. Then she thought she saw something change in Nick's expression, as if she'd caused him alarm. "Oh, come on. I was just kidding. Tigers don't moan."

"What kind of moaning is it?" Nick sat beside her. "Does it sound like sexual moans?"

"Ha. No way. Sometimes it sounds like my clunker of a car trying to turn over and failing, and sometimes there's almost a creepy quality to it."

"Like ghosts?"

"You don't believe in things like that, do you?"

He shrugged. "Why not?"

She leaned back and took a good look at him. "You were a cop. Don't cops go after facts and try to dismiss things that aren't real?"

"Who are we to say what's real?"

Nick was a puzzle. Just when she thought she had him figured out, he said or did something she didn't expect.

"Do you know anyone whose place is haunted?"

Nick laughed. "My brother used to live in an old building a few blocks down Beacon Street. He was convinced they had a ghost. Man, the stories he told me." Suddenly he shut his mouth so hard she heard his teeth click.

"What stories?"

"Never mind. I'm sure they were exaggerated."

"Tell me, Nick. Exaggerated or not, you promised to be straight with me from now on."

His brow furrowed, then he took a deep breath and said, "The ghost was protective of his old apartment. He played pranks on potential renters until he scared them off."

She looked at him askance. "Oh? What kind of pranks?"

Nick shifted, looking uncomfortable. "Nothing *really* dangerous…just unsettling."

If anyone was feeling unsettled at the moment, it was Brandee. She had always wondered why only two of the three floors above the bar were occupied. "Give me an example."

"Oh, he'd flip the lights or the stove on and off. He shifted things out of place a few times…."

Her jaw dropped. "He could move things? Turn on the stove? The electricity? What else?"

"He liked to unplug the TV, start the ceiling fan, or short out the—you know what? Never mind. It's probably just the Balogs doing the nasty, and they don't want anyone to know."

"I guess…" Brandee scratched her head. "Maybe you can stay over some night and hear it for yourself—that is if you're not a heavy sleeper."

Nick massaged her neck and gave her a sly smile. "I can think of an activity to occupy the time and keep us awake."

"I'll bet you're talking about a ten-thousand-piece puzzle, aren't you?"

"Not even close."

"Didn't really think so."

Chapter 10

THE FOLLOWING EVENING, NICK ASKED TO SPEAK to Anthony in his office. Brandee was busy waiting on a table full of rowdy college kids. Thankfully, Ruxandra was nowhere to be seen.

Nick needed to back off and let Brandee take care of herself when she wasn't in any immediate danger. He didn't want her to accuse him of smothering her again. It made him nervous that his mate was human and mortal. It would have been more convenient if he'd fallen for another werewolf, but he hadn't. His heart and soul belonged to Brandee.

As long as she was dealing with mere humans or the paranormal patrons who believed in the peaceful goal of the bar, she'd be fine. So when Anthony came out to get him, Nick sent her a jaunty wave and followed his friend into his office. He closed the door behind himself and sat on the comfortable couch along the opposite wall.

"How's it going?" Anthony asked as he seated himself behind his desk.

"Things have been kind of crazy, but I still want to find out what those goons who kidnapped us had to say when you mesmerized them."

"You were right. They were doing someone else's dirty work. But they couldn't tell me who hired them. It was all arranged by phone. The thugs are from New York.

They said they're Yankees fans and didn't much care what happened to Red Sox Nation. That's all I know."

Nick scratched his chin. "Didn't care what happened to Boston…and they kidnapped a fire mage. That doesn't bode well for the city."

"But because of you, they didn't get away with it."

"I still want to know who hired them and exactly what he had planned. Did you kill the perps?"

"No. I just drained them a little bit and compelled them to go back to New York and never return."

"Okay." *I guess that lead is a dead end. Damn.* "There's something else. I was wondering if you know anything about this building's history."

Anthony leaned back in his chair and interlocked his fingers behind his head. "I know it was built in the early nineteenth century."

"Did anyone die in here?"

"Are you concerned about a spirit?"

"I wouldn't say concerned—yet."

"Sadie said something about feeling a presence. That was a few months ago. She didn't mention anything malevolent, so I didn't think much about it."

"So, it's possible."

"In these two-hundred-year-old buildings, I'd say it's almost probable. But why do you care?"

"Brandee said she hears strange noises sometimes. Some kind of howling or moaning that sounds more supernatural than human or animal."

Anthony's brow wrinkled. "I haven't heard anything like that."

"Did you ever live here?"

"When I first bought the place. I was probably the

only being who could sleep through the renovations during the day—but that's death-sleep for you."

Nick chuckled. "I can see that. What about the Balogs? Didn't they live here before you moved in and renovated?"

"Yeah, I inherited them with the building, and I didn't have the heart to turn them out."

"But you do charge them rent, don't you?"

"Of course. In a way, they're the perfect tenants. They pay their rent right on time, don't want anything in their place updated, and show no signs of wanting to move."

"How do they make their money?"

Anthony shrugged. "Don't know. As long as they give me good checks and aren't running a meth lab, I don't especially care."

Nick paused, unsure of his next question. "I can trust you to keep anything I say confidential, right?"

"Sure. What's on your mind?"

"The Supernatural Council. Ever heard of it?"

"I've heard rumors about its existence, but that's all. Some say it's made up of gods and goddesses who punish paranormals who make them angry. I've never encountered anyone who has any firsthand knowledge."

"Well, now you have."

Anthony's brows shot up. "You met them?"

"Yeah, but if you tell anyone, I'll deny it. I'm not supposed to tell a soul."

"Technically, I don't have a soul."

"Hey, that's right. So I'm in the clear," Nick said.

Anthony leaned forward. "Who are they? What are they like?"

Nick worried his upper lip. "You'll think I'm ready for the funny farm."

Anthony waved away his concern. "I know you, Nick. You're one of the most rational werewolves around. Just tell me."

Nick had to tell someone or he'd burst. Ordinarily he'd tell his twin, but in this case it might be better not to.

Anthony sighed. "If you'd rather not, I'll understand, but I swear on my own grave I'll never tell a soul—or the soulless, even."

Okay, here goes. "The Council is run by Mother Nature, and she calls it GAIA. It stands for Gods And Immortals Association. They're housed in a high rise on State Street. Now, *this* is where things are going to sound weird."

Anthony raised his eyebrows. "Which building?"

"It doesn't matter. You can't access the Council headquarters from the building's elevator. I'm not even sure how I got there or exactly where it's located. The outside architecture doesn't match what I saw on the inside. They just spat me out there on State Street." Nick raked his fingers through his hair.

"What did they say?" Anthony asked.

"I was in deep shit for revealing my true nature to a human, especially getting caught on camera. Mother Nature confiscated the camera, so she bailed me out there, but she made it clear that if I ever screw up like that again, she'll have my hide."

"Fuck."

"Exactly. I told her that you wiped Brandee's memory, but there were a few things I had to explain. I figured we should get our stories straight."

Anthony's jaw dropped. "You told them about me?"

"You were already on their radar. But they seemed glad that I went to you. They believed me when I said I trusted you."

"Whew!" Anthony wiped his brow. "That's a group I really don't want to piss off. I imagine gods must be pretty invincible.

"No shit."

"So what do I need to know?"

"Just that Brandee's mind was wiped of my shifting. She knows nothing about my being a werewolf. However, I had to fill her in on the kidnapping. Apparently the victim told her parents that Brandee helped her get through it, and they called to thank her."

"Christ. How did you explain to her that she forgot something like that?"

"I said the trauma must have made her blank it out. But I wonder if she'd believe that more if you lifted a few of her memory blocks about what happened. Then it would seem as if some of her memories are returning. That's usually how amnesia works isn't it?"

Anthony fiddled with a paperweight. "My power doesn't work like that. I can add new memories of things that really happened if you tell me exactly what you want her to know. But I don't want to spend any more time with Brandee than I have to—for her own sake."

Nick leaped to his feet. "You can't mean Ruxandra is still gunning for her."

"Not exactly."

"What are you going to do?"

"I'll just let Ruxandra hang around for a while and make her see I have no interest in any of my employees. Well, except for Claudia, but that's just between you and me. I'd never put Claudia in danger by pursuing her until Ruxandra is out of the way—permanently."

Nick whistled. "That's quite a gamble. I hope it works."

"It will…for now."

———

"I'm surprised everything got cleaned up so quickly," Kurt said. He and Tory grabbed a table in Brandee's station. "I thought for sure the window would be boarded up for a few days." Kurt leaned back in his chair and asked, "How are you holding up, kiddo?"

"I'm okay."

"So it looks like you're staying here?"

Brandee took her order pad from her apron pocket. "Anthony assured me Ruxandra won't be a problem. Besides, I really can't afford to quit."

Tory shook his head. "It's a damn shame he ever got involved with that psycho bitch in the first place. Do you really believe she won't bother you again?"

"She has no need to. She was jealous because, for some damn reason, she thought I was involved with Anthony. Nick told her we were dating, and she's noticed how protective he is. He's been hanging around a lot, keeping an eye on me. I'm not supposed to know that, though." She winked. "He's keeping a low profile."

Kurt glanced around the room. "He must be invisible. I don't see him anywhere."

"He's in Anthony's office. Probably threatening to have Ruxandra arrested if she tries anything again."

Tory snorted. "Good luck with that."

Just then, the door to Anthony's office opened and

Nick walked out. Simply laying eyes on him made her heart skip a beat.

"So, you and Nick, huh?" Tory sounded skeptical.

No more skeptical than Brandee would have been a couple weeks ago if she'd heard the infamous play-boy had suddenly become monogamous. She still had moments when she wondered if it was real. "I know, I know. You're probably going to tell me to be careful."

"Nope," Kurt said. "Because here he comes."

Nick placed a possessive arm around Brandee's waist. "Are these goons bothering you?"

She assumed he was just kidding. He was smirking at the guys when he said it, and then he sat down with them.

"Not at all. I was just about to take their orders."

"A Corona for me," Tory said. He glanced at the other two. "My doctor said I'm not getting enough vitamin C, and it comes with a lime."

They laughed.

"Hey, it's always a good idea to prevent colds." Kurt ordered one too.

"Would you get one for me too, sweetheart?" Nick asked.

"Vitamin C all around then." Brandee smirked as she made her way to Angie at the bar. When she caught her friend's attention, she ordered, "Three Coronas with limes."

Angie nodded.

As she waited, Phil, another semi-regular, asked, "Is Nick going to be your bodyguard from now on? Doesn't he have a job or something?"

Brandee spoke a little louder than usual because Phil was hard of hearing. "I imagine his workload is just light right now." She leaned closer to speak directly into his ear. "He's not my bodyguard."

"Could have fooled me."

Brandee thought about it and realized Nick hadn't mentioned taking any more cases. She hoped he wasn't turning them down just to keep an eye on her. *I'll ask him later. He'll probably be here after my shift.* That thought was both comforting and annoying.

A couple of hours later, Kurt and Tory had left, and Nick wanted to check out one thing. It would satisfy his curiosity and get him out of Brandee's hair. She was beginning to look at him as if she didn't appreciate his hanging around.

He slid into the booth opposite Sadie. She was shuffling her cards as usual.

"Can I ask you something? I don't need a reading—well, not exactly."

"Did you meet the one-drink minimum?"

"I nursed a beer for an hour or so. Does that count?"

She raised an eyebrow. "Barely. But since you're a friend of Anthony's, I'll allow it. What's on your mind?"

"Is this building haunted?"

"Yes," she said matter-of-factly and stopped shuffling. "Does that bother you?"

"Not unless the spirit is unfriendly. Do you know any details about the haunting?"

"Like?"

"Like who? How many? Why they're here?"

"I don't know any of that. He, she, or they have never given me any sign of wanting to make contact."

"What if he, she, or it doesn't know you're a psychic?"

"More likely he or she is shy and stays out of the bar when there are people here. Why are you interested in this, Nick? Are you concerned about Brandee?"

"Bingo."

"I don't think she's in any danger. I would have mentioned something to Anthony if I was worried."

Nick remembered Anthony telling him that Sadie *had* mentioned it to him. Maybe her nonchalant act was just that—an act.

"Sadie, if I can get you into Brandee's apartment when she and Angie are out, would you try to make contact and see what the story is? I'd feel better knowing everything is okay."

"What makes you think it isn't?"

Nick glanced over at Brandee. She seemed sufficiently busy and wasn't paying any attention to them. "Brandee said she hears moans, growls, banging…"

"Oh, dear. Is she sure it's not the Balogs?"

"What she described didn't sound human."

Sadie stared off in the distance for a few seconds.

"What's wrong?"

"I can't say for sure unless I make contact, but it doesn't sound like the spirit is hanging around because it's comfortable here."

"No, it doesn't."

Sadie began to wave Brandee over.

Nick pulled down her hand. "What are you doing?"

"I was going to schedule a time to go upstairs and check it out."

"No. I don't want to alarm her."

"Too late. She saw me wave to her."

"Then just order a drink. I'll pay for it if you don't say anything to her about ghost busting."

Brandee wove her way through the crowd to their table. "Hi there, Sadie. What can I do for you?"

"Nick generously offered to buy me a drink. I'll have the usual, please."

"You got it. Anything for you, Nick?"

"All I want is to see your beautiful smile."

Brandee rolled her eyes but couldn't suppress the blush invading her cheeks—or the smile.

Nick snapped his fingers. "Hey, I just thought of something."

Brandee tipped her head. "Yeah? What's that?"

"You mentioned you were having car trouble. I'm bored out of my mind just sitting around and waiting for my phone to ring. Why don't you let me take a look at it?"

"My car?"

"Yeah. I'm pretty good with older models. I thought about becoming a mechanic before I became a cop. I might be able to figure out what's wrong with it if I can hear the motor turn over. Why don't you bring me your keys along with Sadie's drink?"

"I, uh…I guess I could do that. It's not like I have to worry about you voiding the warranty."

He laughed and mentally congratulated himself when she went off to get her keys. She called out the order to Angie as she strode by and then entered the back room.

Sadie cast him a sidelong glance. "What are you thinking?"

"Her car keys are on the same ring as her apartment keys. If she doesn't take the time to separate them, I'll be able to let us in upstairs. We shouldn't go outside together, though. I'll take a look at her car while you finish your drink. Then you can meet me at her outer door. Do you know where it is?"

"Yes. It's the next door on the right."

"Correct. So, it's a plan?"

Sadie shrugged and resumed shuffling. "If you wish."

Nick was slightly puzzled by Sadie's reaction, but not enough to get into it. Brandee was returning with her keys even before getting Sadie's drink.

He rose when she approached. She dangled the keys over his open palm. "Here you go. Don't try to fix anything yet. Just let me know if there's something obviously wrong."

"Why not let me fix it if it's something simple? It seems a little silly not to."

She eyed him warily. "You're not going to spend any money on it, are you? Because I don't want you to. It's probably not worth fixing if it needs an expensive part."

He crossed his heart. "I promise not to buy any expensive parts for your hunk of junk vehicle. Which one is it and where are you parked?"

"It's the ancient red Corolla on Revere Street."

"Gotcha. I'll take a look and hopefully have an answer for you in a while." He strode out to the street, hoping he could diagnose the car's problem or sound semi-intelligent about it despite having little experience with cars. Even his cruiser had been taken care of by professionals. Maybe he could move it slightly to make it look like he'd driven it and she wouldn't be suspicious. Then he'd get back to her apartment door and wait for Sadie.

Who knows, maybe I'll even be able to fix the problem. Not just the car's, but the apartment's as well.

Chapter 11

AFTER THREE ATTEMPTS, NICK WAS ABLE TO START Brandee's vehicle. He'd poked around under the hood and finally decided the car was old and tired. Maybe it needed a new battery, but more than likely it needed to be junked. A dealer might give her a hundred bucks for it as a trade-in, but that was being optimistic. After waiting years for his true mate, he didn't want to lose her just because her car broke down in a dicey part of the city.

Nick waited outside Brandee's apartment with his grimy hands in his pockets. The mid-September evening was the first to feel like autumn. At last Sadie exited the bar, wearing her woolen South American poncho.

"Do you still want to invade the girls' privacy?" she asked.

He hesitated, but only for a second. "I need to know Brandee's not living with a poltergeist. You won't rat on me, will you?"

"I told you all my work is confidential. However, breaking and entering costs extra." She winked.

"Fine. Money doesn't matter if it reassures me that Brandee is safe." He opened the outside door. The two of them tromped up the narrow stairway to the second-floor apartment.

At the door, he chose the key he thought was the right one and tried it. The door opened easily. Too easily, in his opinion. He made a mental note to install a dead bolt for Brandee.

Sadie flipped on the light and glanced around the small but neat apartment. "Not bad for the area. I live in a one-bedroom closet. This living room must be about four hundred square feet. Are the bedrooms roomy?"

"I've only seen one, but it's tiny."

Sadie's lips curled up on one side.

"Oh, very clever," Nick said. "Yes, I've been in her bedroom."

She grinned. "Good."

Nick took a seat on the lounger part of the sectional and stretched out with his hands clasped behind his head. He couldn't help smiling when he thought about making out with Brandee on that couch. "Okay, Sadie. Do your thing."

Sadie closed her eyes. "Spirit, if you can hear me, give me a sign."

All remained quiet. Sadie wandered around the living room. "I can sense a presence." Addressing the spirit, she said, "I'd like to know if I can help you." Suddenly, she stopped and cupped her ear. "What was that?"

Nick swung his feet to the floor. "What? I didn't hear anything."

"Shhh! I wasn't talking to you, Nick."

He gripped the edge of the sofa and waited. Then he heard a noise too. It sounded like footsteps.

Suddenly the door swung open and Brandee appeared. Before he could say something, she looked up and shrieked.

Nick rose quickly. "Relax. It's just me and Sadie. We heard—"

Before he could finish his sentence, she threw a set of keys on the floor with a loud crash. "Angie" was spelled out in chunky silver metal. A large brown stain covered Brandee's blouse.

"Oh, my invasion of privacy! What the pluck are you doing in my apartment?"

"I was about to tell you." But what could he say? He didn't want to frighten her by mentioning ghosts. But what other explanation was there, besides a robbery or surprise party? *If only I had a cake and balloons.*

Thankfully, Sadie jumped in. "I was trying to see if there were any spirits present in your apartment. Nick said you described some otherworldly sounds, and I—"

Brandee jammed her hands onto her hips. "And you never thought to ask my permission? You just decided to come up here and look around? Un-freakin'-believable."

Nick tried to reach for her, but she stepped away. "I didn't want to scare you if it was nothing, sweetheart."

"Oh, it's *not* nothing," Brandee said. "You'd probably arrest someone who was in *your* apartment without permission."

"I, uh—well…"

"Give me my keys and get out. Right now. Both of you."

Sadie crossed to the door immediately, but Nick didn't move. He had to get Brandee to understand. The tenuous trust he had managed to reclaim couldn't withstand any more suspicion.

"Brandee, please let me explain. I had to be sure you didn't have a poltergeist or some kind of—"

She stomped her foot. "No, you didn't. You didn't have to poke around my home without my knowledge or permission. *You didn't.* Angie and I have lived here for a year. If the boogeyman was going to get me, wouldn't the spirit or poltergeist or whatever monster is under the bed have made a move by now?"

He opened his mouth to speak, but she shut him down with her continuing tirade.

"I don't know who you think you are. One minute you want nothing to do with relationships, and the next you're taking over my life."

"But—"

"But nothing! I said 'Get out' and I'm *not* going to say it again. Now hand over my damn keys. I have to change my blouse and get back to work. I'm not going into my bedroom until you're on the other side of this door. If you still refuse to leave, I'm calling the cops. Oh, and here's your damn camera." She picked it up off the side table and thrust it at him. He didn't want to take it, but she looked ready to throw it at him if he didn't.

Sadie grabbed Nick's arm and tugged. "Come on, Nick. Sometimes it's better to live to fight another day."

One more look at the murder in his girlfriend's eyes told him perhaps Sadie was right.

Nick handed Brandee's key ring to her. "We'll talk later." He followed Sadie out, and the door slammed behind them—hard.

After the shift from hell, Brandee flopped into the side chair. She didn't want to sit on the couch where she and Nick had almost—forget it. She had to forget Nick Wolfensen.

Sadie's presence is what really threw her. Ghosts? She couldn't see the two of them together in her apartment for any other reason. She needed to talk to someone, bad.

"Ange?" she called out.

Angie rounded the corner, wearing her pajama bottoms and a tank top. She was brushing her shiny blond hair one hundred strokes like she did every night. "Yeah?"

"Can you talk for a few minutes?"

Angie stopped brushing and lowered herself to the couch. "What's up?"

"I need a sympathetic ear."

"Sympathetic is my middle name."

Brandee smiled. "Well, Angie Sympathetic Tripp, what I have to tell you is going to sound weird."

Angie sighed. "Weird is my other middle name. Angie Sympathetic to Weird Shit Tripp. So, spill it."

"Remember when I ran up here to change my shirt during our shift?"

"Yeah, you had a collision with someone's rum and Coke. I remember."

"When I walked in, I caught Nick and Sadie sniffing around our living room."

Angie reared back. "Nick and Sadie? Wait, you gave Nick your keys, but I thought it was to look at your car."

"It was. But apparently he used them to let Sadie in so she could look for ghosts in our apartment."

Angie's jaw dropped. "What the… They were playing ghost busters? Here?"

"Yeah. Sadie said she sensed a presence, and Nick wanted her to check it out to be sure we were safe."

Angie glanced around the apartment. "Oh my God. Did they find anything?"

"I have no idea. I was so mad at them for being here without my permission that I kind of went ballistic and threw them out before they could tell me anything."

"Damn. I wish you'd at least waited to hear what Sadie found."

Brandee couldn't believe her roommate was more concerned with the possibility of unwanted ghosts in their apartment than the actuality of uninvited humans.

"Do you believe in ghosts, Ange?"

She shrugged. "I guess. Do you?"

Brandee gnawed on her fingernail. "I never really considered it until Nick brought up the subject. Mrs. Balog knocked on our door and told me and Nick to keep it down. I confronted her on the loud banging and grunting sounds that come from upstairs some nights."

"I always assumed they were the sounds an old building makes. I've learned to tune out the racket."

"Me too. But what if there's more to it?"

"Oh, crap. Now I'll be sleeping with one eye open."

"I'm sorry. That's exactly what I didn't want. I never thought you'd believe in ghosts. I'll talk to Sadie tomorrow."

"Maybe I should do it. If you went ballistic on her ass…"

Brandee chuckled. "Yeah, I kind of did. I'm still pissed at Nick. I imagine it was his idea, not Sadie's. I know he wants to look out for me, but he overstepped this time."

"Yeah. Sadie kind of goes where the work takes her." Angie resumed brushing her hair. "I can't imagine her coming up here on her own."

"Me neither. I know her nephew owns the building and everything, but I don't think she feels entitled to the run of the place."

Brandee kicked at the floor. "Yeah. I'm really disappointed. I was surprised when he wanted to do the boyfriend-girlfriend thing, but his definition of what that includes is drastically different from mine. He's way too possessive."

"Jeez. What are you going to do?"

Brandee hung her head. "I don't know. What would you do?"

Angie held up her hands and leaned away. "Oh no. No, no, no. You're not going to trick me into giving you relationship advice. I tried to warn you away from him. But when you didn't listen, I decided to keep my opinions to myself. It's all you from here on."

Brandee slumped. "Great. I was hoping you'd tell me to break up with him."

"Why?"

"Because I don't want to, but I think I probably should."

Angie rose. "I'll let you sleep on that. I'm off to bed so I can lie awake and listen to everything that goes bump in the night."

"Sorry." Brandee felt like the worst roommate ever.

Anthony slid into the booth across from Sadie the following night. He folded his hands and didn't say a word.

She stopped shuffling her cards. "Are you angry?"

"No. Should I be?"

"I hope not. I apologized to Brandee and Angie for invading their space without their knowledge. They both seemed to understand it was only to assure Nick of their safety."

"Yes, I spoke to Nick. Meanwhile, they spent a sleepless night, wondering what spirit or spirits might be haunting their apartment. Did you learn anything while you were there?"

"There's definitely something around, but I didn't have enough time to establish communication."

"Could you do it from down here?"

"Probably, after-hours. I think the entity avoids people. If anything, that should make the girls feel safer."

Anthony studied his clasped hands. "Okay, then. I'd like to ask you to stay after closing time tonight. Can you do that?"

Sadie's lips curled slightly. "Is there cash involved?"

"How about not pressing charges? Will that do?"

Sadie let out a big sigh. "All right."

Anthony laughed. "I love your entrepreneurial side, Sadie." And he did. His only known relative was an interesting mix of kooky and clever. What some might call *crazy like a fox*.

She returned to shuffling the cards. "How long should I stay if no one appears?"

Anthony scratched the eternal stubble on his chin. "I think you'd know better than I would how much time to give a shy spirit."

"I'll stay until just after midnight. The bar will have been empty for about an hour. That should be enough time."

"It's a full moon tonight. I'll stay with you to be sure you get home okay."

"It might be best if you stay in your office. I don't want anyone else around to spook the little bugger."

Anthony's eyebrows rose. "Little? Did you get the sense that it might be a child?"

Sadie's brows knit. "Not exactly. It was odd. The only thing I heard sounded like a cough, but from about waist high. I hope I can tell you more later."

"So do I." Anthony rose and strolled toward the bar. He waved over Angie and Brandee.

When the two of them stood close enough to speak in low tones, he said. "I'm going to have Sadie stay after closing. She'll make contact from down here. Hopefully, she'll be able to make whatever is hanging around move on."

Brandee placed a fist on her hip, "If she can talk to the spirit from down here, why did she have to go into our apartment last night?"

"She said it probably avoids people. Since she's never around when the bar is empty, she wouldn't have had the opportunity to make contact with whatever shy spirit could be here. That's another reason you girls should feel plenty safe."

Brandee and Angie stared at each other.

"Do you feel safe, yet, Ange?"

Angie lifted one finger to say, "just a sec," to a patron who was trying to get her attention. "I have to go, but let us know what she finds as soon as you can. I'll feel better when this spirit thing moves on or goes into the light, or whatever it is they do."

She scurried off, but Brandee was still looking at Anthony as if she had more questions.

"Have you heard from Nick?" she asked.

"Uh—yes, but I doubt he'll be in tonight."

"Coward," she muttered and strode off to pick up an order.

⚯

Nick had another case, and just in time too. He needed
something to focus on other than how hugely he had
screwed up with Brandee, and he was getting nowhere
on the identity of Katie's kidnapper. But tonight the
full moon would demand he shift. He only had time for
some basic research on the assignment before he met the
rest of the pack.

This new case was becoming an embarrassment to
the department. It should have been solved by now. He
didn't wonder why they'd finally come to him. It had the
stamp of *paranormal* all over it.

Banks were being robbed by seemingly invisible
perps. Captain Hunter had managed to get some camera
footage from one such heist to Nick.

Nick was scanning the footage over and over. Finally,
he slowed it way down. A faint blur appeared and Nick
thought he knew *what* he was after, but not who. A vampire could move so fast he'd be undetected by the naked
eye or cameras. It fit with the rest of the story too—except
in one important way. Vampires couldn't pull this off during the day, and these robberies occurred only when the
vault was opened. Someone was taking advantage of the
short time it took to load or unload the vault. Unmarked
cash—a few banded stacks at a time—seemed to disappear
unnoticed until the next time the books were reconciled.

Shit. He couldn't slow the footage enough to see
a body or face. Stopping it on a blur only showed a
dull wash of gray. Nick's mind wandered to Brandee.
How she'd worn gray that first night she followed him.
Most of her red hair had been covered by a hoodie. The
memory had nothing to do with the case, but *everything*
reminded him of Brandee.

He glanced at his watch. He had just enough time to hop the train to Newton and meet up with the pack before the full moon. He usually arrived early to visit with his brother and sister-in-law before heading to the wooded area behind the school where the pack shifted. But tonight he'd have to go straight there.

After closing and putting away his computer, Nick's mind drifted back to Brandee. Again. It was probably a good thing he had no time to chat with his brother before the shift. Now he wouldn't have to tell him about finding his true mate, only to screw up royally. He'd wait until he'd repaired things with Brandee. A little voice in the back of his mind said, *If you can patch things up*.

He squashed that thought. He *had to* fix this. Roses, candy, holding a boom box playing a romantic song under her window…he'd do whatever. Hell, if he had to confess all his secrets—including his paranormal identity—to earn back her trust, he'd do it. Mother Nature and the Council be damned. But did he dare take the chance of scaring Brandee to death? He was almost positive she was his one true mate. No one had ever affected him the way she did…and he doubted anyone ever would.

―――

Brandee had managed to talk Sadie into letting her stay in the bar after-hours to watch her communicate with the ghost. Sure, the psychic *seemed* trustworthy, but Brandee wanted to hear the interaction for herself. Sadie could make up anything the next day.

Sadie had insisted that Brandee stay behind the bar. She said, with Anthony in his office and another person around, she wasn't sure the spirit would approach

her. With that in mind, Brandee brought a book with
her and squatted on a footstool behind the bar, out of
sight of any ghost that might appear. It was the best she
could do to be invisible.

The bar had closed at eleven as usual. The staff
had done their rudimentary cleanup. Placing chairs on
top of wiped tables, sweeping the floor, taking out the
trash, and then everyone departed. It wasn't unusual
for Anthony to stay in his office a little longer, but
he always left by eleven thirty or eleven forty-five at
the latest.

Brandee didn't know why he refused to stay open
past midnight like other bars in the city, but she wasn't
about to question her easy hours.

She was beginning to think nothing was going to
happen. It was nearly midnight and Sadie had tried a
couple times to make contact without success.

Then at the stroke of midnight someone spoke.
It was a voice Brandee had never heard before—
definitely not Sadie or Anthony. The strange voice
sounded kind of like someone who had just inhaled a
lungful of helium.

Sadie responded cordially. She didn't sound surprised
or upset, so chances were it wasn't a burglar.

"You'll have to leave—we won't work around you,"
the odd voice said.

"I'm honored that you showed up despite my presence
and that you're allowing me to talk to you," Sadie said.

"Yeah, well, don't get used to it," another voice said.
He also sounded like he'd had a shot of helium—or maybe
like a Munchkin—but the voice was definitely male.

"We wouldn't have shown ourselves, but this place is

a mess. If we don't start soon, it'll take all night to clean it." There was a tsk-tsk noise.

Brandee had an overwhelming desire to peek over the bar. What would she see? Would she see anything at all? Spirits didn't have bodies, did they? Yet one of them had said they "showed themselves." And they mentioned cleaning… What did that mean?

Her curiosity won out. She lifted her head slowly and gazed at Sadie. At first she saw nothing, then she noticed Sadie looking down. Brandee lifted her head a little higher. A sight she never expected to see in a million years met her eyes.

Two little men—the smallest people she could ever imagine—only about a foot high but perfectly proportioned from the back. How did they get in? Did they hide in small spaces like the air ducts during the day and only come out at night when they wouldn't be stared at? Did Anthony hire a tiny cleaning crew to get into the tight spots the staff missed?

They wore green and blue suits and felt hats. The hats nearly covered their hair, but the strands peeking out beneath their brims appeared white.

Suddenly Sadie looked up and spotted her. She shot her a disapproving frown and Brandee ducked down.

"Who else is here?" demanded one of them.

Sadie didn't answer. Brandee heard tiny footsteps running toward her. *Oh, crap.* One of them jumped up on the bar and peeked over. The other appeared in the space beneath the bar where it lifted for the staff to come in and out.

Brandee glanced from one face to the other.

These were no midgets. They had completely black eyes and only holes for noses over fluffy white beards.

Suddenly she couldn't breathe. Were they a product of genetic experimentation gone wrong? Some kind of aliens?

Her vision clouded and her head swam. She knew what was happening but had no desire to stop the sweet oblivion of a good faint. The last thing she remembered was the sensation of her body slumping against the bar.

Chapter 12

"I CAN'T DO THAT TO HER MUCH MORE."

Brandee's sense of hearing returned first. Anthony and Sadie seemed to be having a heated discussion.

"Why not, Anthony?"

"Because she'll wind up with Alzheimer's."

Brandee's eyes popped open. She was in Anthony's office, lying down on his couch. "Who's going to give me Alzheimer's?" she demanded.

Anthony and Sadie whirled toward her and stared. Brandee struggled to sit up, and Anthony was beside her in an instant.

"How much did you hear?"

"You said you couldn't do something to me anymore or I'd get Alzheimer's. What the fudge is up with that? You can't *give* someone Alzheimer's. And where are those weird little guys?"

Anthony patted her hand. "I'm sorry you heard that, Brandee. I wasn't serious about giving you Alzheimer's. I can't really do that. I'm a hypnotist and thought it might be easier for you if I erased your memory of the brownies."

"The Brownies? Why? It wasn't that bad. I even stuck with it and became a Girl Scout."

Sadie tittered. "The 'weird little guys' you saw are called brownies, dear. We didn't realize they were here in the building until tonight."

They were real and inhabited her workplace? What

about her home? She tried not to overreact. Instead she cleared her throat and casually asked, "So, it's still to-night, and I didn't go all Rip Van Winkle or anything?"

Anthony stood. "You were only out for a few minutes."

Brandee began to rise, but Anthony stopped her with a gentle hand on her shoulder. "Sit for a minute. I want to be sure you're all right."

"Why wouldn't I be? Did I bump my head?"

Sadie strolled over and sat in the spot Anthony had just vacated. "I don't think so. I found you sort of crumpled in a heap, but your head wasn't on the floor."

"Then I should be good to go." Brandee's voice wavered a bit, but she wanted to get out of there before anyone did anything *to* her.

"Not yet," Anthony said. "I imagine you have questions. I'd rather you ask us than anyone else."

"Who would I ask? Everyone would think I was crazy."

"Exactly." Anthony crossed to his office chair, rotated it to face her, then sat.

"So what the hell are they—brownies? Where did they come from? Are they some kind of alien?"

Sadie gave her hand a reassuring squeeze. "As a matter of fact, they're very much from earth. They're earth spirits."

Anthony leaned forward and clasped his hands. "They inhabit certain homes. They like to clean places, and as long as a snack is left for them, they're happy to help. But they don't like to be seen. You were very fortunate to get a glimpse of them."

"Ha. If I'm so lucky, why were you trying to make me forget? And what did you mean when you said you couldn't do it to me much *more*? What have you done to me?"

Anthony bit his lip, then swore and grabbed a tissue. A drop of blood was visible. He pressed the paper over the cut until it stopped bleeding, which seemed to take no time at all.

Sadie fiddled with her rings. "Do you remember wanting to stay behind the bar and see if I could make contact with the spirit I detected?"

"Yes. I remember everything before that and up until the little noseless, bearded men found me. Do they come into our apartment?"

"No, and Anthony didn't do any hypnosis with you tonight."

He leaned back. "I'd like to take the memory of the brownies from you for your own good. You absolutely can't tell *anyone* about what you saw. If you don't know about them, you won't let it slip out. I need your permission, however." He glanced at Sadie and she gave a slight nod.

"What would happen if I did let it slip? I'm not saying I would. Anyone I told would think I'm a few bottles short of a six-pack."

"I imagine the brownies would move out—or worse. If curious gawkers came looking for them, they'd be very upset. They're sensitive creatures."

"Worse? Something worse than not getting your bar cleaned for free?"

"If angered, they play pranks on the offender."

"But we'll tell Angie, right? I mean, she'll want to know since she lives here too."

"I wouldn't," Sadie said quickly. "The fewer people who know, the better. We really can't take a chance on word getting out."

"I used to wonder why the place sparkled the next day after a busy night. I just figured you had a kick-ass cleaning crew come in."

Anthony smiled. "And I thought you guys always did a great job of cleaning up after I left."

"You really didn't know about the brownies?"

"I really didn't. The bar opens several hours before I get in."

She faced Sadie. "But you said snacks had to be *left out* for them. We don't leave out any food at the end of the night."

"Apparently they were helping themselves to the peanuts and pretzels. But they did such an excellent job of cleaning up after themselves that we had no idea."

Brandee shook her head. "Crazy." After a brief pause, she asked, "So, is it okay if I go upstairs now? I promise not to breathe a word of this, and I'm really exhausted."

Anthony and Sadie looked at each other, then at her.

Anthony spoke first. "You don't have any more questions?"

"I'm still hoping I'll wake up in my bed and realize the whole thing was a dream."

"I can arrange that," Anthony offered, sounding hopeful.

"No. Part of me thinks this is unbelievably cool and wants to believe in fairy tales."

"What's the other part doing?" Sadie asked.

"Freaking out."

Nick stabbed a sausage and took a large bite. He and his brother were having a big breakfast after their midnight run with the pack. After swallowing, Nick said, "I tell you, Konrad. I really screwed up. I don't know if Brandee will ever forgive me."

Roz entered the room, carrying half of a bagel, and offered him a sympathetic look.

Konrad smiled up at his wife. "Remember when I upset you so badly I thought you'd never speak to me again, honey?"

Roz smirked and sat between the twin brothers at the round table. "What makes you think I've forgiven you yet?"

Konrad leaned back in his chair. "Hmmm…I just assumed you did because you married me, took my name, and moved to the suburbs to live and work at my school."

"Okay, I guess I got over it. But as I remember, you did a pretty good job of groveling."

Nick groaned. "Is that what I have to do? Grovel?"

"Not necessarily," Konrad said. "I left Roz a single red rose and a note. And don't forget, we had telepathic communication. When she refused to answer her door, I simply spoke directly into her mind. She had no choice but to listen to what I had to say."

"How did you two establish that? I wish I could talk to Brandee that way."

Roz chuckled. "Be careful what you wish for. It's not easy to filter your thoughts in the beginning." Then she took a dainty bite of her bagel.

Konrad answered his original question. "My fang accidentally punctured her tongue when I was kissing her. I lapped the spot, so the bleeding stopped and the hole closed. It only took a second. After that, we were telepathic."

"Seriously? I've been so careful not to let my fangs emerge while kissing Brandee." *I shouldn't have tried so hard. Telepathic communication would be proof that she's my mate.*

"Maybe you should continue that way until you're sure she's the one. First you have to fix your screwup."

Roz set down her bagel. "What was the situation, if you don't mind my asking."

"She described some strange noises coming from her neighbor's apartment upstairs. I just wanted to be sure she was safe, so I borrowed her keys for another purpose and then asked a psychic to come into Brandee's apartment with me. I didn't want to worry the girls who lived there, so I didn't tell them about it. We'd just gotten started when Brandee walked in and went nuts—"

"Nick?" Roz interrupted.

"What?"

"You're a numbskull. Why didn't you just tell her what you wanted to do and get her permission?"

"I didn't want to scare her—especially when I didn't know what we were dealing with."

"So instead you terrified her. And let me guess, you were also afraid she'd say no if you asked her permission."

He scratched his head. "Uh, yeah. How did you know?"

Roz gazed at the ceiling. "Men."

"So what should I do?"

"Does she love you?" Konrad asked.

"I think so. She hasn't said it yet, but we were headed in that direction."

"Have you told her you love her?"

"Yes. Although I may not have used those exact words."

Konrad's brows rose. "Wow. I never thought I'd see the day."

Nick groaned inwardly. *If I have to listen to one more asshole disbelieving my ability to commit now that I've found the love of my life…*"Yeah, yeah. Enough about my past, okay?"

"How did she react?" Roz asked.

Nick thought back to the moment he confessed he had been falling for her. "She didn't hate it."

Konrad closed his eyes and muttered something like, "Better than nothing."

Roz steepled her fingers as she thought out loud. "Damn, I remember when I was in her shoes. Let's see…you don't want to wait too long, but you need to give her some time to cool down. How long ago did this happen?"

"The night before last."

Roz nodded. "Okay. Don't wait too much longer. Is there something you know she'd like that you can give her?"

Nick scratched his head. "She needs a new car."

Roz made a soft noise. Something between a gasp and a chuckle. "Uh, no. That's too much, and not quite what I meant."

"Then what did you mean?"

"Does she love something you hate, like ballet or the opera, that you'd be willing to take her to, just to make her happy?"

"Oh, I get it. She loves art museums and galleries. I'm not a fan of that stuff. She likes the beach too, but so do I. I guess what you're saying is, I should take her to a museum? What if she doesn't want to go with me?"

"Try this—get her a membership to the Museum of Fine Arts. It's not cheap, but it doesn't cost nearly as much as a car. In a note, let her know you're willing to go with her because experiences shared are so much better."

"But what if she's still angry and doesn't want my company?"

"Even if she doesn't ask you to come with her right away, she'll think about you every time she uses her membership."

"And eventually she'll realize how much her happiness means to me."

"Exactly."

Nick finished his breakfast and couldn't wait to get back to the city. He was a man on a mission. Operation Scrape the Egg Off His Face.

Brandee had promised Anthony she'd say nothing about the brownies to Angie or anyone, and she *had* intended to honor that promise. Even though she always kept her word, now in the next morning's light she wondered if she'd be able to keep her mouth shut. Her roommate was sipping coffee right across from her at their dinette table.

Brownies? Seriously? The one thing she had to do first was double-check that the incident had really happened. She still wasn't one hundred percent sure she hadn't dreamed the whole thing. That meant talking to either Anthony or Sadie. Keeping in mind Ruxandra's reaction to her, she figured Sadie would be safer.

"You're quiet this morning," Angie remarked over her coffee mug.

"Huh? Oh, I'm just tired."

"You got in late."

Brandee put down her coffee mug. "You heard me come in? Are you still losing sleep over the whole ghost thing?"

"Yeah. I wasn't completely comfortable being here all alone. After you got home, I was fine and went right to sleep. Stupid, I know."

"No, it's not stupid. It's perfectly understandable."

"So what kept you downstairs so long?"

"Uh…" *Crap, now what do I say? I was meeting the things that go bump in the night?*

Angie held up one hand. "Never mind. If it's personal, I understand. I thought I saw Nick heading toward the bar just before I went upstairs."

Whew. I can blame it on Nick even though he never showed up. She wondered why he hadn't. Was he watching to be sure she got home all right? That seemed like something he would do, and she *still* wasn't sure how she felt about that. Having a big, strong ex-cop looking out for her was a bit of a turn-on, to be honest, but she didn't like anyone spying on her. The Balogs were creepy enough. She didn't need her boyfriend…*was* he still her boyfriend?

Angie waved a hand in front of her face. "Earth to Brandee."

Brandee snapped to attention. "What? Did you say something?"

"No. Your eyes were just doing that glaze-over thing again."

A knock at the door was a welcome interruption. Brandee jumped up. "I'll get it."

She tied her robe a little tighter before checking the peephole. Brandee didn't recognize the guy on the other side, so she left the chain in place and opened the door a crack. "Can I help you?"

"Courier. I have a special delivery for Brandee Hanson." The guy waved a manila envelope.

"Do I have to sign for it?"

"No. I'm just paid to hand-deliver it."

"Okay. Job done." She reached for the envelope, and the guy handed it to her through the gap. "Thanks."

"What is it?" Angie asked.

"I don't know." Brandee tore open the outer envelope from the courier service to reveal another envelope inside. A white one with just her name on it. "I don't recognize the handwriting."

"Well, open the flippin' thing. Who knows, maybe it's a big fat check from Publishers Clearing House."

"Funny." Brandee picked up her butter knife and used it to tear open the flap. Inside was a brochure from the Museum of Fine Arts and a letter. "Huh?"

"What is it?" Angie asked.

"It's a brochure for the MFA." She unfolded the letter and read out loud.

Dear Brandee,

> *I hope you're okay. I'm really sorry about invading your privacy, and I'd like to make it up to you. This is a one-year membership to a place I know you'll like. I only want your happiness and always will, no matter how you feel about me.*

> *Nick.*

Angie picked up the brochure. "Huh."

"Yeah, that's what I was going to say."

"I guess he feels really bad. The membership must have cost—"

Brandee slapped her hands over her ears. "No, don't tell me."

"It doesn't say how much he spent. I just know these things aren't cheap. It says you get free admission whenever you want, members-only invitations to special events, discount parking, discount dining…"

"Yeah. It's a really nice gift."

"And you'll like this part. The money goes toward maintaining and improving the museum." Angie looked up at her roommate. "Are you going to accept it?"

"Well, it wouldn't help the museum if I didn't. Nothing says I have to use the benefits."

"Sheesh. You're still that angry?"

Brandee rose and wandered around the kitchen, straightening up. As she was wiping down the counters, Angie spoke again.

"Do you realize you clean when you're avoiding something else?"

A corner of Brandee's mouth turned up. It was really tempting to say something like, "The brownies aren't doing it, so…" but she thought better of it in time. "No. I didn't."

"Well, you do. Not that it's a bad thing, but lately the apartment has been really clean. I think you need to deal with Nick."

Brandee tossed the sponge into the sink and folded her arms. "How can I 'deal with him' when I don't know what I want to do with him?"

"Well, you could start by thanking him for the museum membership."

Brandee sighed. "I thought you weren't going to give me advice."

"Well, you obviously need a little."

"Okay. So, tell me. Should I forgive him or stay mad?"

Angie snorted. "I don't think it works that way. Instead, maybe you should be asking yourself *if* you can forgive him or *if* you're still mad."

Brandee plopped into her chair again. "In other words, you think I've already made up my mind."

"I think you already know in your heart. This isn't one of those things the mind decides."

Brandee covered her eyes in an attempt to shut out her mind, her roommate, and anything else but her heart. She had been avoiding her feelings because she knew her heart was the traitor in all of this. *Stupid heart.*

Chapter 13

NICK FINALLY HAD A PLAN TO CATCH THE BANK ROBBER. It would stretch the department's resources, but that was no longer his problem. Captain Hunter had agreed to meet him at Boston Uncommon as soon as it opened. He had hoped to get his former captain in there anyway. Hunter, being a peacekeeper, seemed to like the concept.

Fortunately, Brandee was scheduled to work, so he might be able to kill two birds with one brunch—so to speak. He hoped she didn't still want to kill *him*.

He found a corner booth as far from the action as he could get. Brandee strolled into the bar, still tying her apron, then halted when she spotted him. He smiled.

She offered a weak smile in return and spoke quietly to Angie, who was cutting up limes behind the bar. Unfortunately, his hearing wasn't quite acute enough in human form to gather what they were saying. Finally, Angie gave his lover a shove in his direction.

Brandee approached him slowly, betraying her uncertainty.

Maybe there's a chance for us.

When she got close enough he said, "Hello, beautiful." He'd let her take the conversation from there, hoping for the best.

"Um…thanks for the museum membership. That was very thoughtful of you."

"You're welcome." Waiting for her next move was torture, but he really wanted to see where she would take this.

"I, um…"

She bit her lip and he couldn't stand it anymore. "Can we try again, Brandee?"

"I guess. I just need you to swear you'll be less possessive and never do anything like that again. Entering my apartment uninvited, I mean."

Hallelujah! She forgives me. "I so swear."

She nodded. "Okay. Can I get you something?"

"Yes, you can." He rose and pulled her against his chest before she could protest. He lowered his lips to hers and kissed her tenderly. She seemed to melt into him. He wanted to howl with joy and relief, but he held himself in check.

The sound of someone clearing his throat nearby interrupted Nick's internal celebration. He reluctantly broke the kiss and gazed over to find Captain Hunter, dressed in blue jeans and T-shirt, sporting a subtle smile. He seemed more amused than annoyed.

"Oh, uh, Ca—I mean, Hunter. I was just…"

Hunter grinned. "No explanation necessary. Is this still a good time to meet?"

"Yeah. Brandee, honey, would you please get me a cup of coffee and anything my friend wants?"

"Coffee for me too, please. Black."

"Sure thing."

Brandee sauntered back to the bar while Nick admired the swing of her hips.

"Damn, she's fine," Hunter muttered.

"And she's mine," Nick countered as he retook his seat.

"Hey, I wasn't talking about poaching on your territory. Is it serious?" His old captain settled into the booth opposite him.

"My mate. She just doesn't know it yet."

If Hunter wasn't one of the werewolves among Boston's finest, he wouldn't have put it that way. Fortunately the captain knew exactly what Nick meant.

"No kiddin'? That's great. From the look of things, you'll be marking her in no time."

Nick smiled. Even though he knew they were a long way from that, the thought warmed him.

And then Hunter brought him back to the present. "Getting down to business…"

"Yeah. The bank robberies. I think I know what you're dealing with. A vamp."

"That's what we thought, but I wanted your opinion—and your help."

"It won't be an easy sting."

"That's why I called you in."

"I can't capture this bastard by myself," Nick said. "We don't know which bank will be hit next, so they'll have to be covered simultaneously."

"Shit. That won't be easy."

"It looks to me like we're dealing with a savvy vampire. This guy knows exactly when the vaults will be opened, so he gets in and out right around the employees without being detected."

The captain scratched his head. "Okay. But why bother? He could only take what he can grab without slowing down."

"I think it's less about the money and more about the mayhem. Someone is either showing off or possibly trying to make a fool of the department. Do you know of a disgruntled vampire?"

The captain snorted. "Isn't that the definition of a bloodsucker? They're all peeved about something."

Nick hated the prejudice he heard among his kind, especially toward vampires. The whole purpose behind this bar was to dispel the stereotypes.

"No matter what the motive is, you hired me to help you put a stop to it."

"What do you propose?"

"The vampire, or whoever, seems to be taking advantage of precise timing—not only when the vault opens, but the front door as well. I'm betting the perp is hanging around outside during the time the vaults are supposed to open, then zooms into the lobby as soon as a customer opens the door."

"But what about getting out? They'd have to wait until someone exits or it would look like the door opened by itself."

"Exactly. I assume the vamp can't slow down, but has to run around and around until the outside door opens again. No one can keep that up for long."

"Bizarre theory."

"But it could work."

"What are you saying? That we should lock down all the banks after the vaults have been opened and closed?"

"That's one way."

"But for how long? And what do we tell the public? 'Oh, sorry. You all have to sit tight for fifteen minutes while we wait for an invisible thief to materialize'?"

"There's another way."

"I'm listening."

"Cameras outside, covering every angle. If he's hanging around out there, then suddenly disappears, and a few seconds later materializes again…"

"Then we get a picture of the perpetrator."

"How do we know how large a distance to cover?"

"That's where it comes in handy to know a friendly vampire or two. Someone who can do a dry run for us."

Captain Hunter straightened. "Are you saying you know someone besides the vamp that owns this place? I can't imagine a bar owner who's trying to unite the factions wanting to get involved in a sting like this."

Nick shrugged. "I might know of someone else."

"Wait a minute. You're not talking about the owner's psycho girlfriend, are you?"

Nick let out a booming laugh. The bar's few early patrons turned their way. He waited until they had gone back to their own conversations and spoke in a low voice. "No. This is someone you've probably never heard of."

"But don't they all cover for each other?"

"Not this guy. He and his wife are virtually unknown to the vampire community, and they'd like to keep it that way."

"I suppose it could work. Can you contact him and set up these dry runs at every bank in the area?"

"I can ask."

"Good. How long do you need?"

"Give me a week. How about compensation? Is the insurance company offering any?"

"I'll ask. Meanwhile, don't offer. Maybe your vampire will be a good citizen and do it for free."

"Ha. We can always dream."

"How about the other case? Are you any closer to discovering who hired the thugs to kidnap the mayor's stepdaughter?"

"Nothing yet. It would help if I could look at some mug shots from New York. I, uh, recognized their accents." Nick had agreed not to tell anyone about Anthony's involvement.

"I'll see what I can do."

"Great."

"Thanks for your good work on both cases, Nick."

"Don't thank me yet. All I have are theories."

"Damn good ones. More than anyone else has been able to come up with. If this one pans out, the chief will be glad we kept you as an important contact."

"And if it doesn't?"

"You'd better hope it does. That's a lot of costly equipment and man-hours, Nick."

After the captain left, Nick finished his coffee and waved Brandee over.

"Another coffee?" she offered.

He rose and fished his wallet from his back pocket. "No. I have a couple leads to follow up on. When do you get off—and can I help with that?" He waggled his eyebrows.

Brandee rolled her eyes. "That was so bad, I'm tempted to pretend I didn't know what you meant."

"But you did." He grinned.

"What makes you think I'm ready to just pick up where we left off?"

He hesitated. "I thought we were making up. Isn't make-up sex the best part of having a fight?" He handed her a twenty and said, "Keep the change."

"You're incorrigible. But Angie isn't planning to go out, as far as I know, so fooling around at my place is out of the question."

"Then I'll take you to mine." He was surprised how easily that popped out. He rarely took a woman back to his place, and yet with Brandee, he didn't even have to think twice about it.

She smiled. "I'd like to see it. I'll bet you have mirrors on the ceiling."

He laughed. "Nope, Not even close."

"Seriously? I figured a horny bachelor would have all the bells and whistles."

"You really do have a bad opinion of me."

She shrugged. "You earned it."

He slapped a hand over his heart. "Ouch. You wound me."

"Hey, I'd be happy to be proved wrong. I get off at five."

"And I'll get you off at five thirty."

She groaned. "I'm serious, Nick. That was really, really bad."

"I'll work on it."

—◌◌◌—

Good to his word, Nick returned at four fifty-five, ready to take her to his place. She made him wait in the bar while she ran upstairs to change. She brushed her teeth and hair, then freshened her makeup. Now, what to wear...

She stood in front of her crowded closet and started flipping through her clothes.

A red silk blouse slipped off its hanger and pooled

at her feet, almost as if she'd had a little "help" decid-
ing. She glanced around, then shook her head. "Oh, my
paranoia. It's just a coincidence."

Even though the thought of supernatural "help" un-
nerved her, she had to agree with the choice. A pair of
black slacks and her red top would work for pretty much
whatever he had in mind. Although the only thing on
Nick's mind seemed to be getting her out of anything
she put on as soon as possible.

She ran to the bathroom and shut the door. Brandee
felt stupid, acting as if someone might be watching, but
she dressed quickly. A pair of gold hoop earrings was in
a dish on the counter so she grabbed them and put them
in as she trotted down the stairs. Anything to get out of
there. The place was giving her the heebie-jeebies.

When she reentered the bar, a wolf whistle greeted
her. Nick quickly strode over. "Wow."

He shrugged into his leather jacket. "Ready, gorgeous?"

"I think so. I didn't know if we were going out before
heading to your place, so…"

Tory must have overheard. "You're taking her to
your lair, Nick?"

He bristled. "It's not a lair."

"Oh, that's right. You're a reformed man now."

Nick leaned over and kissed her temple. "Pay no attention to my hard-up friend, sweetheart. He's just jealous."

"True," Tory said and laughed.

Nick opened the door for her, then called over his
shoulder, "Get your own hot date, Tory."

Brandee liked being valued, but really. "Damn. Oh,
look, now you made me curse. Do you have to act like
you own me?"

Nick looked like he was about to put his arm around her but let it drop. "What did I do now?"

She shook her head. "I don't know. It's just…I don't know." She sighed.

"It's a guy thing. We were just busting each other's chops."

He was right. She was probably being oversensitive. "Okay. Sorry. I'll try not to pay attention to things like that, as long as you don't start getting overly protective and possessive again."

"I'll do my best. Shall we?" He held out his hand to her.

She slipped her hands into her pockets. "Where do you live?"

He paused, then said, "Mount Vernon Street." He tucked his own hands in his pockets and strode off in that direction.

She had a hard time keeping up with him. "Hey, slow down."

He whirled on her. "Which is it, Brandee? One minute you want more of me than I've ever given any other woman, then you complain when I pay too much attention to you. I don't understand. What do you want?"

She reared back. "What the…"

"Yeah. What the…" He jammed his fists on his hips.

He's usually so happy-go-lucky. I've never seen him this frustrated. Brandee blew out a long breath. "Look I can see that you're a little confused."

"A little?"

A young couple veered into the street rather than go around them on the sidewalk.

"It might be better if we discuss this at your place. I-I should tell you something."

He took a deep breath. "Fine."

She reached out her hand. He stared at it, as if unsure what to do. She must have *really* confused him. Later, she'd admit to being a little confused too.

At last he enveloped her hand in his big, warm palm. She smiled up at him and said, "Lead the way."

By the time they arrived at his place, both of them had calmed down considerably. He led her up some stairs with a wrought-iron railing.

"You live in one of these pretty brownstones?"

"Not the whole thing. The building is considered a duplex. I have my living space on the third floor, and the bedrooms are on the fourth floor. The other occupant has the first and second floors." He gave her a sly grin. "I had planned to take you to the top floor and right into my bedroom. But…"

"But we need to talk first."

"Right."

They had to hammer out a few details before they nailed each other. She took one step inside and stopped. His place was breathtaking. She hadn't known what to expect, but this wasn't it. The ceilings must have been at least ten feet high. Period details like the crown molding and exposed brick had been lovingly preserved.

The polished hardwood floors gleamed, interrupted only by two large oriental rugs. An open-concept living and dining room was unusual in these old buildings, but the result made the space seem huge. He must have had it remodeled.

"Wow," she said.

He smiled. "That's the reaction I was going for."

"Did you design this?"

"Partly. I told the architect what was important to me, and he basically rebuilt it from scratch. We recycled the trim and doors, though."

"How long have you lived here?"

"About ten years."

"How could you afford this on a cop's sal—Oh, I'm sorry. I shouldn't ask you that. How rude of me."

He chuckled. "It's okay. My brother and I co-owned a successful business for a few years. Then we sold it. But you don't want to know all that." He peeled off his coat and hung it in a large closet near the entrance.

"You're wrong. I want to know everything about you. I think that's why I've been so…"

"Reluctant to commit?" he supplied.

"Yeah. There may be a couple of other reasons too."

"Well, let's get comfortable and discuss it over a glass of wine."

She nodded. "Sounds good."

He reached the modern kitchen in three long strides and took a corkscrew from one of the many drawers. "Red or white?"

"White, please."

He opened a wine fridge. "How about sauvignon blanc?"

"Sold."

"You're easy."

"Not usually. But you swept me off my feet."

He chuckled. "I'm glad you seem to be in a better mood." He poured two glasses, then handed her one. She followed him to the living area and sat next to him on the sofa.

"Is it okay if I kick off my shoes?"

"Make yourself comfortable."

She did. With her stocking feet curled up under her thighs, she faced him and lifted her glass.

"Cheers," he said.

"You know that's the name of a rival bar, right?"

"Oh, right. Well then, Boston Uncommon! Where everybody knows you're strange."

She giggled, and they clinked glasses.

After each of them took a sip, he asked, "So, how do we start this?"

She knew what he meant. She had asked for this conversation, but knowing where to begin was daunting. *Might as well jump in anywhere.*

"I think we need to talk about what we expect from each other."

He nodded. "Okay. You go first."

Lovely. Now she had to figure out how to put her feelings into words. "I guess I just want a normal boyfriend."

He let out a loud guffaw. "Boy, did you come to the wrong place. No wonder you're disappointed."

"I never said I was disappointed. I just think we went a little too far too fast. Maybe because we've known each other for a while, we thought we knew each other better than we do."

"Hmmm… Okay. I think I get it. You missed the old-fashioned courting thing?"

"Huh? No. I don't need that. I just think we should have gone on a few dates and talked about ourselves—our pasts, our present, and maybe the future."

"Oh, is that what dating is for?" he asked, with a teasing smile.

She rolled her eyes. "Sheesh, I forgot. How would

a player like you know that, especially if you've never done it?"

"I've done it…superficially. I just never got wrapped up in anyone's life before."

"Yeah. I think that's the problem. You got too wrapped up in mine, instantly."

"Hey, when it's right, it's right. Why waste time?" He gave her another teasing grin.

"Stop being charming for five minutes, will you?"

Instead of listening to her, he leaned in for a kiss. And instead of meeting his lips, she raised her glass of wine and took a big sip.

He sighed and leaned back into the loose pillows. "Cock blocked by my own crystal."

"Nick, I'm serious. We need to talk first."

"And I'm serious too. About you. About us. I love you, Brandee. You're the only woman I've ever loved."

Her jaw dropped. "Really?"

"Honest to God."

She couldn't help being impressed and just a little bit flattered. "You're full of surprises."

"You are too."

"Me? I thought I was an open book."

Nick played with a few strands of her hair. "Maybe with a few pages stuck together. You said there were some reasons you were reluctant to be with me."

"Yeah. Well, they mostly have to do with my past. I've been stood up and dumped a few times. I've become kind of cynical when it comes to men in general."

"They were idiots. I'd never do that to you," Nick said.

"I'm beginning to believe you."

"Just beginning to?"

She shrugged. "It's been hard to trust guys after all those disappointments. It might take a little time."

"Was any particular relationship more disappointing than the others?"

How should I answer that? Should I tell him about Darryl? Apparently she hesitated too long.

He backed off from the question. "I'm sorry. It's impolite to talk about ex-boyfriends or ex-girlfriends. Forget I said anything. Suffice it to say you've been hurt."

She nodded and took another sip, relieved that she didn't have to go into it.

"Just tell me this. How long ago did it end?"

"Uh…recently." Her face heated.

He stared at her for a moment. "How recently?"

She squirmed a bit but wanted their relationship built on truth. "A couple weeks ago."

"A couple weeks? Holy… No wonder." He cupped her cheek. "Hey, I'm sorry." A small smile stole across his lips. "But not really."

She had to laugh. "Yeah, your timing was kind of impeccable. I didn't even have time to cry about it."

"Good, because he doesn't deserve your tears."

Sure, it was what she wanted to hear, but she didn't get the sense that he was just saying it to make her feel better. *He means it. And surprise, surprise, I believe it.* Relief washed over her like a warm shower washing away the dirt of her past.

This time when he leaned in, she met his lips. It started with a gentle nibble but didn't stay that way for long. His lips were masterful. He quickly took over with open-mouthed aggression. Before she knew what was happening, she found herself lying supine with his big body over hers. Her head spun. Why did his kisses always affect her so profoundly?

His mouth traveled from her lips to her neck and collarbone. He hastily pushed up her blouse and bra, then kneaded her breast. Her desire spiked and her body screamed to couple with his.

As his mouth latched onto her nipple, she sucked in a deep breath and arched her back. What had they been talking about? What was she going to ask him? All thoughts flew out of her head, except *What's happening to me?* She felt all tingly and hot, as if she was blazing out of control.

She slid her hands into his hair and clutched his head to her breast. A visceral reaction caused her womb to clench. She wanted to take, but she also wanted to give him as much pleasure as he gave her. She wanted to give him—everything.

Nick lifted her and carried her like she weighed nothing. They locked eyes. She was barely aware of ascending some stairs, and then he laid her on soft bedding. He almost tore off his clothes and helped her get rid of hers.

His tongue and lips devoured her like he was starving. The cool, damp trail provided her temporary relief from the burning inside her. She inhaled deeply, dragging in his spicy scent. It made her want to turn the tables and feast on him for a change. She attempted to flip him over, but he was having none of it. His mouth traveled lower.

"Please. Let me…" she begged.

He lifted his head and he was panting.

Knowing she could turn this civilized man into a

primitive beast was such a turn-on. She ran her hand over his sculpted shoulder and attempted to squeeze his solid bicep.

"I need to give you pleasure too."

He licked his lips. "Your response gives me pleasure." His voice sounded ragged, barely contained.

He lifted her legs over his shoulders, opening her to him fully. He lapped her folds from bottom to top. Each time he grazed her clit, she jumped as if an electric shock zipped through her. Her core body temperature grew white hot.

"Nick...Nick..." She couldn't even tell him what she was begging for. She just needed more, *had to* have it.

At last, he concentrated on her sweet spot. Suddenly, a white light exploded behind the back of her eyes. Her breath converted into a blast of air, followed by a scream of release. Ripples of bliss radiated from her core to every nerve ending. Her thighs shook as if she were lying on the epicenter of an earthquake.

She wanted to weep, she felt so good.

At last, he let her legs drop and crawled up next to her with a satisfied smile on his face. He touched his lips to her forehead tenderly, then grabbed something from his bedside table. The rip of foil told her what it was. He applied the condom, then positioned himself between her legs.

He eased himself into her and she closed her eyes to concentrate on the wonderful invasion. Nick buried his hard cock to the hilt.

He began his rocking motion and she rose to meet him. She sighed out loud, feeling somehow more complete than she had moments before.

"So tight…" he ground out, as if forcing the words. "Won't last long." He slowed.

She slapped his butt. "Don't you dare stop!"

He chuckled. "Wasn't going to." He continued to thrust and withdraw, while gazing into her eyes.

It was the most intimate she had ever felt with another human being. This is what all the love songs were about. Every sonnet she had to read in high school suddenly made sense.

"Am I hurting you?"

"God, no." She wondered what would make him ask. It must be the expression on her face. She was experiencing so much pleasure, it overwhelmed her.

"I'm crazy about you, Brandee."

"I-I…"

He closed his eyes, dropped his head, and sped up his rhythm. She couldn't see his face but felt his concentration. Before long, a sheen of sweat formed on his body. Her fingers glided over him and he let out a sound almost like a whimper

Whatever was happening to him, it was at least as profound as her reaction to this coupling.

Shock registered as she realized he was biting her neck. *Hard.* "Ow!" He let go, stilled inside her, and arched. As he jerked with his release, he howled at the ceiling. Actually *howled.*

A few moments later, he collapsed beside her and gathered her to him. He was trembling.

"Nick, what the heck just happened?"

"I'm sorry. I didn't mean to. Instinct took over and I…"

Brandee fought her way out of his grasp and propped herself up on her elbow. She touched the aching spot on her neck and it stung. When she checked her fingers, she saw a small smear of blood. "You drew blood? Nick, what the…"

"It will never happen again. I promise."

"I-I can't believe it happened in the first place." She rolled up to sit on the edge of the bed and searched for her panties in the pile of clothes.

"Don't go." He was on his knees in front of her before she realized he had moved.

"I wasn't going to leave. I just feel like I need a minute. Some emotional breathing room."

"Okay." He handed her clothes to her and dressed himself quickly. "I have something to tell you. Something major."

Crap. Now what? "Will I need another glass of wine?"

"Probably."

Chapter 14

NICK HAD HOPED HIS IMPULSIVE BITE WOULD BRING on telepathic communication. If it did, he'd have proof positive that Brandee was his mate. Since it didn't, he was hoping he hadn't made a horrible mistake. But how could it be a mistake when he loved her so deeply?

He'd waited so long for his true mate. Didn't he deserve one?

As much as he thought he was right and wished it were true, wishing didn't make it so.

"Would you mind if I invited Anthony over?" Nick handed Brandee a glass of white wine and sat next to her on the sofa. "I think I might need his help explaining this." *And his mind wipe might be necessary if you can't handle what I have to say*

"Seriously?" She leaned away and scrutinized him. "You're about to tell me something major, and I have to wait until my boss gets here?"

"I wouldn't ask if I didn't think it was important." He waited an anxious moment or two while she hesitated.

Finally, she sighed and said, "Whatever you think is best."

Nick located his cell phone and stepped into the kitchen to place the call.

After two rings, Anthony answered, "Hi, Nick."

"How'd you know it was me?"

"I'm sitting here with Sadie. She said you might call. Or maybe it was the caller ID."

Nick snorted. "I'm glad you're nearby. Can you get to my place quickly?"

"Sure. Why? Is something wrong?"

"You could say that." He lowered his voice so Brandee couldn't hear him, but Anthony with his vampiric senses certainly could. "I marked Brandee. I didn't mean to, but animal instinct took over. Now I have to explain it to her."

"Crap. How much are you going to tell her?"

"Everything. That's why I need you here. Just in case."

"If it makes you feel any better, she's already aware of one type of paranormal, and she swore not to tell anyone. If she hasn't told you, that's a good sign that she can be trusted," Anthony said.

"Huh? What type?"

"Brownies. Apparently they've been cleaning the bar, but we didn't discover it until the night of the full moon. Brandee was here when they showed themselves."

"Holy shit. What was her reaction?"

"She fainted."

Nick slapped a hand over his forehead and closed his eyes. "Terrific. So what happened when she came to?"

"Sadie and I explained who and what they were. I offered to mesmerize her and remove the memory, mostly so she wouldn't accidentally slip and mention their existence to anyone, but she said no. She said she could keep the secret, and apparently she was right."

"So she knows you can do mind wipes?"

"Yeah, but she thinks it's hypnosis."

"Gotcha. Okay, so she knows about the brownies and soon she'll know about me…and you don't think she'll need your 'hypnosis'?"

"I doubt it."

Nick inhaled a deep breath and blew it out in a whoosh. "Okay. She wants an honest relationship, so I'll give her the unvarnished truth."

Brandee rounded the corner, holding her empty glass, and headed toward the wine fridge. "Something tells me I'm going to need another."

"Crap. How much did she hear?" Anthony asked.

"I don't know, but it doesn't matter. Could you come over? She might need your…talents later. I'll leave that up to her."

Brandee poured a full glass and leaned against the counter. She didn't look like she was going anywhere.

"Yeah," Anthony said. "Just give me a bit of time."

Well, this is it, Nick. You're in too deep to back out now. "Thanks. See you in a bit."

Nick set the phone on the counter and returned to Brandee. He stroked her arms gently and said, "It looks like I might not need Anthony's help after all."

"Oh? What changed?"

"You did."

"Anthony told me you know about the existence of paranormals. And apparently you kept your word not to reveal the secret—even to me."

"I don't go back on a promise, and they made me promise."

Nick placed a hand on the small of her back and escorted her to the living room. "In that case, I'm going to need you to promise again."

"Promise what again? Are you a brownie too?"

Nick reared back and let out his booming laugh. "Do I look like a brownie?"

"Heck no. They were tiny and you're…well, you're huge. You don't mind my describing you that way, do you? I mean, it's not insulting, like saying my ass looks huge, is it?"

"Nope. It's the truth. No offense taken." He chuckled and kissed the top of her head. "Gods, but you're cute — and your ass is perfect."

She smiled and settled on the sofa, then took a sip of her wine. "So, what is it you have to tell me?"

"Promise you'll never breathe a word of it—ever."

"I promise."

She sounded a little too cavalier for his taste. *I have to make her understand.* "I'm serious. You'll have to take this secret to your grave. Do you still want to hear it?"

She set her wineglass on the coffee table. "More than ever."

"Shit," he muttered to himself. "How do I say this?"

"Just say it. And in case you're thinking of holding anything back, don't. Tell me all of it. I need to know you're being completely honest with me."

"I wish my sister-in-law were here. She could put it tactfully as well as truthfully."

"Your sister-in-law? What does she have to do with it?"

"She went through the same thing. My brother had to tell her what I'm about to tell you."

Brandee crossed her arms and looked as if she was getting frustrated. "So tell me already."

Maybe if I tell her the good news first it'll help. "Here's the thing…I'm not exactly human. I'm part wolf, and wolves mate for life. The bite I just gave you marked you as my mate. You'll never have to worry about my straying. My kind is completely monogamous once we've chosen our mate."

She hadn't reacted yet. No screaming. No fainting. No nothing. *Did she hear me?*

"A wolf, huh? Is that some kind of club, like the Lions or the Rotary Club?"

"Uh, not exactly."

She let out a deep breath. "Well, that doesn't sound so bad. At least you're not a werewolf." She chuckled loudly. "Imagine how weird that would be."

Crap. Nick sucked in a sharp breath and sighed. He put his head in his hands and peeked at Brandee from the corner of his eye. *"Brandee…"* She didn't respond to his telepathic thought. *Damn.*

Her eyes grew wide, and Nick reached out and took both of her hands in his. "Yeah. Things just got weird."

Brandee yanked her away. "Are you telling me you're a werewolf?"

Nick nodded slowly. He hoped the sad expression on his face would tell her he wasn't thrilled about it.

She sat frozen. Palpable waves of fear radiated from her. *Quick. Jump in before she faints.* "It won't change a thing between us, except once a month on the full moon I'll be with my pack in Newton. You never have to see me shift into my wolf form if you don't—"

To Nick's surprise, Brandee burst out laughing.

"Oh, my monthly… You really had me going there for a minute."

Puzzled, he sat back and stared at her. She was giggling so hard, tears were leaking from the outer corners of her eyes. *Is that nervous laughter, or does she really not believe me?*

Her giggles slowly subsided. She stared at him. "Nick,

we said we were going to be honest with each other. Brownies are one thing, but c'mon. Werewolves? This isn't funny anymore."

"I'm not joking."

Her jaw dropped. Eventually she said in a soft voice, "And you think I'm your mate?"

He nodded.

She stared at him for a full minute. "Let's say I believe you. If it's true, you can prove it, right?"

Nick mulled over the possibilities—and the consequences. His shift was a hideous thing to watch. Seeing cute little brownies was one thing, but witnessing a grown man pop and contort into a giant wolf was quite another. He had learned not to scream and howl during the transformation, but he couldn't help grimacing in pain. If she truly loved him, she'd probably experience emotional pain *for* him.

"Nick?"

"Brandee, please don't make me show you. It—it's disturbing."

"I need to know."

Nick thought about the time she *had* seen him transform. She couldn't have seen his pain from that distance. He had asked Anthony to erase it from her memory, but perhaps he could undo the memory wipe.

—w—

He gently touched the spot where he'd marked her. "Does it still hurt?"

"Not a lot."

He gazed down at her with a sad-looking smile.

"What's the matter?"

Sweeping her hair behind her ear, he said, "You've just learned I'm a monster. And you're still here with me."

"You're not a monster. You're Nick. I've known you as a person a lot longer than I've known you as a werewolf." *And I'm not convinced you're not delusional yet.*

"You might be in denial. I wouldn't blame you if you were."

A knock sounded at the door. Nick left to answer it, and Brandee was surprised to hear Anthony's voice.

Nick brought Anthony to the living room and faced Brandee, who was still in the open kitchen. "I'll give you a demonstration now that Anthony's here."

"Why does my boss need to be here?"

"I'm just here for emotional support," Anthony said. "Are you ready, sweetheart?"

"As ready as I'll ever be." Her nerves were kicking in, big time, but she wanted to get this over with, so she joined the guys and sat next to Anthony on the sofa.

Anthony looked very serious. "Are you sure you want to see this, Brandee?"

"I'm sure, but first I want to ask you something."

"What's that?"

"When you said you had erased my memory before. Was it *only* the one time Nick mentioned—when, according to him, I saw him shift?"

"Yes. He and I felt it was best if you didn't know about the existence of paranormals. I'm still not one hundred percent sure it's a good idea to fill you in now."

"Why not? Do you think I'll break my promise and tell?"

"Not purposely. It could slip out, though."

Brandee snorted. "How on earth would I let 'My boyfriend is a werewolf' slip into any conversation?"

Anthony smiled. "I guess you have a point."

Nick began to strip. "Last chance to change your mind, hon."

She sucked in a breath. "What are you doing?"

"If I'm dressed when I shift, I'll tear my clothes."

She turned to Anthony. "Have you seen him shift before?"

Anthony shook his head.

"What about Nick's dignity? If he has to gear down to his birthday suit, maybe you should look away."

Nick rolled his eyes. "There's nothing dignified about this process, Brandee. In fact, I should warn you—it's a little painful."

"How painful?"

"I imagine it's similar to childbirth. I'll be fine afterward."

"Really? It's that bad?"

"Well, not quite. It only lasts a minute or so. Considering labor can go on for hours or days, in that way I'm lucky, I guess."

He continued to undress, swiveling so his back was to them before removing his underwear. As soon as he was naked, Brandee heard some cracking sounds. He fell to his hands and knees. Nick's spine seemed to rise, becoming more visible just under his skin.

Dear God! It's just like a horror movie.

Hair sprouted all over, filling in slowly. A few popping noises accompanied a change to his legs and arms. He shivered.

"Stop!" It had to be painful. More painful than he had let on. She grabbed Anthony's arm and shook it. "Stop him. I-I don't want him to go through this anymore."

"I don't know if he can," Anthony said.

A buff-colored tail sprouted from Nick's coccyx. At last, he seemed fully formed. He turned to face them and sat on his haunches. A moment later, he sported what looked like a grin, with his tongue lolling out over one side of his powerful jaw, and he panted as if he'd just run around the block.

She'd never seen a wolf up close. He was magnificent. His coat was a beige color with dark brown markings on his head and around his eyes.

"Are you frickin' kidding me?" Brandee whispered.

"He can hear you, you know. In fact, his hearing is better now than in his human form."

Nick lifted himself to all fours and slowly approached her.

"He—he knows who I am, right?" Then she remembered Nick could hear everything she said and addressed him directly. "You won't take a chunk out of me, will you, boy?"

He shook his head.

"Okay…"

The beautiful wolf moved closer. At last, Brandee reached out a shaky hand and patted his soft fur.

"I'm sure he knows you. You're his mate."

"Yeah, so I heard. He said he chose me." *But why didn't I get a choice?*

"Then you're a lucky woman."

The jury is still out on that.

Chapter 15

THE FOLLOWING DAY BRANDEE DIDN'T HAVE TO work. Ordinarily she'd spend her day off taking pictures or setting up her bathroom as a makeshift darkroom, then experimenting with new artistic techniques. But today, everything had changed. She had no desire to tackle her passion. She needed time to let the recent turn of events sink in. And she needed a change of scenery.

She had explained that to Nick, and he seemed to understand. He suggested she talk to his sister-in-law and gave Roz's phone number to her. Then he promised to leave her alone for twenty-four hours.

Part of her wanted to get away—permanently. Just skip town and live on a beach somewhere down south. But avoidance wouldn't help in the long run. Besides, she loved Nick.

She stared at the phone number in her hand and wondered what kind of woman would knowingly marry a werewolf. Moreover, she had to figure out if *she* was that kind of woman—not that Nick had proposed or anything. Apparently, he knew better than to do that. But this marking thing…wasn't that similar?

She had too many questions and not enough confidants. She took a deep breath and sighed. At least if she talked to this Roz person, she might come away with a little more insight.

Brandee lifted her cell phone and dialed the number she'd been given. After two rings, a woman answered.

"H'lo?"

"Um—hi. My name is Brandee. I'm looking for Roz Wolfensen."

"You've got her."

"Oh. Hi, Roz. I'm your brother-in-law Nick's friend. He suggested I call you."

After a brief hesitation, the woman asked, "You're just his friend?"

"Well, no. I'm his girlfriend—I guess."

"He said you might call and need to talk. Feeling a bit confused?"

Brandee plopped onto her couch. "Man, am I ever."

"Are you okay?"

"Um…"

"Oh, boy," Roz said. "Maybe we should talk in person. Are you free this afternoon?"

"I'm available all day."

"Good. I have an appointment this morning, but we could meet for coffee around one. Do you want to come here?"

"Sure." *That's one way to get out of town and face this predicament at the same time*.

"Good. Do you know how to get to Riverside on the T?" Roz asked.

"That's like the last stop on the Green Line, right?"

"Yup. I'll meet you there."

"I'll aim for one, but with the subway, you never know. If I'm a few minutes late, I'll be there shortly."

Roz chuckled. "Good. I'm glad you said that. If you were late, I might have wondered if you'd just decided to blow town instead."

How did she know what I was thinking? "Yeah, I kind of considered that already."

"So did I. If it's any consolation, I'm very glad I stayed. It gets better."

I hope so.

Nick was having the worst time concentrating. Not good, considering he was about to meet Konrad's old neighbor, Sly—a vampire. Why the hell had he marked Brandee so soon?

He spotted the beautiful brownstone on Beacon Street in which Sly and his new wife, Morgaine, lived. He took the steps two at a time and located the buzzer, but before he pressed it, a woman spoke over the intercom.

"Nick? Is that you?"

"Yeah. How did you know?"

"I'm psychic. Oh, and your brother called ahead. Come on up. When you get to the third floor, we're the door on your right."

The buzzer sounded, and he yanked open the heavy wood-and-glass door. The familiar lobby of white marble and dark mahogany crown molding greeted him. He hadn't been there often, preferring to meet Konrad at obscure restaurants.

His brother had to keep a low profile back in those days for a number of reasons. He had been kicked out of their pack and didn't want anyone to know where he'd gone. But more importantly, he was breaking into Boston businesses so Nick could come in the next day and sell the frightened owners a security system. That was the business Nick had alluded to when Brandee asked how he could afford such a nice place.

Since Konrad had met Roz, the woman who inspired him to "go straight," Nick's leads had dried up. That was fine, though. Now that he was with Brandee, having the extra time to spend with her was more important than money.

Nick took the elevator and found the apartment with 3B in brass letters on the door to the right. He had just raised his fist to knock when a pretty blond opened the door.

Her eyes widened. "My, oh my. You look just like him."

"Konrad and I are identical twins."

"Cool. I'm Morgaine—one of a kind." She chuckled. "Come in. Sly will be up in a moment."

"Oh, I didn't know he was asleep. Don't wake him."

Morgaine laughed. "I meant he'll be coming upstairs. He's in the basement right now."

Nick followed her inside the small but tidy apartment.

"Have a seat. Can I get you something to drink?"

Nick spotted a bottle of red wine. "I don't suppose you could spare a glass of wine."

Morgaine wrinkled her nose. "You don't want that kind. It has blood in it."

Blood wouldn't bother a carnivore like him, but he supposed it must be their food. He'd survive until he got to a coffee shop. "Are you a vampire too?" he asked.

"Yes." She smiled. "Sly turned me shortly before our handfasting…at my request. He had already grieved for one wife. I didn't want him to go through it again."

"Handfasting? Are you witches too?"

"I am. Sly's Catholic. Can you imagine that? A Catholic vampire?"

Nick had to admit these vampires defied all the stereotypes. "So are all vampires capable of being awake during the day?"

"No. There's a secret ingredient in our wine that makes it possible. It also slakes the bloodlust. As long as we get some of it each day, we're almost normal."

"Who's normal?" asked a pale, dark-haired man in the doorway.

"Oh, Sly. This is Nick, Konrad's twin brother."

"No kidding," Sly said. "I could have easily mistaken you for Konrad. How is our old friend, anyway?"

"He's great. He and Roz got married recently."

"We heard. Actually, they invited us to the wedding, but we didn't want to make anyone uncomfortable. I guess some werewolves are still very antivampire."

"I know, and that's so foolish. If you two are interested, you should stop by the bar where my girlfriend works. It's on Charles Street. The place is called Boston Uncommon. It's a safe place for paranormals of all kinds to socialize."

Sly gave her a sideways glance. "It would be good for *both* of us to get out *together*."

She folded her hands in her lap and gazed at them. *There's something they're not saying.* "Oh, well. The place is always there if you decide to give it a try."

"Yes. Thank you for bringing it to our attention," Sly said.

Nick cleared his throat. "Well, on to the reason I'm here. I'm a private investigator working on a case that involves a paranormal perpetrator—possibly a vampire."

"I'm intrigued," Sly said. "How can I help?"

"The perp robs banks while the vault is open and only while it's open. No one sees a thing. I slowed down some video footage and saw a dark gray blur. I thought because vampires can run at speeds that essentially make them invisible, perhaps that's what we were dealing with."

Sly raised his eyebrows. "Did you think *I* might be able to test this theory?"

Nick took in a deep breath and hoped for the best. "Yes."

"Wow." Sly scratched his head and his brows knit. "I haven't flown that often. I'd be willing to try it, as long as everything is arranged ahead of time and I won't get arrested."

"Don't worry. We have the cooperation of the police force. A test will be set up for a Sunday when you're free, not during business hours. Can you do it?"

He shrugged. "Like I said, I can try."

"How about tomorrow?"

"Sure. I'm available."

Morgaine put a hand on his knee. "I don't know, hon. This sounds impossible." She focused on Nick. "How would the thief manage to get in and out of the building without being seen? I can't imagine no one would notice the door opening by itself."

"Good point," Sly said. "Has your video footage captured anything that would account for that?"

"No. That's why I need to test the full theory. I can only imagine he slips in as a customer opens the door, then makes a grab and runs around the perimeter until another customer opens the door."

"I'm sorry, but that sounds crazy," Morgaine said. "I doubt either of us could pull that off."

"Unless he had an accomplice," Sly said. "Someone to open the door and stand out of the way at the precise time the vampire needed to enter, then to reopen it when the vampire needed to leave."

Nick shook his head. "We ruled that out. None of the cameras captured a consistent person at each of the heists."

Sly rose and paced. "If I were to pull this off, I might mesmerize a random customer in the parking lot to open the door at precise times."

Nick sighed. "We thought of that too. The cops set up long-distance cameras covering all angles outside. They didn't capture anything like that in the parking lots."

Sly paused in his pacing. "Did any of the customers look mesmerized?"

"We checked. It's hard to detect a non-blinking person on a video. That's the only telltale sign I could think of."

Sly smiled at Morgaine. "Remember when I tried to mesmerize you and couldn't?"

She chuckled. "Yeah. I wondered what was wrong with you. You kept staring at me and your eyes changed colors. It was bizarre."

"I already knew you were special. I just didn't know it meant you were my *beloved*."

Morgaine grinned back at him. "In more ways than one."

Nick glanced from one to the other. "Your beloved? You say that like it's a special *thing*, like werewolf mates."

"It is."

"I've never heard that term. What does it mean?"

Sly settled next to Morgaine again and squeezed her knee. "There's one special woman for every vampire. Some are never lucky enough to find that person. When it happens, it means, 'Look no further. You've found your equal.'"

"Kind of like a werewolf finding his one true mate."

"Exactly," Sly said.

Nick nodded. "I get it. Konrad and Roz are perfect examples. They can even communicate telepathically."

"So can we," Morgaine said. "Don't worry. We try not to do it when we're with other people unless it's absolutely necessary. It's kind of rude, like whispering behind someone's back."

Nick frowned. "I wish I could communicate with Brandee that way. I don't know why we can't."

After a brief silence, Sly asked, "Are you sure she's your mate?"

Morgaine raised her eyebrows and shot Sly an intense stare. Nick imagined her telling him to keep his big mouth shut.

Sly quickly added, "I'm sorry. I shouldn't have said anything. I know nothing about you two."

Nick leaned back in his chair. "Don't worry about it. I asked myself the same question. Telepathy is a rare thing among my kind, so I'm not worried just because it hasn't happened to us. I knew Brandee was my mate the first time I kissed her." *And now I've marked her as my life-mate, and I won't find another. If she dumps me, I'm screwed.*

Nick rose. "Well, I should get going. Are you still willing to do the dry run of a bank robbery tomorrow?"

Sly chuckled. "I'd be happy to. It sounds like fun.

I've never robbed a bank before." He rose and strolled to the door. "Just let me know when and where."

"I'll call with the details. Morgaine, you're welcome to try it too."

She rose but didn't join them by the door. "No. If Sly can't do it, I certainly can't. I've never flown before. A vampire's powers increase with age."

Nick straightened. "You mean if we're dealing with a very old vampire, he might be able to pull it off, even if Sly can't?"

Morgaine stared at her beloved. "I suppose so."

Shit. Was all this for nothing?

"Look, just so you know, I doubt *any* vampire could pull this off," Sly said.

And if that's the case, it's back to the drawing board.

Chapter 16

ROZ SEEMED LIKE A WONDERFUL WOMAN. SMART, levelheaded, put together…all words Brandee *wouldn't* use to describe herself. But to be fair, Roz had adjusted to the idea of werewolves a while ago, and Brandee'd had less than a day.

"I'm glad you came." Roz opened the door and led her into a cozy apartment.

Roz offered her a seat in the living room and asked if she could get her some coffee or tea.

"Either one is fine, but no milk or cream, please."

"I'll make some tea, then. Are you still freaking out?"

Brandee nodded.

Roz held up one finger. "I'll be back in a flash."

"It's not like you can't take your eyes off me. I'm not going to do anything crazy."

Roz laughed. "I'm sorry. I'm not laughing at you. I'm laughing at myself. You seem to be handling this better than I did."

Brandee stared at her. "Seriously? I feel like a mangled mess of nerves right now."

"I was *so* not handling it well when I first found out. In fact, I was dissolving in big puddles of tears. But that was then; this is now, as they say." She smiled. "I'll get the tea started. Feel free to look around."

Glad Roz had shared that initial reaction, Brandee almost leaped to her feet. She needed to pace, and the wall-to-wall bookshelves seemed like a good place to do that while pretending to look at titles.

Her first impression of the apartment was neat and tidy, but there was more to it than that. A grouping of comfortable furniture surrounded a fireplace, which was clean, but not too clean. The blackened surround meant it had obviously been used, and split wood was stacked in the grate, as if just waiting for a chilly evening.

The book collection seemed well cared for and even loved. The volumes were grouped according to size. A special vase or statue broke up the volumes occasionally. Many were hardcovers, and their creased spines meant all had been read at least once. A few were leather-bound classics. Some she had read, but most she had to admit she'd only heard of. *War and Peace?* Who actually read that?

Apparently these folks did.

Roz returned with a tray of bone china cups and saucers, plus a plate of scones. The kind with clotted cream and jam Brandee loved but rarely treated herself to.

"The water will be ready in a minute," Roz said. She set the tray on the ottoman and sat on the sofa. When Brandee didn't move, Roz patted the empty cushion beside her.

Brandee strolled over and took the seat offered. "Your place is lovely."

"Thank you. Because my husband is the dean of the school next door, we lucked out and were given this place as part of the whole package."

"You must really enjoy reading."

"It's my husband's obsession, but I'm getting into it more and more. We like to curl up—but never mind that.

I'm getting off the topic again. We're here to talk about you and Nick."

"Yes. I can't thank you enough for taking the time to discuss this, uh…situation."

"You must be pretty confused."

"You can say that again. I'd never have believed him if he hadn't showed me."

Roz's jaw dropped. "He transformed—in front of you?"

"I-I asked him to."

"Wait a minute. Back up," Roz said.

Suddenly the teapot whistled.

"Crap. Hold that thought." Roz raced to the kitchen. A couple seconds later, she returned with the teapot and poured hot water into the teacups.

"How did you know what he was? Did he just come out and tell you?"

"No." Brandee remembered the circumstances of being marked and her face began to heat. Would Roz know they'd been making love at the time? *Oh well, it's not as if I have anyone else to talk to about this. A little embarrassment might be worth the insight.*

Roz filled the silent void. "I knew there was a big secret Konrad wasn't telling me, and as I became more and more suspicious, I demanded he tell me what it was."

Brandee snorted. "I didn't have a clue."

Roz scratched her head. "Now I'm the one who's confused."

Brandee worried her lower lip. "If I tell you, promise not to tell anyone else."

"I won't keep secrets from my husband. If he asks, I'll have to tell the truth. But other than that, I promise."

That's reasonable, I guess. I'd ask for the same exception if I was married. "Okay, but if he doesn't ask…"

"I won't offer."

"Good enough." Brandee took a deep breath and blurted it out. "We were making love, and he bit me. I thought it was weird, so I asked him why he did it and he told me. He said I'm his mate."

Roz gasped and jumped to her feet. "He marked you?"

"Yes. That's what he called it."

Roz slapped her forehead and reeled back. "He didn't tell you what he was about to do and get your permission? He just did it?"

Brandee nodded. "He said something about not being able to control himself. He said it was instinct."

Roz balled her fists. "Wait until I see my brother-in-law again—"

"No! You said you wouldn't."

Her shoulders slumped. "Damn. I did, didn't I?"

At that moment, a key rattled in the door lock and an exact replica of Nick walked in. The only reason Brandee suspected it *wasn't* Nick was because the man wore a conservative suit and didn't seem to recognize her.

"Oh, hello. I didn't know we had company," he said.

Roz strolled over to him and gave him a kiss. "This is Brandee, Konrad. Nick's mate."

Konrad's eyebrows shot up. "Did you just inadvertently tell her?"

"Nope. He told her."

"Already?"

Roz frowned. "He *marked her* already."

Konrad's big body thumped into the armchair nearest him. "Holy shit."

"He marked her *and* he shifted in front of her."

"You weren't supposed to tell..." Brandee hoped Nick wouldn't get in trouble for doing things out of order or for *something* he apparently did wrong.

Roz sat on the armrest next to her husband. "I told you that Konrad is the *only* one I'd ever tell. And he needs to know this."

"Why? What did Nick do wrong?"

Konrad gazed at the ceiling. "Everything."

Brandee rose, intending to leave. "I'm sorry I said anything."

"No. Don't be. We—we're just surprised," Roz said.

"Why? Because he was supposed to keep the big, bad secret from me until I got so suspicious I broke up with him?" Raising her voice, she asked, "Is that what he did wrong?"

The Wolfensens must have been speechless. They just sat there with their mouths open.

"Look, he's not perfect, but I love him and forgave him...not only for biting me, but also for hiding what he was. I imagine the two of you love him too. And if *I* can forgive him, then I expect you can too." *Dang, I didn't realize I'd get angry.* Even so, yes, she'd forgiven him for everything. If yelling at his family made her realize that, it was worth it.

Konrad recovered first. A smile slowly turned into a grin. "You're defending him. That's a good sign. As his mate, you can be assured that he'll defend you too."

"Well, duh. He told me the truth. I don't like it, but I can't change it. And it's not like *I'm* perfect."

"Yeah? What's wrong with you?" Konrad asked outright.

"Konrad!" Roz slapped his arm.

"It's okay," Brandee said. "Well, for one thing, I'm severely lactose intolerant. You shouldn't offer me scones with clotted cream. I love them enough to suffer the consequences even though I know what they're going to do to me."

Roz regained her sense of humor, at last, and giggled. "Go ahead. Eat a lot of them. It'll serve Nick right."

Nick waited to meet Sly and Morgaine at the bar the next afternoon. He had hoped he'd have time to talk to Brandee first, but she was busy with a table full of tourists who wanted to chat. Just as she finished up with them, the mysterious daytime vampires entered and spotted him in the booth at the back.

They strode over. Sly removed Morgaine's purple jacket and his long, black coat and tossed them over one of the hooks on the wall. Then they slid into the booth across from Nick.

Sly smiled. "I can't get over how much you and your brother look alike. I almost called you Konrad."

"I'm glad you brought your lovely bride, Sly. I didn't think you were going to come, Morgaine."

Morgaine squirmed. "I might as well confess. I have agoraphobia, although it's getting better. I've been going out short distances with Sly or my cousin, but today will be a major step for me."

"Really? How?"

"I plan to wait here by myself until Sly returns."

Sly glanced around. "This place is cozy enough. She should be okay. Especially knowing this is a safe place for our kind. Trust is a big part of overcoming her fears."

"Fears?" He probably shouldn't have said anything, but he was fascinated by the thought of a phobic vampire. So much for the bad-ass stereotype.

"I also have nyctophobia," Morgaine said. "Fear of the dark."

Nick raised his eyebrows. "Are you going to be all right after we leave? It's late afternoon. The sun might set before we're back."

"I'm fine in a lighted room." She smiled at her husband. "And I'm fine even outside at night as long as I'm with Sly."

Brandee strode up beside them and smiled. "Hello, everyone. Can I get you anything from the bar?"

Nick rose and gathered Brandee into a side squeeze. "Sly, Morgaine, this is my girlfriend, Brandee."

Sly rose and shook her hand. "It's a pleasure to meet you, Brandee."

Morgaine stayed seated but reached out and shook her hand too. "Likewise."

"Nice to meet you both." When Nick gave her another squeeze, Brandee whispered, "I'm working," and squirmed a bit until Nick reluctantly let her go.

He knew she could whisper all she wanted and the vampires would still hear every word, but she didn't know that. He was slightly embarrassed that she hadn't acted as proud to be with him as he was to be with her.

Perhaps Anthony had some sort of unwritten rule about fraternizing with the customers. He didn't know that for sure, but perhaps it was frowned upon.

"So…drinks?" she asked.

"Nothing for me," Sly said.

"Are you sure?" Nick returned to his seat. "How about a nice Bloody Mary?"

Sly rolled his eyes and put an arm around Morgaine's shoulder. "No. I'm all set. How about you, hon?"

"No thanks. We just had a couple glasses of wine before leaving the apartment. Maybe later."

Wine before going to a bar? Maybe that's necessary for her to relax a bit and leave the apartment. I'm glad Brandee doesn't have any phobias—that I know of. He turned to Brandee. "In that case, sweetheart, one butt wiggle as you walk away is all I need."

"You're incorrigible." She winked at him and left.

"She seems like a nice girl," Sly said.

"She is. Talented too. She went to art school but waits tables to pay the bills."

"Oh. That's too bad," Morgaine said. "Too many artists are undervalued. That's where the term 'starving artist' comes from, I guess."

Nick eyed Brandee's retreating backside. "She won't be starving for long. She's very talented."

Sly twisted to look behind himself, then faced Nick again. "So this is the bar, eh? Who here is paranormal? I can't tell just by looking."

"Neither can I."

A tall man with sandy brown hair sporting a bright yellow streak walked through the front door and glanced around.

"Take the guy who just walked in, for instance. I can tell there's something different about him, but I don't know what it is. I've never seen him before."

Sly eyed the same guy and nodded. "I guess you'd have to ask him. Is that how it works here?"

Nick shook his head. "It's not that simple. Sometimes my sense of smell will tip me off. But we get to know each other first, by striking up a conversation like in any other bar. Eventually, when we build a little trust, we reveal what we are. So far, it's worked out well."

"So, do you know anyone that well here?"

Nick pointed out Kurt and Tory, who were leaning on the end of the bar, talking to Angie. "See those two? One's a shapeshifting coyote and one's a wizard."

"No kidding," Sly said.

Morgaine's eyes rounded. "I've never met any wizards. I was a witch before Sly turned me, and now I'm both witch and vampire. Our building is full of shifters but no coyotes."

"I think you'd like them. Want me to call them over?" Nick asked.

"Not yet. I-I need to settle in first."

"You know who you really ought to talk to is that lady over there." He pointed to Sadie. "She's our resident psychic."

Morgaine grinned. "I sensed another psychic in the room. How exciting. Would it be all right if I just go up to her and introduce myself?"

"I'm sure she'd be very receptive. But let her know you just want to talk psychic to psychic. She makes patrons pay a one-drink minimum for readings."

Morgaine laughed. "Now there's a good business move. Is she human?"

"Yes."

"And how about your girlfriend?" Sly asked. "Is she?"

"Yes. Most of the staff are completely mortal human beings."

Sly interrupted. "If you know an older vampire, why didn't you ask him to do this dry run robbery for you?"

"Excellent question," Morgaine echoed.

"He has to stay neutral. If other vampires were to find out he was helping a werewolf catch a vampire, for whatever reason, it could ruin his and his bar's image. He wants this to be a little piece of Switzerland in the middle of Boston."

"I can understand that," Sly said.

Morgaine rose. "I'd like to meet Sadie while you're both still here."

"That's my girl." Sly grinned and slid out of the booth, allowing her to leave them. He watched as she sashayed over to the booth closer to the middle of the long wall. "Whew. I'm glad she seems comfortable here. Now, let's take care of business."

Nick cleared his throat. "I should warn you that the two cops you'll meet today are typical weres. They might not be as friendly to vampires as the patrons here are."

"Is there anything I should do or not do while I'm around them?"

"Chances are it won't matter. Prejudice is one of those words that perfectly describes itself. You'll be prejudged. Don't bother trying to change minds that have been made up for centuries."

"Then should I go through with this at all? If I'm unsuccessful, won't they think I'm just trying to throw them off to cover for a fellow vampire?"

"Maybe. But you're not doing this for them. You're

doing it as a favor to me. And as I understand it, my brother saved your life once. I can explain that to them."

"Right," Sly said. "I guess they'll see it as an 'I owe you' kind of thing. What they don't realize is I used to catch crooks as a regular thing."

"I seem to remember Konrad saying something about that. He called you the Vigilante Vampire."

Sly chuckled. "It was the only way I could slake my bloodlust and make myself useful at the same time." He glanced over at his wife and smiled. "But those were the days before Morgaine. I had only darkness inside before I met that girl."

"Well, we should get going."

"Yes. I don't want to leave Morgaine too long."

"Give me a minute to talk to Brandee. I'll meet you outside."

"No problem." Sly rose, grasped his jacket, and headed for the door. He stopped to kiss his wife on the way.

Nick watched them and couldn't help being a bit envious. Morgaine had allowed her husband to turn her into a vampire so they could be together forever. In fact, according to her, she begged him to.

Would Brandee ever agree to be turned? Somehow he doubted it. If she didn't like the bite that marked her, she really wouldn't care for the deeper wound needed to turn her.

Nick grabbed his leather jacket from the peg where he'd tossed it. Brandee was waiting at the bar for an order, so he strolled over to her.

"I have to go, sweetheart. Would you keep an eye on Sly's wife? She's a little skittish. Call me if you need us to come back."

"Huh? Why would we need you to come back?"

"It's not my right to reveal someone else's, uh, limitations. Let's just say she doesn't get out much. This is kind of a test for her today."

Brandee looked confused. "Okaaay." She glanced over her shoulder to where Morgaine sat. "She looks perfectly happy talking to Sadie."

Nick took a look at the two psychics who seemed to be having an animated, friendly conversation. "She does seem fine right now. But if Sadie gets busy, she might have to move to another table and that would leave Morgaine all alone."

"Well, whatever her problem is, don't worry. I'll do my best to make her feel at home and comfortable."

Nick smoothed a stray lock of red hair behind her ear. "I know you will, babe. Just be your charming self." He tipped up her chin to kiss her. "I'll be back soon."

She gave him a quick peck. "I hope so."

<center>~~~</center>

When Nick and Sly ambled up to the closed bank, the captain and a lieutenant were already there, leaning against a Range Rover. They were wearing plain clothes and waiting with arms crossed…stern expressions on their faces. The parking lot was illuminated by streetlights, and the shadows cast made the cops' faces seem even more severe.

"Sly, this is Captain Hunter and Lieutenant Lupo," Nick said, hoping for the best.

Sly extended his hand. "Gentlemen."

The two large cops ignored him and focused on Nick.

"Are you sure he's trustworthy?" the captain asked.

Nick knew he'd have to bluster to get through to his captain. Hands on his hips, Nick practically growled, "He's not associated with any vamps other than his wife. He's willing to stick his neck out for absolutely no reward. He owes my brother his life, so he didn't even hesitate when I asked for his help. Is that trustworthy enough for you?"

He spoke to Hunter as he'd been spoken to anytime the captain wanted to make a point. It felt strange being in a position to do so. Maybe being a "civilian" wasn't all that bad.

Captain Hunter's bushy eyebrows jumped up, then settled as he smiled slowly. "Good enough." He extended his hand toward Sly. "Thank you for your willingness to help us."

Sly nodded and shook the captain's hand.

Lieutenant Lupo didn't offer his hand, and Sly didn't bother waiting for him to. However, the two nodded to each other.

"Is this bank ready to go?" Sly asked. "No alarms are going to go off, right?"

"The bank manager left the door keys in my care but can't be here for obvious reasons. Naturally we don't have access to the vault, but we've stashed something just outside of it. The cameras are active, and we'll take the footage with us when we leave."

"So you want me to do this as if I were the real thief? Move fast enough to avoid detection by the cameras?"

"If you can." Lupo smirked at him.

Sly glanced around the parking lot. "Are cameras covering the outside as well as the inside?"

"We've got a few extras," Hunter said. Sly noted that

he wasn't told where they were. He took a deep breath. "I'd like a guarantee in writing that I won't be arrested or prosecuted for what I'm about to do."

Lupo snorted. "Talk about trust—or lack of it."

Hunter held up a hand. "I don't blame you for being suspicious. But you have my word."

Sly pulled a contract from his inner coat pocket. "Just sign this and I'll be good to go."

The three werewolves all stared at each other.

Nick cleared his throat. "He doesn't know we're always good to our word. Just sign—"

"Give me the damn thing," Captain Hunter said as he ripped it from Sly's grasp.

As soon as Hunter had signed the promise, Sly tucked it in his coat pocket and said, "Thanks." Then he took off his coat and handed it to Nick.

"One of you will need to open the door, and I'll try to get around you without touching you. If you were ordinary-sized people, I'd probably fly over your heads, but I don't want to take the chance of accidentally giving you whiplash."

"I'll do it," Nick said.

"You realize there's more than one door to go through, right? The first one just leads to the ATM. I'll need two of you opening both doors at the same time."

"I'll take the other one," Lupo added. "But what are the chances of a vamp waiting for two customers opening the doors at the same time?"

"Pretty good, actually," Nick said. "People tend to hold a door open rather than let it slam in the face of someone who's entering right behind them."

"True." The captain nodded. "Okay, let's do this

as if Lupo's going in first and holding the door for Wolfensen."

The weres all approached the unlocked doors and opened them. Nick kept an eye on Sly. Suddenly he disappeared and Nick felt a slight wind rush past him. Then another. He could have blamed the first on a breeze, but the second was more like a gust of wind. *That's odd. He couldn't have moved so fast that he'd be in and out already, could he?*

Sly suddenly reappeared in the parking lot, but he wasn't alone. He was lying atop a flapping body, which held a linen sack.

"Get off of me, you jerk."

Nick couldn't believe his eyes. A rail-thin body covered in gray fur lay pinned to the pavement. Its voice sounded like a woman who'd been smoking for forty years.

"What is it?" Lupo asked.

"I have no idea," Hunter answered. "In my twenty years on the force, I've never seen anything like it."

"It's strong," Sly said, as the stick figure struggled.

"For fuck's sake, I'm not an 'it.'"

"What are you?" Nick asked.

The figure let out a defeated sigh and after a long pause answered, "I'm a whirling dervish."

"A whirling *what*?" all three werewolves asked at once.

"Whirling. Dervish," the figure enunciated.

"I thought that was some kind of Turkish dance," Sly said.

"The dance was named after us. We're not well-known in this part of the world."

"No shit," Lupo said.

Sly glanced up at the captain. "So what should I do with him? Or are you a her?" he asked the dervish.

"I'm a female, and you should let me go."

"Why were you robbing the bank?" Nick asked.

"What else am I going to do to get money?" she asked. "There aren't many jobs for blenders with fur."

"Why do you need money?" Sly asked.

"I just want to go home. I was captured back in Turkey. We live in some pretty inhospitable mountains, but a group of determined hunters managed to sneak up on us. They caught me and shipped me in a crate to this—this place. I was in some kind of a lab, but I escaped. Now I need the money to ship a crate home—with me in it."

"How did you know the bank would be open? It's a Sunday," Captain Hunter said.

"I didn't. I was hiding up there." She pointed to a stand of leafy trees that would have provided cover. "And I was waiting for the bank to open. It had to sometime, right? And what's a Sunday?"

Nick couldn't help feeling sorry for the poor dervish. How frightening it must have been to wind up in a crate and be shipped across an ocean. He shuddered to think about what the lab was going to do to her.

"How did you learn to speak English?" Captain Hunter asked.

"The night lab technician taught me. He seemed different from the rest of them. Kinder. It was as if he knew I was someone, not something. The others were classifying me as some new kind of animal."

Each wolf glanced at the others, probably all thinking along similar lines. They had been treating a fellow paranormal creature as a human would have treated them, if the unthinkable happened and they'd been captured in their alternate form.

After a long silence, Sly cleared his throat. "I hate to repeat my question, but what are we going to do with her? I can't spend days or weeks lying on top of her while someone decides."

"I guess we'll have to help her get home," Captain Hunter said.

Nick thought he heard Sly let out a sigh of relief.

"But how will we do that?" Lupo asked. "And what if she escapes again the minute the vamp stands up?"

"The 'vamp,'" Sly said tensely, "will tackle her again. But I doubt she'll take off if she knows she's going home and not just back to the lab."

"We can't afford to have a paranormal being in a human lab," Hunter said. "If they discover what she really is, we're all at risk."

"Hello? I'm right here," the dervish interrupted. "Do I get to voice an opinion?"

"Of course," Nick said quickly. He was well aware of the way cops thought. They might not even listen to her if they believed they knew what to do. The plain truth was that no one knew exactly what to do. Five minutes ago they didn't even know what she was, but together they might come up with a viable plan.

"The guy on top of me is right. If one of you big lugs will help me get home, I'll be more than happy to cooperate."

After a brief hesitation, Captain Hunter said, "You can get up, Sly. We'll help the lady get home to the Turkish mountains safely."

"Glad to hear it." Sly rose gingerly and then extended

a hand to the hairy, thin female. She rose to her full height of about five feet and brushed herself off.

"Lupo and I will take her to my place," Hunter said. "From there we can find her a crate and some food. What do you eat?"

"Goats," she said. "Goat's milk and goat cheese will do, I guess. Anything will be better than the nuts and berries they tried to feed me at the lab."

"Sly, would you mind coming along just in case?" Hunter looked at the whirling dervish apologetically. "We don't really know you yet. I'd feel better if we have someone who can keep up with you if you run."

She shrugged. "You'll learn."

"Sure," Sly said. "But I can't stay. As soon as she's safe, I have to fly. Literally." He chuckled.

"I'm sorry to hear that," Hunter said. "I have another problem I was hoping you could help me with. We have a woman in custody for shoplifting. She put up quite a fight last night. I'm pretty sure she's a vamp."

"Really? Was she conscious during the day today?"

"No. That's another reason we suspected it. I have to hold her until we can get the store to drop charges. Right now she's in solitary with only paranormal cops watching her."

"She'll be up soon. I guess I can talk to her. What's her name?" Sly asked.

"Ruxandra."

Ruxandra? Shit. Anthony's ex-girlfriend? "Don't worry about your wife, Sly," Nick said. "I'll make sure she's okay."

"Thanks. In that case, captain, I'll help you out for a short time. I still need to get back quickly, though."

"Much appreciated."

Sly waved, and just as they were about to walk away, the captain called out, "Hey, Nick."

He halted. "Yeah?"

"I spoke to a friend of mine at NYPD. He'll try to help you ID the perps you were looking for. Maybe they can lead you to the guy who hired them."

"Great! Thanks. Can you call me with the details?"

"I'll email them. There's no confidential information. Just his name and the department's phone number."

"Does he know about our unique qualities?" He didn't have to talk in code since everyone within earshot was either a werewolf or a vampire. But it was a good habit to keep just the same.

"Nope. He's completely, um, normal, so don't mention anything about a paranormal aspect."

"Thanks. Good to know."

Chapter 17

Seeing that she was alone, Brandee stopped by Morgaine's table. "How are you doing?"

The woman looked a little pale.

"I-I'm okay."

Not exactly convinced of that and having no customers needing anything at the moment, Brandee sat across from her. "Would you like to talk?"

The woman gave her a weak smile. "I'm sorry. I don't want to be a bother."

"You're no bother. Heck, you won't even let me get you a glass of water." She smiled hoping to lighten the woman's mood, but it didn't seem to help.

Morgaine leaned toward her and whispered, "You must be a remarkable woman."

"Me? Remarkable? Why?"

"Well, you're human."

Stumped, Brandee didn't respond.

Morgaine leaned in closer and lowered her voice even more. "Before I was turned, I was a witch, but I'd still have been nervous mingling with other paranormals—even in a place like this. To think there's a wizard over there. Witches and wizards don't get along, but here I am only ten feet from one. If that's not amazing enough, I can't imagine being in here with no superhuman powers at all."

Powers? A place like this? Witches and wizards? Brandee cocked her head.

Morgaine continued in her low whisper. "Because you're human, you must feel somewhat vulnerable, right?"

"Uh, I guess all humans feel that way from time to time." Maybe this Morgaine person *was* a little insane. *Thanks for dumping a crazy woman on me, Nick.*

Morgaine smiled. "Exactly. That's why I can't help admiring your courage."

"Uh, okay. Thanks."

"And, as I understand it, you're not the only one. A bar full of paranormals, owned by a vampire, with a largely human staff."

Brandee blinked and rose slowly. *Careful, don't upset the lunatic lady.*

Morgaine quickly covered her mouth with both hands. "Oh! I'm sorry. Is that a nonpolitically correct term? Do you call us something other than paranormals here? I'm new to this whole world. I don't mean to be rude."

Great. She thinks she's an alien. Better play along. "Oh? What planet are you from, exactly?"

Morgaine's eyes widened, and then she laughed. "Ha. Good one."

Brandee shook her head. "Let me get you something from the bar. Seriously. It's on me."

"Well, that's kind of you, but I try not to drink alone."

"Hey, I'd join you, but I'm working." *Unfortunately. I sure could use a glass of wine right about now.*

"I know. Well, thank you for checking on me. I really am all right. I just can't get over this being a safe place for paranormals to mix and mingle."

"What exactly do you mean by paranormals?"

"Oh, there I go again. I just don't know what other

word to use. Supernaturals? What do you call vampires, werewolves, and shapeshifters collectively?"

Brandee almost said "myths," but this woman was deadly serious.

"Customers, I guess."

Morgaine slapped the side of her head. "Of course. You make no distinction. That's very PC of you."

The outside door opened and Brandee spotted Nick as he walked in. *Oh, thank God.* But the woman's husband wasn't with him. Tough noogies. She was going to confront her boyfriend, and if the woman freaked out, so be it.

—⁓—

Wow. Brandee looks furious. She marched over, grabbed Nick by his collar, and led him to the back door. If he hadn't come willingly, he had the feeling she would have screamed at him in public.

"Nick, what the hell?"

"Shhh. What's wrong?"

Brandee lowered her voice, but the tone was unmistakable. If yelling in a whisper was possible, she was doing it. And she'd said "*hell*," not "heck."

"The crazy lady you stuck me with said Boston Uncommon is full of paranormals. When I asked what she meant, she said vampires, werewolves, and shapeshifters. Oh, she also mentioned a wizard and said she was a witch. I thought you and your twin were some kind of oddball mutation. Like X-Men. She seems to think the world is full of them, and this bar in particular. She even said the owner is a vampire. Is she talking about Anthony?"

"Calm down, sweetheart. Trust me. There's nothing to be upset about. I'll straighten this out." He strode to Morgaine and sat opposite her.

"You have Brandee scared out of her wits. What did you tell her?"

Morgaine blinked. "Oh, my Goddess. She didn't know about the bar? I got the distinct impression that she knew."

"She knows what *I* am, but she thought Konrad and I were the only ones."

Morgaine's hand covered her heart. "Oh no. I thought she was offended because I was using some kind of politically incorrect term when I mentioned paranormals. My psychic senses rarely let me down like that. Maybe because I was so nervous and she was so calm, I didn't pick up the right vibe."

Fuck. "She said you told her about the owner being a vampire. Is that true?"

Morgaine laid her head in her hands, covering her eyes. "Dear Goddess. Yes, I'm such an idiot." As she lifted her head, a red tear shimmered in the corner of her eye. "I'm so sorry. What can I do?"

Nick looked over at the bar and saw Brandee whispering frantically to Angie. Angie's eyes were growing wider by the second.

"Damn. First of all, don't cry. I don't know how we'd explain bloody tears."

Morgaine grabbed a napkin and dried her eyes. Then she swiveled enough to see what Nick was looking at and gasped. "She's not telling the other human employees, is she?"

"I don't know. Angie is her best friend and roommate.

I need to make sure she's not confiding in her. Sit tight. Sly will be back soon."

"Is he okay?"

"Yes, he's fine. He's helping the police with another situation."

"Why him? Why not you?" Morgaine trembled and her breathing appeared to grow shallow and quick, as if she were hyperventilating.

"I'm not supposed to be involved in police business anymore. It's complicated." *Not as complicated as what's going on in Brandee's head at the moment, I'm sure.* "I'll be right back."

Morgaine rested her head on the table. "Oh Goddess."

Nick didn't think he should leave her like this, but he had to get to Brandee before any more damage was done. Sadie's reading had just ended, and her customers were pulling cash out of their wallets.

"Sadie," Nick called. "Can you come over here for a moment? It's important."

She rose and grasped the money held out to her, then hurried over to Morgaine and laid a hand on her shoulder. She was already speaking to her calmly and reassuringly, so Nick left them and stalked toward Brandee.

She skirted the bar before he got there and waited on a table.

Damn it. She's avoiding me. He took a seat at the bar next to the man with the yellow streak in his hair. "Angie," he called to the bartender.

She didn't make eye contact.

Finally, Nick cleared his throat. "Angie. Can you get me a beer, please?"

She nodded but still didn't look at him.

Shit. What did Brandee tell her? He turned to the guy next to him and said, "Did you happen to hear what the redheaded waitress was whispering to the bartender a minute ago?"

"Not completely. She said something about needing to talk about her boyfriend and a woman. I heard the words 'loony tunes,' I think." He chuckled. "If that's you, my friend, I'm sorry. It sounded like she was upset. I hope it's just a misunderstanding of sorts."

If only.

Brandee had managed to avoid Nick for quite a while, but she had finally run out of customers to wait on. *And here he comes. Crap. Just once I'd like to have a few minutes to mull over situations on my own without his running over to tell me how I should feel about everything.*

She grabbed a rag and began to wipe down a table when he appeared next to her.

"We need to talk, Brandee. Meet me by the back door."

"I'm working."

He set his fists on his hips. "You were working when you dragged me over there because *you* wanted to talk."

Crap, crap, double-crap. "It was important."

"Are you saying you're the only one with something important to say?"

Her face heated. "No."

"Okay, stop scrubbing the table before you wear off the varnish, and come talk to me."

He stalked off, acting as if his command was to be instantly obeyed. She was tempted to ignore him and go about her business, but she couldn't do that forever.

Sooner or later, she'd have to talk to him. *Might as well get it over with*.

She tossed the rag aside and followed him to the back door. Crossing her arms over her chest, she asked, "What's so important?"

"What did you tell Angie? She won't even look at me now."

"That's private."

"Did you mention what Morgaine said to you?"

She shrugged. "What I talk about with Angie is between me and Angie."

Nick raked his hands through his already tousled hair. "I need to know you didn't break your promise."

"I didn't break my promise."

He stared at her as if he had doubts. "When can *we* have a private conversation? We need one—soon."

"Not here and not now."

His big hands touched her arms and rubbed them, surprisingly gently. "I wouldn't let anything happen to you, sweetheart. You know that, right?"

Her defenses lowered a bit. "I really don't know what to think. Look, I didn't tell Angie about you."

"Then why is she giving me the cold shoulder?"

"I don't know. Maybe because I was upset that you brought the crazy lady here. Where's her husband, anyway?"

"He's helping the police. See how easy that was? You just open your mouth and tell the truth."

She rolled her eyes. "Why is he helping the police?"

"He witnessed a crime."

"Oh." She thought about pursuing that further, but she really needed to get back to work and she didn't want to give him time to ask more questions. "Why don't you call me tomorrow? I don't have to work until the evening."

He dropped his hands. "Are you sure you didn't say anything about me?"

"I didn't divulge your secret, if that's what you mean. I just said you had weird friends."

"They're only acquaintances."

She let out a deep breath. "Fine. Now let me get back to work. We'll talk tomorrow."

"What's wrong with tonight? I don't want you assuming things or spreading rumors."

"I'm already tired. I'd rather not talk until I can give you my full attention."

His lips thinned. "I'd rather talk tonight."

She sighed and he finally acquiesced.

"Fine. Call me if you change your mind and want to talk tonight. Otherwise, I'll call you in the morning. When do you wake up?"

"Depends."

He stared at the ceiling. "Give me strength." At that moment, Nick's cell phone rang. "Wolfensen." He held up one finger, meaning she should wait. She rested a hand on her hip and huffed.

He turned his back to her. "Damn it! When?"

Whoa. Something must have really upset him. She rarely saw him lose his cool like that.

He scrubbed a hand over his face. "I'll get right on it and see what I can find out. Yeah. I'll call tonight. Meanwhile, keep her inside. Okay, bye."

Brandee tipped her head. "Bad news?"

"I might as well tell you. You're probably going to

find out anyway. Someone made another grab for your cousin Katie. This time they didn't get her, though."

"Oh, my Lindbergh baby! Who's doing this?"

"That's what I have to find out."

"Please, let me know if there's anything I can do to help."

Then he leveled his gaze at her. "Yeah, there is. Be there when I call you at ten tomorrow morning. Don't even think about avoiding me."

She saluted. "Yes, sir."

Chapter 18

ANGIE LANDED ON THE COUCH WITH A THUD AND kicked off her shoes. "Is it my imagination, or was today weirder than usual?"

"It was weird," Brandee answered without hesitation. She flopped onto the lounging part of the sofa and leaned against the fluffiest pillow.

"Good. I mean, I'm glad it's not my imagination. I think I've lived in the city long enough to distinguish between regular weird and *really weird*. You know?"

"Lots of things seemed odd when I first moved here to go to school. But after a few weeks, nothing surprised me anymore."

"Yeah, that's because you went to art school with the freaks."

"Gee, thanks."

"Don't mention it. I'm just saying it took me a little longer to become shockproof. For instance, today at the bar a grown man had wide, bright yellow streaks in his hair. That would have struck me as bizarre when I was a kid, growing up in the burbs, but all I said to the guy today was, 'Great hair. Where do you get it done?'"

Brandee chuckled. "Yeah, I noticed him too. Nice-looking guy. So where did he say his stylist was?"

"He didn't. He said it was natural."

"Are you kidding me?" Brandee laughed. "Yeah, right. And I'll bet he can fly too."

"I don't know about that, but I took a good look at the roots and didn't see any. I really want to know where he goes for his color. I like my highlights, but you can tell they're not natural. Even five minutes after my hairdresser finishes with me, I have dark blond roots."

"I hope he comes back. Then we can keep an eye on that regrowth. If the roots never show, maybe he's telling the truth. I'm beginning to believe all kinds of crazy things."

Angie waved the comment away. "He was the least of today's weirdness. What was with that woman who talked about vampires and whatnot? First she just hung around without ordering anything, and later she was whining to Sadie. Did Nick ever tell you how he knew her or what mental hospital she escaped from?"

"No. He said they were just acquaintances. Apparently her husband witnessed a crime or something and had to talk to the police. So maybe she was talking about the crime. I didn't ask Nick the details. I just wanted to end the conversation and get back to work."

"Yeah, you two had a couple of intense-looking discussions. What were you talking about?"

"I can't tell you."

Angie reared back and stared at her. "But you tell me everything!"

"I-I shouldn't."

Angie tossed her hands in the air. "Oh, great. Another foul-weather friend."

"What do you mean?"

"It seems whenever a woman finds a boyfriend, he replaces me as best buddy and confidant. Suddenly the woman has no time for me, she starts keeping secrets—"

"That won't happen with us."

"Oh yeah? Then what were you and Nick arguing about?"

"He wanted to know what I said to you, and I said it was private. How hypocritical would I be if I told you about my conversations with him?"

"Not to worry. That's the best friend's privilege."

"I don't think…oh, heck. I might as well tell you what I can."

Before she had a chance to open her mouth, the door buzzed.

Angie hopped up. "Who could that be?"

Brandee had a sinking feeling she knew exactly who it was. "Don't answer it right away. Better yet, let me."

Angie halted. "Why? Do you think it's Nick?"

"Yes." She levered herself up and crawled off the lounger.

Angie shrugged. "Whatever. You can invite him up if you want to. I'm going to my bedroom to read."

Brandee waited until Angie left the room and the buzzer sounded a second time. She pushed the intercom button and yawned loudly, then she tried to make her voice sound as if she'd just been woken out of a sound sleep. "Who is it?"

"Nick."

"What do you want?"

"To come up. I have something to tell you about your cousin."

Shit. If he needed her help with Katie and she turned him away, she'd never forgive herself. She buzzed him in before she could talk herself out of it.

When he knocked on her door, she realized her little sleepy ruse would have been more effective if it was later at night and she was wearing pajamas.

Oh well. Too late now. She opened the door and he strode in.

He looked her up and down. "I thought I got you out of bed."

"No. I fell asleep on the lounger."

He eyed her suspiciously. "Really?"

Crap. We promised to be honest with each other. "No, but I *am* tired."

He snorted. "We need to talk."

"If it's really about Katie, fine. Have a seat."

"I'll start with that."

"Oh, my ulterior motive…I knew it." She took a seat on the sofa.

Nick eased himself into the armchair. "Look, I have to go to New York for a couple of days. It's for the case. I thought we could have that other talk before I leave. I want you to have peace of mind."

That makes sense. "Okay. Go ahead and tell me what you have to say."

He cleared his throat. "First I need to know what you think you heard and what you believe or disbelieve."

"Sheesh. I have no idea what I believe anymore. I didn't think I'd ever believe we had brownies in the bar or that you were a werewolf. But I've seen those things with my own eyes. Now I have a question for you."

"Okay. I suppose that's only fair."

She rolled her eyes. "Gee, ya think? Anyway, my question is…if Anthony is a vampire—and I'm not saying I believe that—or if there are any of these other *things* the crazy lady mentioned, does that mean the employees are in danger?"

"First of all, let's call them 'beings' instead of things.

They may not be *human* beings, but they're real and they have feelings too. Second, she's not crazy and her name is Morgaine."

"Whoa. Back up. You said she's not crazy? They're real?"

"Some paranormal beings are real. You've already seen that for yourself."

"Yeah, but I'm not in danger from brownies as long as I ignore them or leave them a treat if I want them to clean the place, right?"

"I don't know much about brownies. Never met one. But if that's what Sadie told you, I'd believe her. She knows more about what goes on here than most of us give her credit for."

"Is *she* human?"

"Yes. One hundred percent. She's a good example of how safe you are. If she hangs around as much as she does, the clientele must be perfectly harmless. Right?"

Brandee mulled it over. Sadie had a good little business going there. Would she put herself in danger just to make a few bucks and drink for free? *Uh, maybe.*

"Look, Nick. I'm more open-minded than most, but come on. I need to know the rest of the staff is safe. Are there any paranormal employees? And if not, don't they deserve to know the truth and make the choice to work there or not based on this important info?"

Nick took a deep breath. "You know Anthony. He wouldn't put any of you in danger. Hell, he came looking for you when he thought you were in trouble. He'd stick his neck out for any one of you. I think you're safer at Boston Uncommon than at a normal bar."

Her brows knit. "If you say so. So what was that

business about Anthony being a vampire? Does he drink blood? Where does he get it?"

"Whoa. Slow down. It's not my place to talk about Anthony. It's up to him to answer your questions in whatever way he sees fit."

She leaned toward him. "In other words, there *is* something paranormal about him, and you don't want to tell me what it is."

"I never said that."

"Come on, Nick. Honesty, remember?"

"And yet you want your personal business with friends to remain private. Doesn't that go both ways?"

She blew out a frustrated breath. "Fine. Maybe I'll ask him if I can be sure Ruxandra's not around."

"This is your lucky day. Ruxandra's in jail."

Brandee's surprise was only overshadowed by her relief. "What did she do?"

"Shoplifting. I can't talk about the details, mainly because I don't know any, but I doubt it'll go to trial."

Brandee let out a surprised laugh. "Shoplifting? Ruxandra? I knew she was nuts, but why did she have to shoplift? Was she trying to fill her closet with another pair of designer shoes? Maybe she had to add a fur coat to close an empty space?"

Nick rose. "Who knows why she did it—*if* she did it. Innocent until proven stupid, right?"

"Hmmm…Sometimes I wonder if I'm innocent or stupid."

He took her hand and helped her up. "You're neither. You are one amazing, incredible, beautiful woman who I'm lucky to have in my life. I'll call you from New York."

"You'll be careful, right?"

He smiled. "Always. By the way, there's another thing I forgot to tell you about my unusualness. Is that a word?"

"Oh nuts. What is it?"

"Don't worry. It's a good thing. My kind is very hard to kill. We don't even stay injured for long."

"Are you saying you're immortal?"

"We're not immortal, but we age very slowly."

"So, that means you must be a lot older than you look."

"Uh, yeah. You could say that."

"So, am I dating a guy who could be my father's age? My grandfather's?"

"Try your great-grandfather's. This year I turn one hundred and one."

"Get out."

"I'm not quite ready yet…I should at least get a kiss before I go."

"No, I just meant it as an expression, like 'get out of town.'"

"I'm about to,"

She rolled her eyes.

He chuckled. "I knew what you meant." He took her in his arms and kissed her tenderly. When their lips separated, he tucked her head under his chin. "I'll miss you."

"I'll miss you too."

"When I get back, we'll go to the museum."

She grinned. "Really? You'd go with me?"

"Of course. You deserve a treat after today. I'm sorry 'the crazy lady,' as you called her, upset you. She really was in the right place—although I can't tell you about her either."

"Well, if you put it that way, maybe you can buy me lunch too."

"Definitely."

She tipped up her chin and he kissed her again. "I'll see you in a couple days," he said and left.

As soon as the door closed, a pale-looking Angie peered around the corner. "Is he gone?"

Startled, Brandee jumped. "Yeah."

"I didn't mean to eavesdrop, but I heard some…things."

Uh-oh. "What things?"

"Things that will keep me from falling asleep— ever again."

"Ange. You'd better come over here and sit down."

Angie moved hesitantly, sat on the sofa, and folded her hands in her lap.

"What did you hear exactly?" Brandee asked.

"Something about Anthony being a vampire, brownies cleaning the bar, Ruxandra shoplifting, and your boyfriend being a werewolf."

Brandee flopped onto the sofa next to her and blew out a deep breath. "So, basically the whole conversation."

"Yeah."

"How could you hear all of that from your bedroom?"

"I was on my way to the kitchen for a drink. You asked if Anthony was a vampire, and I remembered you said the crazy lady was talking about vampires, so—"

"So you stopped right there and listened to every word."

"Brandee, how could I not? *You* wanted to know if we were in danger, so why wouldn't I?"

Brandee covered Angie's hands with hers. "Did you hear the part about how we're safer at Boston Uncommon than at a normal bar?"

Angie withdrew her hand and began biting her nails.

"Stop that. You've been doing really well not biting your nails. Don't start now. You're almost ready for a manicure."

"Why would I care about a manicure if I'm about to die?"

Brandee leaned back and studied her friend. Angie's face reminded her of a child who had had a nightmare and needed to be assured there were no monsters under her bed. If only Angie *were* a child, Brandee could make up an antimonster spray.

"We're not about to die. How long have we worked there? A year? If something bad was going to happen, wouldn't it have happened by now?"

Angie shrugged. "Who knows? Maybe Anthony was getting his blood from Ruxandra, but now that she's out of the picture…"

"I need to talk to Anthony."

Angie put her hand on Brandee's knee. "Don't bother. If he wanted us to know, he would have told us. And if he doesn't want us to know, wouldn't he just lie?"

"When has Anthony ever lied?"

"I don't know, but come on. If you were a vampire, wouldn't you lie about it?"

"I'm not even sure there *are* such things as vampires. Like I said, I need to talk to him before I assume anything. Do you believe they exist?"

"I saw a documentary about people who adopt the lifestyle. I've never seen Anthony during the day—ever. Claudia is always in charge when we open. Do you think he sleeps in a coffin?"

Brandee laughed. "Are you kidding me? You've been watching too many movies."

"Hey, some of those people in the documentary did."

"Well, so what if he does? It's none of our business where he sleeps—or with whom, right? I thought you were as open-minded and tolerant as I was."

"Was?"

"Am," Brandee corrected. "I am."

"I guess you must be, if your boyfriend is a werewolf. By the way, where did you get that purple bruise on your shoulder?"

Brandee immediately yanked up her blouse's collar closer to her neck. "It's nothing."

Angie crossed her arms. "Then let me see it."

"No."

"If it's really nothing, why won't you let me see it?"

Brandee had to think fast. How could she deflect the conversation without outright lying? "It's my business what kind of tattoo I get, isn't it? Besides, you're one to talk. You have a tattoo."

"Yeah, it's a butterfly at the bottom of my back. No one sees it."

"Some people call that a tramp stamp, you know."

Angie gasped. "Do not."

"Do too."

"Are you calling me a tramp?"

Brandee hesitated a moment too long.

Angie's lips thinned. "Nice work deflecting the conversation and pissing off your roommate at the same time, Brandee."

"I wasn't. At least I didn't mean to."

Angie rose. "I'm going to bed."

"It's only eight o'clock."

"I'm tired. Good night." She stormed off to her bedroom.

Brandee didn't know whether to be relieved or terrified.

⁓

Thanks to Captain Hunter, Nick was receiving the full cooperation of the New York Police Department in Manhattan. He'd already identified two of the suspects—"boss" and "Mr. M."—and after some intense interrogation, they finally gave up the name of the person who'd hired them: Martin Rossi.

Though Rossi had been a fake name, Nick had enough info to track the guy to his home in the Hamptons.

Thrilled by a real ID, he decided to relax a moment and call Brandee. He missed her like crazy and figured she might be missing him too.

"Hello, beautiful. How's my favorite waitress?"

A long pause on the other end of the phone started the hair on his arms tingling. "Brandee, what's wrong?"

"It's Angie. She took off."

Nick raked his fingers through his hair. "Shit. Why?"

"She may have overheard our conversation the other night. I tried to reassure her, but she just didn't act the same way after that. She went to bed early and mad. That's not like her. When I woke up yesterday, she was gone."

"People sometimes act angry when they're really afraid. You do that too sometimes."

"You noticed that, huh?"

"Yup. You didn't confirm anything we talked about, did you?"

"Um, not really."

Fuck. Mother Nature is going to fry my lying ass.
Nick tried to control his voice. "What do you mean?"

"Well, I told her I couldn't elaborate on anything I had promised to keep a secret. It might have been better for all of us if I had."

"But you would have broken your promise if you did. Is Anthony out looking for her?"

"Yes, but so far he's had no luck. He tracked her to the bus station, then lost her scent there."

"Her scent?" Nick wondered what Anthony had said, *if* she confronted him.

"Yeah. I guess the crazy lady wasn't so crazy after all. Anthony told me all about himself. He wouldn't confirm any of the other stuff, though."

"What other stuff?"

"Wizards, witches, shapeshifters, that stuff."

"Are you okay?"

"For some reason, I am. I don't know if Anthony did his hypnosis thing on me or not, but he convinced me I was perfectly safe like you said, even safer than at a normal bar."

"What do you mean you don't know if he hypnotized you or not?"

"Well, he said he didn't. He offered to—again. But I'd rather know an awful truth instead of believing a pretty lie."

Nick didn't quite know what to say. On one hand, he was proud as hell of her. Anthony had told her he was a vampire, and she didn't flip out. On the other, Anthony had told her he was a vampire. He was sure Anthony must have impressed upon her how important keeping *that* secret was, but Nick didn't dare leave anything to chance.

"You're keeping his secret just as vigilantly as you're keeping mine, right?"

"Of course. How can you even ask that?"

"Sorry." What else could he say? Anything more would sound as if he didn't trust her. Mother Nature was the bigger threat. *What a choice. Being dropped into an active volcano or solving an important case? It's not like I can solve anything if she fries me in lava.*

"I'm coming home."

"Did you solve the case?"

"For now. At least I have the information I need."

"Good. So Katie's out of danger?"

"I didn't say that. I need to talk to her parents and the Boston police, but I'd rather do it in person. Don't worry, sweetheart. We'll get this guy."

"I hope so. Be careful, okay? I couldn't stand anything happening to you. Especially because…" Her voice trailed off.

"Because?"

"Well, I wasn't very nice to you at the bar a couple days ago. When you didn't call yesterday, I was afraid I had blown it. I thought maybe after you thought about it, you decided I wasn't worth the trouble and wanted to break up with me."

"There's nothing you can do to make me leave you."

"Really?"

"Honest and truly."

He heard her sigh on the other end of the phone. "Hurry home."

———~~~———

Mother Nature ambled into Boston Uncommon and took a good look around. It appeared fairly ordinary—like any other neighborhood watering hole. Low lighting gave it an intimate feel. Several high stools surrounded a well-polished wooden bar. A few tables took up some of the floor space between the bar and the booths. It wasn't very large. It would only seat about thirty if it was packed.

She slid onto a stool. It might have been difficult had she'd worn her flowing robes, but she dressed in twentieth-century casual clothing. Big blond hair and a white suit with shoulder pads. The last time she had been out in the world was the eighties, so she hoped her getup was still in style.

A male bartender spotted her and came right over. "Wow. You look just like that chick on *Dynasty* reruns. What was her name? Crystal something?"

"I have no idea what you're talking about."

"Oh. Sorry. What would you like?"

"I'd like to get polluted." She smiled to herself. *Mother Nature walks into a bar and says, "I want to get polluted." All I need is a punch line.*

"I hope you're not driving."

She snorted. "I don't use cars—ever. Now get me…" She glanced around at what the other patrons were drinking. A girl at the end of the bar held a martini glass with bright green liquid in it. *Green is my favorite color. I'll go with that.* "One of those green things." She pointed to the girl's drink.

"One appletini coming right up."

Mother Nature turned to the guy beside her. "So, what's your story?"

"I'm kind of new in town. The name's Drake Cameron. I'm a firefighter." He stuck out his hand.

She grasped it. His hand was so hot it could have burned her, and she dropped it right away.

"Yikes, you're hot."

He smiled. "Thank you. You're not bad yourself."

She rolled her eyes. "I didn't mean hot-looking, you idiot. I meant actually scorching."

He lowered his voice. "I didn't hurt you, did I?"

"I'll survive. You must be a dragon. And you need to get laid."

His eyebrows rose. "You know?"

"Well, duh. Your skin is excessively warm and your name is Drake. Plus you have those yellow streaks."

"Yeah, it's a family trait."

Who do you think gave them to you, stupid? "So, new in town, huh? Where did you come from?"

"My family is from Scotland and Ireland, originally. I came here when I was a lad. Now I'm back for good."

"I see." *Why was I not aware of a dragon in Boston? And what's he doing here? I thought they were all in places that reminded them of home—like the mountains and rocky coast of northern New England and the Maritime provinces. That cretin Balog is falling down on the job.*

A waitress dropped her tray on the bar a few feet away. "Another White Russian for Sadie and a dirty martini for her customer," she said.

Dirty martini. That's what I should have had to get polluted. Gaia chuckled to herself.

The bartender set Mother Nature's appletini in front of her and glanced over at the waitress. "Sure thing, Brandee."

Ah, there's the human I'm looking for.

———— ∾ ————

Brandee sensed someone staring at her. She expected it to be a guy about to make a pass. It wasn't unusual, especially if a patron had had too much to drink.

She stuck a hand on her hip and whirled to meet the person's gaze. Oddly, this time a female was staring at her.

"You like working here?" the woman asked outright.

Who is she? Some kind of activist who thinks waitresses are demeaned? The satisfaction police? Or just a retro-looking lesbian?

"Yeah. I like it fine."

"Liar," the woman said.

"Excuse me?"

At that moment, Nick strode in and hurried over to her.

"Miss me?" he asked.

Before she had a chance to answer, he swept her into a bear hug—or was it a wolf hug? When he released her, she smiled up at him. "Yes, I did."

"When are you free? I want to track down Angie before…"

He didn't have to finish his sentence. She knew what he wanted to say, but he seemed to have stopped talking for another reason. His eyes were opened so wide she could see the white surrounding his blue irises, and he was staring at the retro woman as if in shock.

Brandee looked from one to the other. The woman was glaring at Nick. An audible gulp emanated from his throat.

Oh, crap. Is this an ex-girlfriend? Wait a minute…he doesn't have any of those. Not if all he had were one-night stands.

"What's going on here?" She studied her boyfriend's face. It seemed frozen in fear. "Nick? Are you all right?"

"I, uh—I'll let you know later."

He approached the woman slowly as she slid off her bar stool. "Mother, I mean..."

Gaia grabbed the collar of his leather jacket and led him out the back door.

Mother?

Chapter 19

"THIS IS THE SECOND TIME YOU'VE FUCKED UP, Wolfensen. What did I say would happen if you ever revealed any more about paranormals to a human again?"

He glanced up and down the alley, looking for an escape route. "I-I don't remember."

"That's convenient, isn't it? Let me remind you." She waved her hand in a circle and something like a movie became visible in that space. He saw himself standing there, being upbraided by Gaia. Her image said, "If you ever expose the existence of paranormal beings again, I'll send you to Mount Vesuvius and go all Pompeii on your ass. You get me?"

The movie dissipated into the air in a curl of smoke.

"Oh, yeah. Now I remember," he said, despite a sudden dry mouth.

"Good. Well, guess what?" She raised one hand.

"Please don't. I'm afraid there's another breach, and I have to take care of it."

Her jaw dropped. "What do you mean by another breach?"

Even if she's pissed, my punishment can't get much worse. He took a deep breath and spit it out. "My girlfriend's roommate overheard us talking. Now she's in the wind. We need to find her and—"

"I know all this. Why do you think I showed up?"

"Oh. I guess I thought it was because I marked Brandee as my mate."

"You what?" she roared.

Crap.

The back door opened a crack and Brandee peeked out. "Is everything okay back here?"

Mother Nature continued to stare at Nick but snapped her fingers in Brandee's direction. "Come here, girly."

Brandee stiffened and didn't move.

Gaia whirled on her. "Now!"

Nick shouted, "Hey. Don't talk to my mate that way."

A sinister smile played across the ancient one's lips. "Aren't you the brave fool, Nicholas Wolfensen."

Brandee stood in the doorway and appeared like she didn't know where to go or what to do. She glanced over her shoulder as if she wanted to run back to the safety of Boston Uncommon.

"Go back inside, sweetheart. I'll take care of this."

She nodded and disappeared back inside.

Nick folded his arms and stood with his feet shoulder width apart. If Gaia was going to punish him, so be it. But she'd better not drag Brandee into it. "She hasn't done anything wrong."

"Then how did her roommate find out?"

"I told you. It was an accident. We were talking and her roommate overheard."

"Maybe you shouldn't be talking about the supernatural. Or if you absolutely must, maybe you should be someplace where you won't be overheard."

Another idea occurred to Nick. If they were *living together*, they could talk freely all the time.

Then Mother Nature continued, "Either that or I could see you both put into solitary confinement."

"Don't. Brandee would never divulge our existence on purpose."

Gaia folded her arms. "How do you know that?"

"She promised not to."

"Oh well, that's all you had to say. I mean, look how well humans keep their promises." She snorted.

Nick began to pace. This conversation wasn't going well, but then again, he hadn't been sent to Mount Vesuvius yet. "I can fix this if you'll let me."

"How?"

"Brandee knows her roommate better than anyone. We'll find her, bring her back, and have Anthony compel her to forget."

"Where is Anthony, anyway?"

"He'll be here soon. The sun is just beginning to set."

"So, who's in charge when he's not around?"

"A human. Claudia, the manager."

"Is she aware of the bar's seedy underbelly?"

Nick raised his eyebrows. *Seedy underbelly? Is Gaia reading too many crime novels?*

Mother Nature stomped her foot. "I asked you a question."

"As far as I know, none of the other employees are aware of the bar's paranormal patrons or its paranormal owner."

Mother Nature's tense posture relaxed slightly. "That's good. By the way, what the hell is a dragon doing here?"

"A dra..." Nick suddenly remembered the unusual guy with the yellow-streaked hair. *Of course! The guy's a dragon.* They all had unusual markings to denote what family they belonged to, or so he'd heard. He'd never met a dragon. At last, another piece of the puzzle fell into place for him. *Who would want a fire mage like Katie?*

"A fuckin' dragon," he muttered.

Gaia tipped her head and squinted. "What's rolling through that hairy skull of yours?"

"I've been working a case. It involves a paranormal kidnapping, and now everything is making sense. Please. I need your help. You can't send me away now."

"Of course I can."

In a flash of light, Nick felt himself ripped from the fabric of reality. An instant later, he stood on an island the size of his living room populated by exactly one palm tree.

"Crap."

Another blinding flash of light later, he was back in the alley. He glanced around and then down at himself. Other than feeling a little queasy, he seemed okay. The sun was still setting, so no time had passed to speak of. But where was Mother Nature?

The back door to Boston Uncommon opened and Brandee peeked out. She scanned the alley. "Is everything okay with you and your mother?"

"My mother?" He couldn't suppress the cathartic bubble of stress release. It began as a chuckle, turned into a guffaw, and before long he was bent over laughing.

A sudden flash of lightning and boom of thunder interrupted him. He straightened up and wiped his eyes. "She's a mother, all right, but not mine."

"Good. 'Cuz I don't think she liked me."

"She'll be all right as long as you keep your promise and we can find Angie."

Brandee's eyes rounded. "Angie? What does she want with Angie?"

Nick scratched his chin. "She wants us to find her and bring her to Anthony so he can hypnotize her. She has to forget what she heard. And there's another thing."

"What's that?"

"She thinks it would be best if you moved in with me. We'd be much less apt to be eavesdropped on."

"Angie wasn't eavesdropping, she was just—wait a minute. What did you say?"

"I said she'd like you to move in with me." He smiled. "I'd like that too."

Brandee's lips started to lift in a smile, then quickly returned to neutral. "Let's wait on that. First we need to find Angie. I'm not gonna move anywhere without telling her."

Nick didn't want to get his hopes up, but it was too late. He was already delighted. Wolves wanted nothing so much as to snuggle up with their mate and make loads of pups. "So you're considering it?"

"Yes. No. I don't know yet. Don't confuse me."

He grinned to himself. *Soon enough, dear Brandee, you won't be confused anymore.*

—◆◆◆—

Nick tried to act casual as he took the empty seat next to his suspect. He stuck out his hand. "Hi, my name's Nick Wolfensen. I forgot to introduce myself when we talked before."

The guy he believed to be a dragon stared at Nick's hand but didn't shake it.

"My name's Cameron."

"Cameron, what?"

He hesitated before answering. "Drake Cameron."

"Can I buy you a beer, Drake Cameron?"

"Nah. I'm good." He lifted his nearly empty mug.

Nick got comfortable on his stool. "You're new here. Do you live or work in the neighborhood?"

The guy chuckled. "I work here. Can't afford the pricey real estate on a firefighter's salary."

"You're a firefighter, eh?" *That makes perfect sense. Who'd be more comfortable around a fire than a dragon?*

"Yeah. Are you Canadian?"

Nick tipped his head back and laughed. "No. Canadians aren't the only ones who say, 'eh,' I guess."

Drake shrugged. "Oh. I have some Canadian relatives. Just thought I'd ask."

"What part of Canada?"

"Nova Scotia."

"Ah, New Scotland." He gave the guy a knowing look, hoping he'd continue down that road. Instead, he changed the subject.

"The guys from the firehouse usually frequent another bar in the neighborhood."

"Don't say Cheers."

"Why not? I mean, that's not the one they go to, but what's wrong with Cheers?"

"Tourist trap. So, where do they go and why aren't you with them?"

"I heard about this place. Thought I'd try it out."

Nick noticed he'd conveniently avoided the first question. *Damn. If he doesn't come back here, I'd like to know where to find him outside of his firehouse.* "So, what do you think of Boston Uncommon?"

"The bar or the concept?" The guy's green eyes seemed to glow for a millisecond.

Nick's eyebrows lifted before he could school his expression. "Both."

"I like it."

"Me too. I hope I'm not being too nosy, but the glow in your eyes...does that mean what I think it means?"

Drake leaned away from him. "Depends on what you think it means. I'm not in love with you, if that's what you're thinking."

Nick let out another booming laugh. "No. See her?" He pointed to Brandee. "She's the love of my very long life."

The guy nodded but seemed unsure about how to continue. Nick needed to find a way to give him an opening.

"So, are your people long lived too?"

Drake looked at him askance. "Uh, yeah. Very. Yours?"

"We don't live forever, but we're hearty stock."

Drake nodded. Nick hoped that meant he had ruled out vampires from the list of possible paranormals.

At last Drake leaned in and lowered his voice. "Have you heard of this bar's reputation as a safe place for paranormals?"

"Yes," Nick said, relieved. "I'm friends with the owner and several of the regulars. Would you like to meet some of them?"

"Yeah."

Nick called out to Tory and Kurt. "Meet me at the back booth. I have someone to introduce you to."

The two regulars glanced at Drake and nodded. All four of them moved to the farthest booth, near the back door. Sadie's booth was empty, and only one other was occupied by customers. Thankfully, it was the booth closest to the front, so they would be able to speak freely. Supernatural hearing would allow them to whisper and be heard by their companions without fear of eavesdroppers.

When all four of them were settled into the booth, Nick proceeded with introductions.

"Drake Cameron, this is Kurt Morgan—wizard, ex-military helicopter pilot—and Tory Montana—shapeshifting coyote and high-end real estate developer."

Drake's eye's rounded. "Cool. I'd shake your hands, but mine are very hot at the moment. It's been a while since I had a chance to blow off steam, if you know what I'm talking about."

Wizard Kurt chuckled. "Dragon, huh? It sounds like you need a girlfriend."

"Don't we all?" Tory said. Then he pointed to Nick with his thumb. "Except this guy. You could take notes from him. Had a different girl every weekend."

"Until recently," Nick added quickly. "I finally found my mate."

"The waitress?" Drake asked.

"Yeah." He smiled at her and when she looked up, he winked.

She started heading over to their table. "Shit. I didn't mean to wave her over. Can I buy you guys a beer?"

Tory laughed. "You won't find me turning that down."

"Get a pitcher," Kurt said.

"Might as well. Something tells me we might be here a while. I have a few questions for our new friend."

Drake raised his eyebrows but didn't comment.

Brandee approached the table with a pleasant smile. "Can I get you gentlemen anything?"

"Yes," Nick said. "A pitcher of Sam Adams and four frosty mugs—plus a kiss for me."

"Hey," Tory interjected. "If she's giving out kisses, I want one too."

"And me," Kurt said.

"Forget it, guys," Nick said quickly. "You'll settle for the beer and your nuts. Touch her and you'll forfeit the ones between your legs."

"Nick!" Brandee jammed one hand onto her hip.

"It's all in good fun, sweetheart," he said and chuckled.

Tory drummed his fingers on the table. "Don't worry, Brandee. He'd have to catch us first. I hear big lugs like him are pretty slow on their feet."

"Don't count on that," Nick said with a growl.

"I'd better go place your order before I get hit with one of those testosterone bullets flying around," Brandee said and walked away.

The guys chuckled.

"So, you said you have questions for me?" Drake reminded him.

"Yeah. Some of us have become good friends. We help each other out when our talents are needed," Nick began.

"Ah. So you want to know what my special abilities are?"

"To start."

Again Drake seemed surprised. But instead of becoming defensive, he simply answered the question.

"Well, in dragon form I can fly, and naturally, I'm fireproof."

"Do you breathe fire, like in the myths?" Tory asked.

"I personally do not. Some dragons still do, but it's such a destructive force, it's been socialized out of us."

Nick tipped his head. "Socialized out? In other words, you can, but you prefer not to?"

Drake shifted uncomfortably. "The Asian dragons still breathe fire. They seem to have more self-restraint and can handle having the ability. Unfortunately, some of the European dragons abused the privilege and it was taken away—at least from my family."

"By whom?" Kurt asked.

Drake shrugged. "Don't know. If it occurred over centuries we'd simply blame evolution, but it was sudden. Right after the Chicago fire. I have to assume a dragon had something to do with setting it."

And I'd have to assume Gaia had something to do with the sudden evolution.

"You seem like a straight-up guy, Drake. I'm going to level with you. I'm a werewolf and a paranormal private investigator, and I've been working on a frustrating case recently. I might be able to use your help."

Drake shrugged. "Sure. What can I do?"

"Let's take a walk. Tory? Kurt? Would you mind drinking our beers for us?"

Kurt smirked. "It'll be a hardship, but we'll try."

Drake accompanied Nick to the Boston Common. They located a bench far from anyone else, and after evaluating the spot for privacy in every direction, they sat.

"I'm going to get right to it," Nick said. "Do you happen to know a dragon who goes by the name Martin Rossi?"

Drake scratched his head. "No. I—" He suddenly fell silent, then tipped his head back and groaned. "Yes.

Dammit. I do. I have an uncle in New York who goes by that alias sometimes."

New York. It fits. "What's his real name?"

"Irwin." Drake leaned away and shook his head. "You don't want to get mixed up with him. He's the reason I came to Boston."

Nick raised his eyebrows. Was Drake working for his uncle in Boston? Or afraid of him and hiding here?

"What can you tell me about him?"

Drake bit his lip and hesitated. At last he let out a hot breath. "My uncle has his own brand of 'family,' kind of like the Mafia. I may be related to him by blood, but he wouldn't hesitate to off me, if you know what I mean."

Nick nodded. "So you're hiding out from him here?"

"Yes. I'd heard Boston had more than its share of paranormals. Something about the old places reminding immortals of their home cities back in Europe. Not that it looks anything like my native Scotland. I had hoped to locate some other dragons—ones like the family I grew up in, not the distant uncle's family in New York. Do you happen to know of any other dragons?"

Nick sympathized with the guy hoping to locate others like himself and wished he could help, but Drake was the first dragon he'd met. "No, sorry. So I guess your uncle's so-called family must not have a presence in Boston if you're here."

"Not as far as I know. But why are you looking for him?"

"He might be behind a kidnapping I'm investigating." After Drake's long hesitation, Nick decided he needed reassurance. "Don't worry about talking to me. I won't let anyone know we spoke."

"Don't be so quick to promise that. If he gets wind that either of us is involved, he wouldn't hesitate to hold your girlfriend hostage to get what he wants."

Nick's spine straightened. "You'd never tell him about Brandee, would you?"

"Of course not. I want nothing to do with him."

"How would you feel about helping to put him behind bars?"

Drake let out a snort, followed by a small curl of smoke. "If I can do it without being seen, heard, or identified in any way, I'd love to."

"You probably can. I won't ask you to *do* anything. I just need to know his habits, his weaknesses. Anything I might be able to exploit."

Drake leaned back and stretched his long legs in front of him. "I didn't stay with him long. My parents obviously had no idea what he was like, or they'd never have sent me to live with him in the first place."

Nick suddenly had a glimmer of hope. "So, can you tell me anything about him?"

"Yeah. I can give you his address, but the place is a fortress. You can't just waltz in there and take him out in cuffs."

Nick already had the address but didn't have time to check it out. "Any security I can get around?"

"On rainy days the guards are inside. He has attack dogs and they'd be in too."

"So all I have to do is get him to come outside by himself in the rain. Sure. That should be easy." Nick didn't mean his sarcasm to be so apparent, but nothing about this case was easy.

"Wait. I've got it," Drake said.

"I'm listening."

"He has a driver. The limo goes in for service once a month. It goes to a car wash once a week. I think if you could meet his driver alone, you could arrange a bribe."

"What makes you think the driver would give him up?"

"My uncle is a hard man to work for. I personally witnessed him yelling at his driver for driving too slow, too fast, getting stuck in traffic, you name it."

Nick wished he knew more about this driver. He wished he knew more about Drake, for that matter, but his instincts were telling him Drake was on the up and up.

"What's his name, and do you know when and where he gets the limo serviced?"

"His name is Tom and I rode along a couple of times, just to get out of the house. If he's going to the same one, I can tell you where it is. I don't know if he's using the same schedule, though."

"Doesn't matter. I can call the place and say I don't remember the exact date and time of the appointment, and I have to be sure it doesn't interfere with something else that has to be scheduled."

"That might work."

"Does the driver have a distinctive voice or accent?"

"He's a New Yorker with a low-brow Brooklyn accent. His voice isn't that unusual. A little higher than yours, maybe—and not gravelly like mine."

"I can work with that." Nick stuck out his hand. "Thanks, friend."

Drake took his hand and shook it. "I wish you the best of luck. You're going to need it."

—⁓—

Angie strolled along the shore of Star Island, part of the Isles of Shoals off the coast of New Hampshire. The morning sun hid behind the clouds and a cool September breeze matched her mood. She had been there with her mother when she was a kid. The place was equipped with a very basic inn and offered personal retreats. The rooms were spartan, almost dormitory-like. It seemed like the perfect place to get away, feel safe, and have minimal distractions—which Angie needed desperately to sort out her jumbled thoughts.

She tucked a stray hair behind her ear and mulled over calling Brandee. She was still mad at her, but that didn't excuse the anxiety she was probably causing her best friend.

She fished her cell phone out of the pocket of her aqua windbreaker. Brandee was her number one on speed dial, reminding her just how close they were. Her mother was second and Boston Uncommon's manager, Claudia, was third.

She hit speed dial and waited for only one ring before Brandee answered.

"Where the hell are you?"

No "Hello, how are you?" Shit, I suppose I don't deserve it. "Hi. Before I tell you where I am, I want you to know something."

"What's that?"

Angie found a boulder and settled herself onto a relatively flat spot. "I'm sorry for worrying you."

There was silence on the other end.

"I think I know why you kept Nick's secret to yourself. You've always had this misguided loyalty thing going on."

"Misguided?" Brandee's voice rose.

"Maybe that wasn't the right word, but dammit, Brandee, what do you call someone who invites a Lycan into her apartment and doesn't tell her roommate? I assume you've seen enough werewolf movies to know there's a crap-load of danger involved."

"Nick is nothing like the werewolves in movies. He knows exactly who I am, even when he's in wolf form. He's very protective, so I know I'm perfectly safe. He even let me pet him."

Angie chuckled. "I think you guys are way beyond that point. I can't believe he transformed in front of you."

"It was the only way I'd believe him."

Angie hugged her windbreaker closer. "Weren't you afraid? I mean, sure, he probably told you he wouldn't eat you, but how did you know?"

"I trusted him. And Anthony was there, just in case."

"What good would Anthony be if a werewolf attacked?"

"I wasn't worried about Nick attacking me. And Anthony wasn't there to protect me. He was there for moral support, and because he knows how to hypnotize people. He and Nick thought I might want the memory erased."

"I guess you didn't. You seem to remember it pretty well."

"That's right. I didn't. It's a terrible thing to witness, but it's even worse to go through. I don't know how he stands it without screaming his head off. Anyway, if I want to stay with him for the long haul, I ought to know what he has to deal with."

Angie didn't know what to say to that. How could Brandee even consider being with Nick anymore? Her roommate was a little too tolerant of people's eccentricities, and that was one thing Angie both admired and disliked about her.

Angie took a deep breath. "Honey, I'm not telling you what to do, but don't you think you ought to consider what your life would be like with and without a werewolf in it?"

"I have. More to the point, I've considered what my life would be like with and without *Nick* in it. I love him so much, Ange. Wolves mate for life. I don't like the idea of throwing away a love so true and unconditional, that he says there's nothing I can do to drive him away. I love that. You know what my story is."

She had her there. Brandee had big-time abandonment issues. Not only did her parents get divorced, but her father wanted nothing to do with her afterward. Her mother had a string of boyfriends, and after a while, Brandee learned not to get too attached. Her own dating life wasn't much better. She'd been dumped in just about every way—in person, over the phone, stood up, text message…and for about every reason a creative guy could think of.

Her latest had said he was being transferred to Switzerland and didn't see the point in carrying on a long-distance relationship. *Ouch.*

"Okay. I get it. Nick is part of your life, and it's nice to have somebody to count on besides me."

"Can I still count on you?"

Angie's spine stiffened. "What do you mean? Just because I had to get away and think over a life-altering piece of information, you can't count on me anymore?"

Brandee sighed. "It's not that. I mean, can I count on your discretion? I promised Nick and Anthony never to reveal what I know—to anyone. Can you make that promise? Because if not, you might want to have Anthony hypnotize you and remove the information."

"So, I guess Anthony has that mesmerism thing that vam—" Angie spied a couple of kids playing on the rocks nearby. This conversation could get awkward if she was overheard. "Why? Did he offer?"

"He offered to do that for me, so I assume he'd include you too. It's *that* important that no one know. Can you imagine what would happen? People would panic. They'd be suspicious of everyone who was a little different. Hell, some paranormals might even wind up as lab rats."

Angie's friend spoke the truth—never more so than now. "Look, I guess you're right, and I'll consider your crazy suggestion, but I have to go. My privacy is about to be compromised."

"Before you go, please tell me where you are."

"I'm on Star Island. The season is almost over, so I have to leave soon anyway. The last boat back is tomorrow."

"Good. You'll come back tomorrow, then?"

"I only paid for one night, so I might as well come back today. Do you think I still have a job and a place to live?"

"Yeah, at least I assume you do, if you want 'em."

"Anthony won't fire and evict me?"

"I doubt it. He was worried about you, but he didn't seem angry."

"Okay. Tell Claudia I'll probably be late, but I'm coming."

"Thank God! Can I pick you up at the ferry dock?"

"Do you think your rust bucket will make it all the way to Portsmouth?"

"Maybe. If not, Nick said he's good with cars…"

Angie rose. "Oh no. You're not bringing him along, are you?"

There was a long pause on the other end of the phone.

"Brandee, you and I need to talk alone first. Maybe you, me, and Anthony." She strolled away from the kids, who had stopped to study a tide pool. They probably had parents nearby watching them. She lowered her voice. "Does Claudia know about the bar?"

"I don't think so."

"Sheesh, are you sure? She's been there for what… four years?"

"At least. She waitressed to put herself through BU's business school," Brandee reminded her.

"I wonder if she would have stayed if she'd known…"

"Probably. I think she has a crush on Anthony."

"Uh-oh…"

"Don't even think about it, Ange."

"Think about what?"

"Telling her."

Angie set a hand on her hip and huffed, "I told you I wouldn't tell."

"Promise?"

Angie crossed her fingers behind her back, as if her friend could see her. "I promise."

Chapter 20

ABOUT FIVE HOURS LATER, ANGIE SHOWED UP AT the bar. Brandee spotted her from across the room and rushed over. She threw her arms around her friend, not knowing whether to hug her or hit her. Hugging seemed like the safer option. She squeezed a little harder than necessary, though.

"Angie! I'm so glad you're back."

"Then don't squeeze the life out of me."

Brandee let go and Angie glanced over at the bar.

"I see Kathie is filling in for me."

"Yeah, Claudia called her in. We were lucky she was available because she usually has classes in the afternoon."

Claudia approached the pair with an unreadable expression. "Angie. We need to talk." She tipped her head toward the office and Angie followed. Angie glanced over her shoulder at Brandee, biting her lower lip.

"Would you like me to come too?" Brandee called. Robin would be able to handle being the only waitress on duty for a while. She was a bit of a ditzy blond, but she could always knock if she needed help.

Claudia just said, "Nope," and kept walking.

Brandee wished she could tell her friend it would be all right, but she didn't know what was going through Claudia's mind. She hoped Angie would receive no more than a stern talking-to. That much she deserved.

Brandee went back to work without giving it much

more thought. She wiped down a table and was about to get Sadie another drink when the office door burst open.

Claudia appeared shaken. "Emergency staff meeting," she called.

Emergency staff meeting? When had they ever had one of those? Brandee had a sinking feeling in the pit of her stomach. Sadie aimed a concerned frown at the office but continued to shuffle her cards.

Shit. What did Angie tell her?

"Kathie, can you hold the fort for a few?" Claudia asked the part-time bartender.

"Sure."

That meant Brandee and Robin were the "staff" needed in the meeting. As if her feet had just met a bad alchemist and turned to lead, Brandee took her time getting to her destination.

Kurt slid off his bar stool as she passed. "I'll watch the place, kiddo," he whispered.

"*Now*, Brandee," Claudia snapped.

Shit.

She made it into the room and shut the door behind her. Angie stood with her back to them, hugging herself.

Brandee hated that her best-case scenario was *only* Claudia calling them in to say Angie had been fired for taking off without notice. Somehow she knew it was more than that. Waaay more.

"Ange?" When she didn't turn around, Brandee went to her friend and laid a hand on her shoulder. "Are you okay?"

Angie shook her head, then looked away.

"Uh-oh," Robin said. "We're not all getting raises, are we?"

Claudia let out a deep breath. "This is serious. Everyone have a seat."

Brandee took the chair closest to the door just in case her worst fear came true and she had to barricade everyone inside. How the hell she'd accomplish that, and what she'd do afterward, was anyone's guess.

"Angie, do you want to tell everyone what you told me?"

"No," she said in a small voice.

"Uh, that wasn't exactly a request," Claudia said.

When Angie didn't follow through, Claudia sighed. "Okay. First off, everybody, don't say anything to Malcolm and Wendy about this when they come in. I'll need to consult Anthony when he gets here, but I'd like both of you to tell me what you know."

Oh, no. Please say anything but, "Paranormals are running around the city and calling Boston Uncommon home." As calmly as Brandee could, she asked. "Know about what?"

"Angie?" Claudia waited until Angie folded her arms and turned away. "Oh, for the love of…Angie seems to think our bar is full of what she calls 'paranormals,' in other words, vampires, werewolves, and—"

Robin leaped to her feet. She screamed and bolted before Brandee could get up and block the door.

"Oh, crap! Angie, how could you?" Brandee couldn't wait around to hear her answer. She ran after the frightened waitress.

Kurt grabbed Robin around the waist and lifted her off the ground.

She thrashed in his arms. "Let me go! There are vampires and werewolves after us." She tried kicking him. "Let. Me. Go!"

The dozen or so customers seemed stunned. A few rose and moved toward the door.

"Stop," Sadie yelled above the din.

Everyone froze and gave the fortune-teller their rapt attention.

Sadie laughed. "You can't honestly believe there are such things as vampires and werewolves. I don't see anyone 'after us,' do you?" She held out her arms and swiveled from side to side. "Everyone, take your seats and finish your drinks. I'm sure when the poor girl calms down, she'll realize there's been some kind of crazy misunderstanding. Maybe someone's playing a joke on her."

Most of the patrons joined her in an amused chuckle.

Brandee took advantage of the momentary distraction to call Nick. She tucked herself in the ladies' room, making sure she was alone.

"Wolfensen Investigations."

"Where are you?" she whispered.

"Not far from Boston Uncommon. The mayor's office. Why?"

"Angie told."

"Fuck—I mean, shit. I mean—I'll be there in five minutes."

The line went dead and Brandee returned to the bar, hoping Nick would know what to do.

Nick ran inside Boston Uncommon, half expecting to find total pandemonium. What he didn't expect was a bar full of frozen bodies, but that's what he saw. Humans in various poses, most of them staring in one direction.

"Jesus, it's about time you got here," Kurt said.

Nick followed Kurt's voice and found him in the center of the action, holding a frozen waitress.

"What the…"

"Sorry. It was the only thing I could do. Claudia over here…" Kurt tipped his head to point to the manager, who had her hands on her hips and was leaning forward with a frown on her face, "was demanding I let Robin go. But she was the one screaming 'vampire' and 'werewolf' and trying to run for the door."

"So you froze time?"

"Not so much time as physics. I created kind of a slow loop, but only in the bar. As far as these folks know, they're still having a good time, just laughing and drinking with their friends. Interrupting the time-space continuum has far-reaching consequences. Never mind. Wizard stuff. Would probably make your head explode."

Nick's back straightened. "Are you calling me stupid?"

"No, not at all. Look, I barely understand it myself. Just help me! I've been holding this chick for several minutes, and my arms are starting to shake under her deadweight."

Nick grabbed Robin under her arms, which allowed Kurt to step away.

"Why didn't you just put her down?"

"Do you see the position she's in?"

Nick chuckled. Her arms were shooting out in front of her and her legs looked like she was in a roadrunner cartoon. Kurt pulled an empty chair away from one of the tables and Nick lowered her into it. *She doesn't look natural sitting there, but at least she won't fall on the floor when she, uh, thaws?*

"So, now what?" Nick asked.

"I don't know. We can't leave everyone like this until Anthony gets here. It's a couple hours to sundown, and people will probably be missed in that amount of time. I don't want nosy cops coming down here to investigate. No offense."

"None taken."

"But what else can we do? The patrons and staff need Anthony's mesmerism to have their minds wiped."

"You can't do that?"

"No. Wizards and witches aren't allowed to do certain kinds of mind control. A suggestion or a bit of influence is okay, but we can't obliterate a person's free will. This snafu is apt to take more than influence. We need memories totally erased. Nothing can be left to chance."

"We need a vampire," Nick said.

"Exactly. But how do we keep everyone out until Anthony gets here?"

"I know someone." Nick grabbed his cell phone. Morgaine answered after one ring.

"Uh, hi, Morgaine. Is Sly there?"

"He's upstairs babysitting his grandson."

Shit. "Is there any way you can take over for him? I need his help. It's an emergency."

"Of course. He can be with you in a few minutes."

"The sooner the better," Nick said.

"Where are you? I'll send him as soon as I get upstairs."

"Boston Uncommon."

"He'll be there in about five minutes."

Sly was there in three. Nick heard the door rattle, made sure it was Sly, then unlocked it and let him in.

Sly didn't need to ask what was wrong. He gaped at the frozen bodies everywhere and asked, "What can I do?"

Nick let out a deep breath. "Thanks for getting here so quickly. The bar's real identity came out, and a waitress was about to run into the streets screaming it to the world. Kurt's a wizard and managed to stop her—and everyone else."

Sly slapped a hand over his eyes. "Crap. This all happened because of what Morgaine told your girlfriend, and we're responsible, aren't we?"

"No. Brandee didn't do this. But she and I were talking where her roommate overheard us. Now, my girlfriend is cool with everything, but her roommate freaked out and told the manager. The manager told the rest of the employees and this one," he pointed to Robin, "was just about to spread the alarm, Paul Revere style."

Sly chuckled. "Good thing you had a wizard handy."

"Daytime watch over the paranormals is sort of my unofficial job," Kurt said.

Nick smirked. "You mean you're not an alcoholic? I thought you spent every day here because you liked to drink."

"Well, there's that too."

Sly circulated around the bodies. "So which ones actually know?"

Kurt took a deep breath. "All of them heard the waitress screaming about vampires and werewolves. The psychic over there," he pointed to Sadie with his thumb, "told everyone the waitress had misunderstood something or lost her mind. One or the other."

Nick spoke up. "Sadie knows about the bar, but she's always been fine with it. She's related to Anthony. I don't want her memory wiped. Same with Brandee's." He had already located Brandee in the back hall to be sure she was there and okay, but upon closer inspection, he saw the horrified look on her face and thought, *Oh, hell. I'll deal with that later*.

Kurt shook his head. "This is a logistical nightmare."

Sly held up a hand. "Not to worry. I like a challenge. Now, can you both take Sadie and Brandee out back? Kurt, as soon as you unfreeze them—or whatever you do—Nick can explain to them what happened. I'll need you back inside to help me unfreeze one person at a time."

"But won't each one I unfreeze and you mesmerize see it happen to the next one?"

"Nope. I have a plan."

"While you're out there, I'll get the problem waitress here all straightened out, so you might as well unfreeze her now."

Kurt waved a hand at Robin and she slumped into the chair. A moment later she looked up, startled. Before she could say anything or look around, Sly caught her eye. Her jaw went slack and she stared at him without blinking.

"That's a good girl," he said softly, as if speaking to a frightened child.

While Sly did his thing, Nick lifted Sadie as if she were a sack of grain and carried her out back. Kurt acted as lookout, and fortunately, no one was around. Then Nick went back for Brandee.

Kurt waved a hand over both women and slipped back inside.

Sadie and Brandee moved gingerly at first, stretching and groaning, as if they had arthritic joints trying to function first thing in the morning.

"What happened?" Brandee asked. She glanced back and forth. "And what are we doing outside?"

"Kurt had to freeze the action."

Brandee set a hand on her hip. "Oh, terrific. Another paranormal. What is he? The wizard?"

Nick was about to say she'd have to ask him, but Sadie jumped in.

"Yes, dear. Kurt is a wizard. He hangs around for just such occasions as this one. I'm very glad he was here. Even if…" She stretched her shoulder and something popped. "Ow."

"Oh, my Oz. So what's going on in there now, Nick? And you never said why we're out here."

"Because Sly is mesmerizing each person one at a time and erasing their memories of what happened. Because you both can be trusted, he's not wiping your memories."

Brandee smiled. "You finally trust me?"

He tipped up her chin and looked into her eyes. "Absolutely."

He was about to kiss her when she asked, "Where's Angie?"

He sighed. "Getting her memory reset with the rest of them."

"Good," she and Sadie said in unison.

Relieved, Nick smiled at his mate. "I'll be back before closing time, sweetheart. Can I take you to my place after that?"

"I guess so. Will Angie be all right?"

"We'll make sure she is." He glanced over at Sadie. "You should probably tell Anthony what happened so Kurt can continue to keep eyes on the place."

"I will. I'd also like to know why your vampire friend Sly is out and about during the day. If there's a trick to it that he can share, Anthony could really use that information."

Nick shrugged. "You can ask. In my experience, vampires are pretty secretive, but Sly seems very different from most vampires."

Without wasting any more time, Nick grasped Brandee's shoulders and gave her a quick kiss. "Stay here until Kurt says it's time for you to go back in. I have to get back to the mayor. He must be wondering why I took off."

"You didn't explain?" she asked.

"Nope. If you say you need my help, I'll be there as fast as possible. I'd say as fast as humanly possible, but..."

"Got it. All is well." Brandee slapped his butt. "Now get going."

Chapter 21

A FEW MINUTES LATER, KURT POKED HIS HEAD OUT
the back door. "It's safe for you ladies to come in again."

Brandee looked at him in a whole new way. He had
never seemed that different from the other regulars. He
was ex-military—at least he *said* he was—and looked
the part. Tall, muscular, with a buzz cut, clean shaven,
and tattooed with the words "Semper Fi." Now she wondered who he was semper fi'd to. Anthony? Maybe they
had one of those "You saved my life; now I owe you my
faithful service forever" stories.

Sadie let Brandee lead the way. She followed Kurt
through the short corridor past the restrooms and glided
around the bar. Everything *appeared* normal. Folks
were drinking and chatting. Robin was happily waiting
on tables, and Claudia watched Kathie mix a margarita.
Angie was nowhere to be seen, however.

Claudia caught sight of Brandee and strode over to
her. "There you are. When did you take up smoking?"

"Huh? I don't smoke."

"Oh, Kurt said you must have gone out back for a
cigarette."

"That's my fault," Sadie piped up. "I needed to ask
her something privately."

"Oh. Well, it's starting to get busy. That table by the
window has been waiting a while."

"I guess I'd better get back to work then," Brandee

said with forced cheerfulness. "Do you know where Angie is?"

"Angie?" Claudia glanced around. "No. I haven't seen her."

Wow. That mind-wipe thing really works.

Sadie shot her a smile and returned to her booth where her tarot cards sat in a neat pile.

On her way toward the table of thirsty customers, Brandee caught sight of the front door opening. When she saw who it was, she froze.

Darryl walked in, looking as perfectly put together as he always did. He could make business casual look formal.

He strolled over to Brandee. "There you are. Angie told me I'd find you here."

"Angie?" *Duh. Talk, mouth. Ask him what he wants in a tone of voice that means "as if I care."*

"Yeah, Angie. Your roommate? I tried dropping in on you at home first."

Leave it to Darryl to try to make her feel stupid. Nick would never talk to her like that.

"I'm working, Darryl."

"I'll be quick. I know I left without much of a good-bye, but that's because I thought ripping off the Band-Aid would be easier."

Yeah, for you.

"But that was a mistake," he continued, heedless of her need to wait on tables. "I want you to come to Switzerland with me." He held his arms out to her as if she should jump into them and let him carry her away to a better life.

Oddly enough, a few weeks ago, she'd have done just that.

"Things have changed a bit since you've been gone, Darryl. Why don't you have a seat and when I'm not so busy, I'll fill you in."

He frowned and let his arms drop.

Brandee made her way to the table and said, "What can I get for you?"

"It's about time," the female half of the couple answered.

Brandee was about to apologize when a tap on her shoulder interrupted her train of thought. She pivoted. Darryl stood right behind her, arms crossed.

"I don't think you heard me," he said.

This time the male customer spoke. "Lady, can you fight with your boyfriend on your own time? We're dying of thirst here."

She returned her attention to the table. "He's not my boyfriend, and I'm sorry about the wait. What would you like?"

"What kind of imported beers do you have?"

"I'll get you a list."

Darryl followed her to the bar. "We need to talk."

She grabbed the wine and beer menu and returned to the couple without answering or even looking at him.

"Damn it, Brandee. This isn't the way I pictured it."

No shit. You thought you'd be greeted like a returning hero, you vain asshole.

She handed the menu to the couple and said, "I'll be right back."

"I'd rather you wait," the female customer said. "Who knows when you'll make it back here."

Brandee bit her tongue and stood there, hoping Darryl would find a place to sit and leave her alone until she could talk—before she stuffed a wet rag in his mouth.

At last she had the couple's orders and took them to

Kathie. Brandee lingered, rather than walk away, since there were only two bottles to be opened.

Again, Darryl approached her. This time his smile was back in place. "I missed you, baby. I know you must have missed me too and you're probably mad, but I'm back now and I'm ready to work it out."

Brandee rolled her eyes. "I didn't have time to miss you. I have a new boyfriend. He asked me out about five minutes after you dumped me."

The first opened beer landed on her tray, soon followed by the other.

Darryl laughed. "There's no way that's true."

She tried to maneuver around him. He grabbed her arm and the beers toppled over, hitting the floor with a smash. Beer flew everywhere, hitting her legs as well as a customer's pant leg.

"Oh, I'm sorry!" she said to the customer and grabbed a handful of napkins for him.

Darryl made a sound of disgust and walked away. "I'll wait over there." He pointed in some direction, but Brandee didn't see which one and didn't give much of a damn.

She cleaned up the mess and carried the couple's two new beers to them carefully. She hadn't dropped a drink in over a year. Now her record was sullied, thanks to dumbass Darryl. How could she ever have thought he was Mr. Possible?

Brandee was relieved when Nick showed up fifteen minutes later. He strolled over, gave her a meaningful smile, and asked, "How is everything, beautiful?"

She threw her arms around Nick's neck and kissed him full on the mouth. He happily returned the enthusiastic greeting.

When she stepped away, she slapped Darryl up the backside of his head and said, "See? I told you he was real."

Darryl rose to his full five-foot-ten height and looked up at Nick…waaaay up. Apparently he decided he was no match for the six-foot-three, broad-shouldered, good-looking guy, so he tossed a dollar on the table and quickly walked out the front door.

Nick eyed the dollar. "Big tipper," he said with a smirk. "Why didn't he believe I was real?"

"Long story. I'll tell you later tonight."

"Speaking of which, I may have to meet you at your place. I have a couple of things to get out of the way first, and those will probably take me until past closing."

"Okay. I'll see you whenever you get there."

Nick scanned the bar and lowered his voice. "Where's Angie?"

"Home, I think. I haven't had a chance to call her yet."

"Good. Sly told me what he told her, and you should know so you can play along."

"Okay."

"She and Claudia think Anthony gave her a couple of days off because she had been working so hard and deserved it."

"I guess that will explain why she went to Star Island. Maybe she thinks it was a mini-vacation instead of a freak-out retreat."

"Probably. If Anthony needs to reinforce anything later, let him know."

"I will. I guess I'll have to wing it in the meantime."

Nick cupped her cheek. "That's my girl." He leaned down and gave her a quick kiss before heading out the back.

—᠁—

Brandee dragged herself upstairs to her apartment that evening, totally exhausted. She suspected it was more emotional than physical. *Talk about bizarre days*.

When she opened her door, she was hit with the most amazing cinnamon aroma. *Yippee! Angie's been baking*.

She entered the kitchen just as Angie pulled something out of the oven. It looked as good as it smelled.

"What did you make?"

"Bread pudding. Want a piece?"

"Thanks! I had a crazy day. I can use a bit of comfort food." Brandee was grateful that Angie always cooked with lactose-free ingredients so she could share nummy things with her.

"That bad, huh? I'm glad I had the day off, but if you needed me you could have called."

"Nah, the new part-time bartender was happy to have the hours. I was just a little overwhelmed mentally. Guess who showed up?"

Angie said, "Wait, don't tell me. Brad Pitt, and you're overwhelmed from crawling after him, starstruck, trying to lick his shoes."

Brandee would have laughed, but it took too much energy. "No. Almost as unbelievable, though. Darryl."

"Darryl? The guy who wasn't into you enough to continue your relationship long distance?"

"That's the one."

Angie cursed. "Someone buzzed the intercom and asked for you. If I'd known it was him, I'd have said you moved to Hawaii. What did the douche bag want?"

"Me. He said it was all a big mistake and he wanted me to move to Switzerland with him."

"Ha. I hope you sent him packing—literally."

"Even better. Nick showed up." Brandee touched her lips and smiled.

"And?"

"Darryl took one look at his replacement and ran."

"Poor baby." Angie chuckled. "I know I wasn't always supportive of Nick, but I see how he treats you, and believe me, you upgraded quite a bit."

"Thanks. I agree."

"Did you ever find out why he quit the police force and became a PI?"

"Uh, yeah. It had something to do with his identical twin being accused of some high-profile art theft. Even though his brother was acquitted, there was still suspicion hanging over his head like a big black cloud."

"Is that because of the twin thing? Did people see his brother's picture in the paper and think it was him?"

"Yeah, partly, and because the thieves wore Boston Police uniforms to get past the security guards, some people *still* think he was involved somehow. By the way, he's coming over sometime tonight. Don't bring it up, okay? I don't think he likes to talk about it."

"Don't worry. I'll be cool. Speaking of cool…" She pointed to the bread pudding. "I'll cut up this bad boy while it's still warm. Would you like a scoop of lactose-free ice cream on it?"

"That's really sweet of you. Thanks."

Brandee was ravenous and the bread pudding was incredible, so she savored a piece. "Oh, Ange, that's like the Fourth of July in my mouth!"

Angie chuckled. "Eat up. I made way more than we need."

Half an hour later, Brandee was starting on another piece while waiting for Nick. When the door buzzed, her mouth was full, so she just pushed the button to let him in without using the intercom.

She waited for the knock on her door and opened it without looking through the peephole, confident that it was Nick. To her surprise, in walked Darryl.

"You didn't ask who it was. How did you know it was me and not some rapist?"

Brandee nearly choked. When she could speak, she said, "I thought you were my boyfriend."

He set his hands on his hips. "And I thought you were my girlfriend. How could you just throw away a year with me for a couple weeks with some big, blond, hairy ape?"

"Ape? You don't even know him." Her stomach growled and roiled. She clapped a hand over her rounded abdomen. "Oh crap." *I know these symptoms*. She had an awful feeling there might have been some kind of milk in the bread pudding. She could already feel the bloat beginning to distend her stomach.

Darryl stepped back and eyed her belly. "Shit." He pointed to it. "Is that from us?"

He thinks I'm pregnant! Brandee was about to rip him a new one, but when she opened her mouth to speak, she burped instead. "Oh, my Pepto…"

"Uh, yeah. Never mind, Brandee. You have a new guy in your life now. He can deal with your—problems." Darryl turned on his heel and practically ran out the door. His footsteps pattered quickly down the stairs.

What an ass. Nick would never do that.

She thanked her lucky stars that she found true love before settling for—for what? She realized she didn't even *like* Darryl. Why on earth did she think she might have a future with him? Was avoiding loneliness more important than learning what love really was, even if it took a while? Talk about a close call!

Brandee didn't know whether to laugh or cry. She opted for running to the bathroom when she felt the inevitable about to happen.

As soon as she was seated on the throne, she yelled, "Angie!"

A few seconds later, Angie answered through the door. "What's the matter?"

"Did you use milk in the bread pudding?"

"What? Of course not, I know better than to…"

Brandee couldn't hold it in without immense pain, so she let out a loud burp.

"Oops. Let me check."

As Nick rounded the corner onto Charles Street, he thought he saw Brandee's ex-boyfriend fleeing from her apartment. He chuckled to himself, wondering what his little spitfire had said to scare the guy off like that. He could hardly wait to find out.

He jogged the rest of the way to her apartment, opened the outer door, and hit the intercom buzzer. He waited a while before Angie finally answered it.

"Nick? Is that you?"

"Yeah. Brandee's expecting me."

"I know, but she's a little, um…under the weather at the moment."

She looked fine at the bar. I hope she isn't crying over that asshole. "All the more reason to let me in. Whatever it is, I can help take care of her."

"I don't think she'd want you to do that right now."

"Angie," he said in a controlled tone, but one he hoped broached no argument, "open this door and let me in."

"Or what? You'll huff and you'll puff and blow our four-story brick building down?"

Nick almost gasped. Did she still know he was a wolf? Was she protecting her roommate from him? A growl escaped.

He pressed the intercom again. "Angie. Let me in. I mean it."

"Oh, all right, but you're going to wish I hadn't."

What the hell could be wrong with her? He yanked the door open when the unlocking mechanism buzzed and took the stairs two at a time. He arrived at the second floor before Angie had a chance to change her mind. He pounded on the door a little harder than he meant to.

Angie opened it with the chain still linked across "Jeez, calm down. She's not dying or anything."

He balled his fists. "Angie, let me in. I need to see her."

"You can't. She's in the bathroom, and you *really* don't want to go in there." She lowered her voice and spoke behind her hand. "Not without a gas mask."

Nick's eyebrows shot up. *All of this because of a little gas?* He gentled his approach. "Just let me talk to her through the door."

Angie sighed and closed the door enough to remove the chain. "Fine. But I guarantee she'll be embarrassed. Don't say I didn't warn you."

Nick stalked to the bathroom and stopped just short of the door. "Brandee, honey? Are you okay in there?"

"Nick?"

"Yes. Angie said you were feeling ill. I need to be sure you're all right."

"Yeah, I'm just…indisposed at the moment."

Her voice sounded okay. At least she didn't seem shaken up.

"I can wait," he called.

"I don't think that's a good idea."

"Why not?" He glanced over his shoulder and saw Angie coming up behind him.

"She's lactose intolerant, and I accidentally used the regular milk instead of the lactose-free stuff in my bread pudding. The recipe called for four cups and she had two pieces."

"Oh." He chuckled. "Christ, you had me worried. I thought she was really sick." *Is that why her ex-boyfriend ran off? Afraid of a little gastric distress?*

"Sweetheart," he called through the door. "Don't worry about me being put off. I love you no matter what. You believe that, don't you?"

After a brief pause, Brandee answered. "Yeah, but I don't want to ruin the romance right away. I'm not feeling very sexy."

"I don't expect you to feel sexy all the time."

He heard a soft sigh on the other side of the door. Then she called out, "Go into the living room and get comfortable. I'll be out as soon as I can." Her sentence was punctuated by a long, muffled burp.

"Hey, Brandee?"

"Yeah?"

"You're adorable."

—᭡ᥩᥩ—

After a large dose of Pepto and a few more good burps, Brandee hoped her symptoms were under control. She pattered out of the bathroom and curled up on the sofa next to Nick. He looped his arm around her shoulder.

"Hey, you. Feeling better?"

"I might still need to jump up and run to the bathroom in a hurry, but I'll live."

"I'm very glad to hear that."

Nick leaned in for a kiss and she gave him a quick one. Burping during a kiss was about the least sexy thing she could imagine. *Now, to change the subject.* "How's Katie?"

"She's getting antsy being indoors all the time. She has a tutor so she won't fall behind at school, but she misses her friends."

"I can imagine. Her parents won't even let me take her to the mall. Are you getting any closer to catching the culprit?"

"Yes. I can't tell you any more than that right now." He shot a meaningful look her way, and she figured it had something to do with Angie possibly overhearing the conversation.

He looped her hair around his finger. "So, what did you say to make your ex-boyfriend run out of here like his heels were on fire?"

"I didn't get a chance to say anything. He saw my bloated belly and assumed I was pregnant."

Nick swore. "And he took off? Left you to fend for yourself and an unborn child?"

She nodded. *Nick wouldn't run from responsibility like that. He's too honorable and would probably propose marriage on the spot.*

Nick smiled. "For what it's worth, I'd be thrilled if I found out you were carrying our baby."

Whoa.

It was better if she changed the subject back to something safe—even if it was gross. "I can't believe you waited this long for me. I must have been in the bathroom for half an hour."

He swept her hair behind her shoulder. "You're worth waiting for. Besides, if we're going to live together, I can't let a little upset tummy get between us."

Wow. He really is in it for the long haul. She couldn't believe her luck. Before she could make a terrible mistake, a truly devoted guy had shown up and swept her off her feet, and now he wanted to make a life with her. The idea was thrilling, but going all-in so soon still felt like a big risk. Caution tamped down her momentary excitement.

She chuckled. "You might want to slow down, cowboy. Even though I'm glad you know what's wrong with me, and it doesn't seem to faze you."

"Of course not. And why wait? I know you're the one, sweetheart."

But am I sure you're the one? Everything had moved so fast. Brandee could feel their relationship deepening. However, only a few weeks ago, he was still One-Night Nick, and she would never have guessed him capable of living with any woman, never mind her. Anyone would say she was nuts for considering it. Still, she wasn't like most people.

Brandee knew she had her issues, like anyone else, but she was worthy of a loving relationship. In that department, she hadn't had much luck. Of course, she didn't have Nick before. Comparing him to any of her past boyfriends, Darryl included, made her very glad none of them had worked out.

She lowered her voice again. "I haven't mentioned it to Angie yet, and now is not the time."

"When, then?"

"It would be ideal if she had a boyfriend too, or at least another roommate."

His eyebrows lifted. "I don't think I can wait that long." He leaned in and nuzzled her neck. "I want you in my bed."

His nose tickled her and she giggled. "At least wait until we can have sex again."

"Why can't we have sex now?"

She burst out laughing. "Are you kidding me?"

"Look, nobody's perfect. Not even me." He grinned. "Well, I wouldn't wish my condition on my worst enemy."

"How did you get it?"

"I was born with it. It's inherited. I'm half Irish and half Finnish. Unfortunately due to a genetic mutation, about ten percent of Finns have it." She lowered her voice. "And now you know we're both mutants."

He laughed. Whispering in her ear, he asked, "Did Angie remember anything other than what Sly told her?"

"No," she whispered back. "I think her memory's back to the way it was before she found out. Now we have to be extra careful not to discuss the *w* and the *v* words while she's around."

"Think you could make it to my place?"

Her eyes rounded. "Tonight?"

"Yeah. We have stuff to discuss, and I have to go to New York again."

"No way."

"Why not?"

She smirked. "I'm not ready. I'm *barely* in control of my, um, situation. Any minute now…" Her stomach started to roil. She jumped up and ran to the bathroom, tossing a "See? I told you" over her shoulder.

Nick laughed. "You're *still* adorable."

Chapter 22

NICK WAS GLAD DRAKE HAD BEEN RIGHT ABOUT Martin Rossi's limo driver. The guy was more than willing to take a bribe.

"So, I guess all we have to work out is how you'll deliver him to me and when."

"Hey, I don't want him knowin' I had any part in dis. If you can figure out a way to stop me as I'm drivin' him somewheres, den, you know, you can grab him and take him in for questioning or whatevah."

"I'm not a cop and even if I was, I wouldn't have any jurisdiction here."

"Yeah, yeah. Well, how you get him is your problem. I can tell you when I have him in my car without any bodyguards, my route, and when we'll be on the road. Maybe you can set up a roadblock or somethin'."

Nick didn't know how strong dragons were. If a werewolf could overpower him easily, yes, a roadblock might work.

"In your opinion, would he be helpless to defend himself against one powerful man? Is that why he has bodyguards? Or would I need a small army to bring him down?"

The guy shrugged. "I ain't never seen him in a fight. He pays people to do his dirty work."

"It sounds like I can take him." *I'd better call Drake to be sure.*

The driver looked up and down, obviously sizing up Nick. "Yeah. You're a big dude. You could probably wrestle him to the ground. But he'll yell for me to help him. If I don't, he'll know I sold him out."

Nick thought about the predicament for a moment. "How are your acting skills?"

The guy laughed. "Well, I ain't never been in a play if dat's what you mean."

"If it looked like you were coming to his aid, and I pretended to hit you, could you act as if I had knocked you out?"

Light dawned in the man's eyes. "Yeah, yeah. I get it. Den it would be you against him, and I'd be off da hook."

"Exactly."

"Yeah. I could do dat. Hell, I could even take some actin' lessons. Maybe after I lose my job I can become a stunt man or somethin'."

"That's a great idea!" *That's a terrible idea. People have to practice for years to do that sort of thing.*

Nick dug a paper out of his pocket. He had already written the number of his disposable cell phone on it. "Here's how you can reach me. Do you think he'll be going somewhere in the next few days?"

"Yeah. He visits his mistress every Tuesday and Thursday."

"Perfect." Nick felt even better about doing whatever he had to in order to get this guy. He had little sympathy for a man who cheated on his wife.

The limo driver shuffled his feet. "So, we have a deal?"

Nick extended his hand. "Absolutely."

The guy shook it.

"Oh, one more 'ting. You said you'd pay me in cash. I want a down payment."

"Right." Nick had expected that. He removed his wallet and peeled off five hundred-dollar bills. "I believe half up-front is customary. The other half on delivery."

"Yeah, and make sure he doesn't see you givin' me the other half."

"I'll tie him up and blindfold him before you," Nick made air quotes, "'wake up.' I'll have the money in an envelope and I'll toss it into the limo."

"Okay. You sure you can pull this off?"

"Unless he has superhuman strength I don't know about, yeah. I'm sure."

The only thing I'm not sure about is what'll happen to him once I deliver him to the mayor and police commissioner. Then he thought of Gaia. If only he could get her to zap this guy to an island the size of a postage stamp!

The following day, Nick kept his cell phone on, anxiously waiting for the driver's signal. At last the text arrived, alerting Nick to the limo's route and status. He drove his rented van to the rendezvous point and blocked the road with large crates. As a werewolf, he had the strength to toss them out of his way as if they were empty shoe boxes.

The limo approached the barrier and slowed to a stop. The driver honked his horn. *He probably wants his annoyance to look good for his boss.* Suddenly the driver stepped out of the vehicle.

Wait. This isn't the scenario we agreed upon.

The driver had probably forgotten or become

confused. He didn't seem very bright. Nick approached, figuring he'd pretend to knock him out first. *Oh well. Either way, it'll work.* He took a swing, but instead of going down, the driver ducked. The back door swung open and two bodyguards rushed out.

Fuck. I've been double-crossed.

After a long struggle, the three of them managed to get Nick to the ground and pinned. They zip-tied his hands behind his back. Fortunately, Nick managed to ball his fists before the ties were secure. That would leave a bit of wiggle room when he relaxed his hands.

The driver laughed. "You thought I'd turn over my boss for a measly thousand bucks? He paid me twice that much to turn the tables on you."

With a lot of grunting, the goons managed to drag Nick to the limo and force him inside. The boss wasn't even with them.

The driver took off in reverse, turned the car around as if he'd had stunt driving experience since birth, and roared off.

Shit. "Where are you taking me?" Nick asked.

"Shut up," was the only answer he received from one of the bodyguards.

Nick's next thought was about Brandee. What if he never made it back home? Would she think he'd abandoned her? She couldn't, right? Even with her abandonment issues, he'd made it abundantly clear he'd never leave her. Hadn't he?

The thought that he might hurt her, regardless of how unintentionally, gave him a sudden surge of strength and he kicked out, hitting one of the bodyguards square in the jaw.

"Ow! That hurt, dickwad."

The other one pulled a weapon while the first guy rubbed the back of his neck. "We was supposed to bring you to da boss alive, but accidents happen. Don't try that again, or this gun might *accidentally* go off."

Shit. Shit. Double shit.

———∾∾∾———

Nick was refusing to walk to his doom. If they insisted on taking him into the mansion, they'd have to drag his deadweight up the stairs. *Deadweight. That's what I'll be anyway, if I can't get away.*

Tired of trying to lug him across the manicured lawn, one of them said, "Hey, why don't we just stuff him in the gardener's shed for now. We can tell the boss we've got him stashed and ask for further instructions."

"Dat's a good idea," the driver said. "I'll get da key. Can you two hang on to him while I'm gone?"

The only thing his cohort said was, "Hurry."

Nick had an opportunity, but was it the right one? The men had at least one gun, maybe more. How far would he get? He couldn't shift in front of humans—no matter what. But it sure would be fun to see their faces as they came face to face with a vicious werewolf.

He'd let them lock him in the shed. That way he'd have the privacy he needed to shift. Whenever they opened the door again, he could leap over their heads and run. He'd been clocked at speeds of up to forty miles per hour. He'd be long gone before they got into a car, and he could avoid roads.

Nick felt a little better having a plan that involved his superior senses. He'd be able to hear them coming and he'd be all ready to spring. They wouldn't be expecting anything of the kind and would be flustered for a few precious seconds. Enough for him to get away.

And now that a crime had been committed, he could enlist the help of the local police. Were werewolves on the force in the Hamptons? It was a remote possibility. They tended to make good cops, so many went into law enforcement—at least in Boston. That might be too much to hope for here in a beach community.

He still didn't know if dragons had superior strength or not. He'd tried to reach Drake yesterday at the fire station, but he was off for a few days. He wasn't at Boston Uncommon and Nick didn't have his unlisted home number, so he'd had to go with what he already knew. Drake had said he could fly. Would the boss shift and fly over the city to locate a wolf on the run? How would one explain a giant dragon in the sky? He might get away with it at night, so Nick hoped he could break out before the sun set.

There were too many possibilities for things to go wrong. He'd have to stay sharp and ready to change his plan at a moment's notice.

That evening, Brandee paced the floor of her apartment. Holding her cell phone in one hand, she stared at it for the dozenth time.

"You can't make it ring by looking at it, you know," Angie said.

"Something must be wrong. He always calls by now to ask how my day was and tell me he loves me."

"I'm sure he just forgot." Angie patted their small dining table. "Please sit down and eat something."

"I can't. My stomach is in knots."

"Well, there's nothing you can do about it, so you might as well try to relax."

Brandee halted and glanced up. "Wait a minute. Maybe there *is* something I can do."

"Like what?"

"Go downstairs and talk to the guys at the bar. Maybe one of them knows something. Where he went, what he was planning. Maybe they can help find him and bring him back."

Angie gave her a pitying look. "It's a long shot."

"But it's worth a try. I *can't* just sit around and do nothing. Why did it have to be my evening off? Work might have distracted me a little. Now I'll be obsessing about it all night."

"Why don't you set up the darkroom and do some of your experiments? If I need to use the bathroom, I can always go downstairs."

"You make me sound like Dr. Frankenstein."

"I want you to find something constructive to do with your time. Hell, I wouldn't even care if you decided to sew together human body parts if it would help you stop obsessing."

Brandee thought about the time Nick had told her he was stronger than most men and, as a wolf, could run much faster. *If he is in trouble, he'll be able to get away, won't he?*

Angie rolled her eyes. "Okay, okay. I can see the wheels going round and round in your brain. Talk to the regulars. But what if it's really just that he forgot to call? You're going to feel like a total ass."

"So? I'll feel like an ass. A lucky ass. I'm willing to risk it."

Nick had walked into the shed under his own power. As soon as he was alone, he shifted. As always, the transformation was painful, but he avoided making any more noise than necessary. He imagined someone might be outside, guarding him. A small window let in the rapidly fading light, but it was too small for a full-grown man to fit through. The building itself was built of cinder blocks, probably reinforced with rebar. The door was some kind of metal. The window was his only option.

Perhaps in his wolf form, however, he could fit through it.

He used his superior sense of hearing to determine if the guards were outside or not. He heard no conversation, but there were other noises. Nothing easy to identify. It could be a squirrel, for all he knew.

He crept toward the door and tried his sense of smell. Nothing. That didn't mean much either. The wind could be blowing the other way.

Could he break the window and jump out?

Suddenly he heard voices in the distance. *Someone is coming.*

This would be his chance to put plan A into action and hope he didn't need a plan B—because he didn't have one.

Before long, the padlock rattled. He positioned himself a few feet away from the door so he could rush them, get a little momentum, and then spring over their heads. It wasn't exactly a neat and tidy plan, but it should work. At least he had the element of surprise—if not utter shock—going for him. How they would explain to their boss about the switch between a six-foot-three human and a buff-colored wolf was their problem.

The door creaked as it opened. Nick spotted the two guards from before, and there was a third man, but not the driver. It was Martin Rossi or Irwin, or whatever his name was today. He sported the same yellow stripe in his hair as his nephew Drake had. Nick didn't give them even a split second to realize they were dealing with a new animal and adjust their strategy.

He rushed at them, leaped into the air, and heard gasps as he took off running across the lawn. Suddenly a shot rang out.

Nick felt a hot poker stab him in the butt, and he yelped. He couldn't afford to stop or even slow down. He dashed toward the tall hedge that separated the dragon's property from the one next door. Instead of leaping over it, he dove for the small opening near the roots. Even with a few more scratches and throbbing hindquarters, he kept going—pressing on to the relative safety of the nearest Long Island police station.

Getting shot was no picnic, but now he had rock-solid evidence of an attempted murder. That should get Martin behind bars, at least temporarily.

Kurt and Tory sat at one of the tables, drinking frosty mugs of beer. Brandee chatted with Malcolm and waited until the back booth was open before approaching them. When the couple who'd been sitting in the desired booth finally got up to leave, she strode over to the wizard and shapeshifter.

"Can I talk to you two?" she asked.

"Of course. Have a seat," Tory said.

"I'd prefer the back booth, if you don't mind moving."

"Whatever the lady wants," Kurt said.

When the three of them were settled in the booth, Brandee waved away Wendy, who was about to come over. "I've got it," she said, trying to sound cheerful. She picked up a cocktail napkin and wiped off the table.

Wendy gave her an appreciative smile and practically skipped off to another table.

"Guys, have either of you heard from Nick recently?"

The two paranormals glanced at each other, then gave her their full attention. "No. Why? Haven't you?"

"No, and I'm afraid something is wrong."

At that moment, Sadie strode into the bar. *Her* booth was occupied, so as she stood surveying the place, Brandee waved her over.

She smiled and approached their booth.

Brandee scooted over so the psychic could join them.

"What's wrong, dear?" Sadie asked immediately.

"Is it written on my face or did you pick up something psychically?" Brandee asked.

"Both," Sadie answered.

"I usually hear from Nick a couple times a day. But today…nothing. I know he went to New York on a case, and I'm afraid something's happened to him."

Sadie nodded and drew out the velvet pouch she always carried her tarot cards in.

"You're going to do a reading?" Brandee asked incredulously.

"Sometimes just drawing a single card will speak to me, and I can follow the psychic energy from there."

Brandee remembered the time Sadie drew a single

card for her, and up came The Lovers. The card had
sparked her prediction that Brandee was about to embark
on a relationship, and immediately Nick walked into her
life. Maybe the cards really did speak to Sadie. In that
case, Brandee hoped the cards were talkative today.

Sadie shuffled while the group waited in silent anticipation. Finally she fanned out the cards in a neat arc.
"Form a question and then draw a card."

Brandee thought about how to word the question so
that she'd get the greatest amount of information. She
didn't just want to know that he was safe, because if the
answer was "no," she needed to know how to help him.

"Can I make it a two-part question?"

"Depends. Are the questions related?"

"Yes."

"All right. Let's hear it."

"You don't usually ask people to voice their questions. I've heard you tell them to think of one, but not
to ask it aloud."

Sadie smiled. "That's to impress the tourists. They're
always thrilled when I answer the question and they
didn't have to tell me what it was. You and I can cut
through the bull."

That was the first time Brandee had ever heard Sadie
refer to what she did in a semi-derogatory way. She
might have been concerned, but she knew Sadie was
simply referring to her process, not to her psychic gift.

"I need to know if Nick's in trouble, and if so, how
we can help." Her finger circled the air to include the
others at the table. They seemed to understand—at least
no one interrupted and said to leave them out of it.

Sadie nodded toward the cards. Brandee had almost

forgotten she needed to draw one. Her hand shook slightly as she reached forward. How would she know which one to choose? She wasn't psychic.

Brandee withdrew her hand and said, "I can't. You do it, Sadie."

Sadie raised her brows but didn't argue. She pulled a card from the lineup and flipped it over. On it was a heart with three swords piercing it.

Brandee gasped. "Oh my…" There were no words for the fear that sliced through her at that moment.

Sadie was quick to say, "It's not as bad as it looks. Although at this moment it may mean sorrow and pain, there's a positive view in the end. Right now there's upheaval, separation, disruption, and conflict. That's the worst part. He's probably worried about you and his not being here to reassure you.

"However, it also means the clearing of the obsolete to make way for what is to come. Establishment of something better. Had the card been upside down, an eventual defeat would be indicated. This card is telling me that, yes, he's in trouble, but he will overcome this on his own. What you need to do is trust that. Trust *him*."

Brandee covered her face with her hands. All she'd heard was that Nick was in trouble and nothing could be done about it.

Sadie placed a hand gently on her shoulder. "It's going to be all right. You need to believe that."

Brandee stared at Sadie. "And what if I don't? Is that going to affect the outcome?"

Sadie paused for several moments, as if trying to choose her words carefully.

"Brandee, dear. What we believe always impacts the energy around us. Look up the law of attraction online or in the library. It may sound odd at first, but think of it this way: it's one way you can help Nick."

She hung on that thought. "Okay. I do want to help Nick. So are you saying that the law of attraction will tell me how to do that?"

"Yes. That's exactly what I'm saying."

Brandee nodded. At least she could do *something* to help. "Thanks, Sadie. I owe you one."

Sadie smiled. "Well, you know what I like as payment for my services."

Brandee kissed the old woman's cheek. "One White Russian, coming up." She waved to Wendy to get her attention and tried to think positive thoughts.

Nick was in too much pain to think about finding clothes and going to the police department. He figured the hospital would be less annoyed by a naked man with a bullet in his butt. How he'd explain it would be interesting.

Getting the bullet out right away was important too. Werewolves heal rapidly. He really didn't want to explain why he'd waited until it was healed over before he sought treatment. He could always ask the police to take his statement at the hospital.

He'd managed to locate the nearest hospital by following the signs, then he shifted outside the emergency room and walked in, covering his genitals with his big hands. Even so, the nurse behind the partition seemed startled and took off.

Great. Just great. She's probably calling security.

Moments later she returned with a hospital gown, practically threw it at him, and said, "For Pete's sake! Put this on."

Nick did as he was told and fastened it in the back.

"I don't suppose you have your insurance card on you," she said, smirking.

"You supposed right. I don't have insurance. I'd say I'll pay out of pocket, but…"

She finished his thought by rolling her eyes. The woman handed him a clipboard and told him to fill it out, then have a seat in the waiting room.

"I'd rather not sit down. I've been shot in the hindquarters."

"Oh! Let me get the triage nurse to take a look."

"Aren't you a nurse?

"No. Just an intake professional."

"Oh. You seemed blasé enough to be a nurse."

She snorted. "I've seen it all from my little window, mister. I'll get you in as soon as you fill out the form."

"Do you think you could hurry? This thing hurts like a mutha."

Nick felt good about his choice to come to the hospital rather than the police department. He might have been arrested for indecent exposure there. Now he was being treated like a normal naked guy who just happened to walk in with a gunshot wound in his tush.

The triage nurse came out to take a look at his butt, then asked him to follow her before he'd had a chance to fill out the form.

"I'd like to ask someone to call the cops for me. I need to report the bastards who shot me."

"Oh, don't worry. We report all gunshot wounds to

the police. It's New York State law. Sherry's probably calling them now."

"Efficient," he said.

She didn't follow up with any more conversation. Just led him to a room and instructed him to lie on the gurney, facedown, of course.

"Of course," he said and took the prone position.

She peeled back the gown and said, "It looks like it's stopped bleeding. When did this happen?"

"Ah…" *What would sound realistic?* "I don't know. It was a while before I could locate the hospital, so a couple hours, at least."

"I'm surprised you're not moaning in pain."

"Nah. I'm tougher than I look."

"I'll be back with the doctor. In the meantime, keep working on the form."

He had laid the clipboard on the nearby table, so she handed it to him along with the pen and left him alone with his form.

Let's see, do I want to give my real name? And what do I use for an address and date of birth? He had to think about that for a while. He and Konrad had been born on December 12, 1912. They had agreed on a more recent year to go with their looks, but was it time to update it? Did he look older than he had thirty years ago?

Crap. This is harder than I thought. He moved on, figuring he'd come back to that stuff. Next of kin. That was easy. He filled in Konrad's name and phone number. Konrad was his *only* kin. Their parents, both human, had died long ago, and they'd lost track of any extended family they might have had. He and Konrad had been running away from home at age ten when they came across a pack shifting in the woods under the full moon.

The only reason the pack turned them instead of killing and eating them was because the alpha at the time had stopped them. *Stop ruminating, and get the damn form finished.*

Name of primary-care physician? None. Insurance? Self pay. Place of work? Self-employed. *Okay, now back to the difficult questions.*

A partial truth was always easier to admit to than a downright lie, so he wrote down his name as Nicholas Wolf. *Close enough.*

Again he thought of Brandee. Would she want to keep her maiden name, or would she want to become Mrs. Wolfensen like his sister-in-law Roz had? He shook his head as if to clear it. *The crazy things I think about. She might not even want to speak to me when I finally get to talk to her.*

Now they wanted his address. He couldn't use his own. Maybe the bar? He almost laughed out loud as he pictured writing down *Boston Uncommon* as his address. They'd probably believe he belonged in an asylum since he'd walked in stark naked.

He fudged the rest of the form and hoped no one would check his facts until he was out of there. He signed his fake name with an illegible scrawl and stuck the pen into the gap at the top of the clipboard.

The nurse returned to take his blood pressure and temperature, start an IV, and check his wound again. It had already stopped bleeding, as she'd noted before. Maybe she just wanted another peek at his butt.

"The doctor will be here soon. Hang in there," she said, and left.

The pain had settled into a dull throb. He hoped the doctor would be able to just dig it out right there in the emergency room instead of scheduling an operating room for the following day. By then, it would be too late.

Chapter 23

BRANDEE'S PHONE FINALLY RANG. "PLEASE BE Nick, please be Nick," she chanted, running to the kitchen where she'd left it to recharge.

She grabbed it and didn't recognize the number but answered anyway, shouting, "Hello," a little louder than necessary.

"Brandee?"

"Oh, Nick, thank goodness! Are you all right?"

"I will be. I just had a little trouble down here and I thought you might be worried. I wasn't able to call for a while."

"Oh, my MIA. Of course I was worried. It's been two days with no word at all."

"I'm sorry, sweetheart. It couldn't be helped. I'll tell you all about it when I get back."

"Nick, what did you mean when you said you *will be* all right? Does that mean you're not okay right now?"

"Not exactly. I got shot in the ass. Fortunately my hide is pretty tough so the bullet was shallow. Digging it out was painful and the drugs they gave me didn't work at first. So they gave me more and that knocked me out for quite a while. When I finally woke up, I had to give the police my statement, pick some dudes out of a lineup, and talk to a DA about getting the judge to set no bail. My perp was a flight risk—literally."

"You were shot in the... Oh, my shit! Where are you now?"

"At a cell phone store. My brother paid for the new phone with his credit card, and he's wiring me some money so I can get home on the train. I called you as soon as I could."

"What happened to your phone? And your money?"

Nick's voice lowered to a whisper. "I had to shift to get away."

"Away from what? Or who? The dudes in the lineup?"

"Yeah. Like I said, I'll tell you everything when I get back."

"I had Sadie do a reading and she said you were in trouble. That was two days ago, and I've been going crazy ever since. I wanted to send Kurt and Tory after you, but no one had the faintest idea where to look. Sadie suggested I use the law of attraction to think you into a safe situation, so I borrowed a book to learn how, but it's easier to read about it than actually do it. I could barely think straight."

"I'm sorry you were so worried. I'll make it up to you when I get back. There's just one thing I need to take care of first, then I'll come straight to your place. Are you working tonight?"

"Yes. Thank goodness you called. I was so preoccupied last night I kept dropping stuff and couldn't remember an order to save my life. The night before, I tried to occupy my mind by working in my makeshift darkroom, but I lost track of time and overexposed everything."

He sighed on the other end of the phone. "I'm afraid my job is going to put me in danger from time to time."

"Then get a new job."

There was silence on the other end.

"Nick?"

"I'm here."

"I've been meaning to ask…why do you always call me sweetheart? Not honey or baby."

"Because you have the sweetest heart I've ever seen. People show who they are in a million little ways. An ex-cop notices these things. You're the one who'll grab the map from behind the bar and show lost tourists how to get around the city. You always speak up when you talk to Phil because you know he's hard of hearing. You've even taken money out of your tips to help a customer pay her bill when she came up short."

"Oh. You saw that stuff?"

"Yeah. The fact that you didn't know anyone was aware is even more telling. You obviously weren't doing it for brownie points."

She chuckled. "I'll never think about 'brownie points' in the same way since meeting the cleaning crew."

"Yeah, they're worth their weight in Pine Sol. I should go, though. We can talk about everything later. Meanwhile, I told my brother I need some clothes and he wants me to call him as soon as I have something picked out."

"What? Did you say you need clothes? What are you wearing now?"

"The hospital loaned me some scrubs."

"Oh." She chuckled. "I pictured you at the cell phone store stark naked with your hands over your… you know."

"Yeah, I know. That's how I walked into the hospital."

She gasped. "You're kidding."

"Nope."

"Oh, my naked ape."

"Hey. Are you calling me an ape?"

"Hell no. I just say the first thing that pops into my head. Sorry." She lowered her voice. "Maybe I should have said, 'Oh my naked wolf.'"

"Or, 'Oh, my nude model.'"

———~~———

Nick stood opposite his brother in Konrad's Newton office. Mother Nature's reaction to humans, especially those who knew about paranormals, had been bothering Nick for some time. He hoped Konrad could shed some light on the subject since his wife was completely human.

If Konrad had met Gaia before, he might know how to handle her. Konrad was always the brains and Nick the brawn.

"Bro, I've got to know how you cleared Roz with the Supernatural Council."

"The what?" Nick's brother leaned forward and clasped his hands on top of his desk.

"You've never heard of GAIA? The Gods and Immortals Association?"

Konrad's brows knit. "No. Should I have?"

Nick stuck his hands in his pockets and paced. "Shit. I thought the society was just a rumor until I saw its members for myself. You've got to swear to keep what I'm about to tell you in the strictest confidence."

"Of course."

Nick went on to explain what happened the night Adolf Balog took him to the mysterious building that housed GAIA. He described its paranormal leader,

Mother Nature, in detail, including her temperament. Then he shared her threat and ability to carry it out.

In typical Konrad fashion, he seemed to consider what Nick had told him seriously and thoughtfully. Then he nodded and muttered, "Mother Nature seems like a real asshole."

Nick laughed. That was just the kind of remark he needed. But even though it relieved the tension slightly, he was puzzled about his brother's lack of knowledge.

"I thought you knew everything about the paranormal world," Nick said. "Hell, I thought you knew everything about everything."

"What gave you that idea?"

Nick scratched his head. "Oh, only because you've read every book you could get your hands on and seem to know it all."

"Are you calling me a know-it-all?"

"Kind of." Nick was quick to add, "In a good way."

"Well, I knew nothing about this society. And fortunately, they seem to know nothing about me."

"Lucky you. So you never had to fess up and tell them Roz knows about us."

"No. Now I'm beginning to wonder why not."

"Me too. Shit. I had hoped you could tell me how to get in touch with the Council and how you managed to get their approval to marry Roz."

"Nope. Sorry, Nick."

"Have you ever wondered why you and I wound up with human mates instead of other wolves?"

Konrad shrugged. "I imagine it's because we were human in the first place. Had we been born pups of two werewolf parents, we might have had a pack mate."

Nick nodded. Leave it to his brother to be logical.

"So, getting back to the Council. Where did you meet when Adolf took you to them?"

"Good question. There's an office building on State Street where they supposedly hang out, but I'll be damned if I can find the right floor. There was a glass bubble and sky overhead, so you'd think it would be easy to locate, but it's impossible."

"Why do you want to get in touch with Mother Nature? It seems to me you should avoid her."

"I'd like to get her blessing as far as Brandee is concerned. I know for a fact my mate can be trusted with our secret. I need to make Gaia understand that before I propose. I don't want Brandee to wind up a widow just because I was too chicken to clear it with a deity."

Konrad rose and took over pacing for Nick. "I wonder if I'm off the hook or not. My only excuse is ignorance. I couldn't have told Gaia about Roz since I didn't know about the existence of the Council back then—thank God—or gods and goddesses, or whomever." Konrad slapped his brother on the back. "You're a braver man than I."

"I was kind of hoping you'd come with me. If I can even find them again."

Konrad's jaw dropped. "You want me to face an angry goddess who you pissed off by doing exactly what I did, but somehow I got away with it?"

"Well, when you put it that way…"

———ᴠᴠᴠ———

Nick sought out Adolf Balog before going to the bar to see Brandee. After all this, he wanted to give her some *good* news.

He walked into the small foyer that housed the buzzers for each apartment. Instead of pressing two for the second floor, he pressed three for where the Balogs lived.

"Yah," a female voice said.

"Mrs. Balog. I'm looking for Adolf."

"Adolf? Who are you and what do you want with my son?"

Nick heard Adolf's voice in the background but couldn't make out what he said.

"It's Nick Wolfensen. I need to talk to him."

Adolf's voice said, "I'll be down in one minute."

Whew. He had the feeling Mrs. Balog wouldn't let her precious son speak to a werewolf.

A few moments later, the young man opened the door, but instead of letting Nick in, he stepped out and closed the door behind him.

"What can I do for you?"

"You can take me back to GAIA."

Adolf reared back and started at him. Finally he asked, "Are you sure? I mean, she doesn't exactly welcome visitors."

"It's not a social call."

"Okaaaay. May I ask what it's about?"

"It's personal." Nick thought he saw the kid's eye twitch.

"Hmmm… When did you want to do this?" Adolf asked.

"As soon as possible."

The kid shuffled his feet. "I need to go upstairs for a few minutes. Meet me back here in five."

"How about if I meet you in the bar? I need to see my girlfriend, just to touch base and let her know I'm okay."

Adolf's eyes narrowed. "Is your girlfriend Ruxandra?"

Nick almost burst out laughing, but he managed to swallow it. "No. Why would you think that?"

"Because she's the only paranormal in there at the moment."

I wonder how he knows where she is. "I thought she was in jail."

"They couldn't make the charges stick."

"How do you know all this?"

Adolf clammed up. He shoved his hands in his pockets. "Do you want to see Mother Nature or not?"

"I didn't mean to rattle you. I was just curious. Yes, I'd like to see Gaia as soon as possible."

"Fine. I'll meet you in the bar."

Nick nodded and left the strange young man to his preparations—whatever they were. He couldn't wait another minute to see Brandee anyway. He walked through the door to the bar and spotted her immediately.

She was waiting on a table full of locals, and as if she sensed him, she glanced over her shoulder. She squealed, set down her tray, and ran over to him.

Jumping into his arms, she yelled, "Nick, I've never been so glad to see you."

He crushed her to his chest and then remembered not to squeeze too hard or he could squash her like a bug. That would be an awful way to say, "Hi, honey, I'm home."

She leaned back enough to smile at him, then mashed her mouth to his. He had no idea how long they kissed. He felt slightly dizzy afterward, as if he hadn't taken a breath for a while. Perhaps he hadn't.

Ruxandra sauntered over to them. "At least someone in this dump is happy."

"Nice to see you too, Ruxandra," Nick said. He set Brandee on her feet. "Sweetheart, I just wanted you to know I'm back. I have one more thing to take care of. I hope it won't take long, but if it does, I don't want you to worry. I'm fine."

She rubbed his biceps. "I missed you so much, Nick."

"I missed you too."

Ruxandra spun on her heel. "I'd better go before I vomit."

As soon as they were alone again, Brandee lowered her voice. "Does it hurt?"

"The wound? Nah. I'm all healed and good as new. How are things around here?"

"About the same. As you can see, Ruxandra's back, and Anthony is hiding in his office most of the time. Other than that, everything's okay."

"Good. I'll be back as soon as I take care of this one important matter."

She looked as if she was about to pout. "Is it dangerous?"

What could he say? If Mother Nature was in a bad mood, it might be. He didn't want to lie to Brandee, but he couldn't afford to tell her the whole truth either. Besides, he didn't really know what the truth was at that point.

Nick brushed a strand of hair behind her ear. "I should be safe enough." *And if I'm not, I'll get the hell out of there before she drops me into an active volcano.*

Brandee gave him a smile that looked as sad as it did happy. "Don't be long." Then she drew a fingernail down his chest and a sly smile replaced the sad one. "I have a special welcome home planned."

Please be sex. Please be sex. Please be sex. "I won't be a minute later than I have to be."

Nick didn't know if he'd even be allowed to see the deity, but if perchance an audience was granted, lingering was the last thing on his mind.

———

Adolf opened the door to the bar but just stood in the doorway.

That's right. The kid isn't old enough to drink. He's probably never been in here. Again, Nick wondered how Adolf knew what went on inside the bar. Maybe he watched customers come and go from an upstairs window. *Yeah, that's probably it.* But a niggling feeling told Nick that might not be the whole story.

He kissed Brandee good-bye, then strode to the door and out onto the sidewalk.

"Ready?" was all Adolf asked.

"As much as I'll ever be." Nick steeled himself for whatever the kid had to do to transport him to the Council.

Instead of magic dust, the kid just walked off toward the nearest side street and rounded the corner. Nick kept up with him easily. They walked uphill, and Nick guessed they were going to the mysterious office building on State Street.

When they finally got there, Adolf opened the outer door and, with a swooping gesture, indicated that Nick was to enter first.

Instead of following him in, the kid just said, "Get in the elevator. Press the button for the top floor, and good luck."

"Aren't you coming with me?"

Adolf worried his lip. "I don't think so."

"Are they expecting me?"

Without answering, the kid let go of the door and rushed off.

"What the…"

Nick's stomach suddenly felt as if he'd swallowed a flock of hummingbirds. He straightened his back, lifted his chin, and said, "I can do this."

At that moment, the elevator door opened. *Shit. Are they listening?*

He concluded they probably were and moved slowly toward the elevator. The doors remained open, as if waiting for him.

Everything will be all right. This is for Katie and Brandee. Mother Nature will see that as altruistic, right?

Stepping into the elevator, he continued his mental pep talk. Before he could push the button, however, the doors slammed shut and he took off like a rocket.

"Holy…"

When the rapid ascent stopped, his feet felt like they'd left the floor for a second. The doors whooshed open, and he paused a moment to take in the scene before he stepped out.

The glass dome overhead, the white-robed gentlemen strolling and talking to each other, plus the forest in the far-off area indicated he'd found what he was looking for.

It's go time.

He stepped off the elevator prepared to ask one of the gods where Gaia might be when the woman herself came out of her forest and strode over to him.

"Nick Wolfensen, brave soul. What on earth would bring you here again?"

"Gaia, I need your help in two different matters."

"Two?" She shouted so loudly that some of the gods stopped talking and stared at them.

"The first is something you'll want to know about right away."

"Don't presume to tell me what I want. Just state your business quickly so I can spit you back out onto the sidewalk as soon as possible."

Like gum. His mouth went dry, but he had to press on.

"Gaia, there's a dragon on Long Island who is in police custody at the moment, but they won't be able to hold him forever. He's dangerous. I discovered his plan when I was protecting a fire mage here in Boston. He hired some thugs to kidnap her so he could use her for her ability."

She crossed her arms over her chest. "Lovely."

That's all she has to say? One sarcastic word?

"I'm well aware of this dragon. He set the Chicago fire. That's when I took his power to breathe fire away. Now you're telling me he hasn't learned his lesson and wants to burn down Boston too?"

"Yes, ma'am."

She raised one eyebrow.

"I mean, Goddess. He must have wanted revenge on you, and he was ready to use an innocent to do it. The girl hadn't even come into her power yet. She was just about to when he nabbed her."

"I see." She began to pace.

Nick wondered if she "saw" at all. Did she *have* to rely on mortals to be her eyes and ears on the street? Were her powers that limited? And if Mother Nature was his target, how did the dragon know she was based in Boston?

"Did he know the Council hangs out here?"

Her lips thinned. "Yes. I had him brought here for his punishment. I should have sent him back where he came from, but I was busy and angry, so I just spit him out on State Street and let him find his own way home."

"I thought you could just poof anybody anywhere. You did it with me."

She threw her hands in the air. "I have to be everywhere at once. Taking care of this, stopping that. Why can't people just fuckin' behave themselves?"

She halted and slumped over as if discouraged. When she straightened, she took a deep breath. "Wolfensen, I'm glad you came to me with this. I don't know what your other question is, and I don't care. This takes priority over, well, everything. I just let a dam break for this, so in case you were wondering, no, I can't do it all. But I can and will deal with what's-his-name."

"Martin Irwin."

"Yes. I had forgotten. Well, Martin's ass is grass. I'll be back momentarily."

She disappeared into thin air. Nick didn't quite know what to do. Should he wait for her? Or should he just leave and forget the other matter?

One of the gods strolled over to him. It was the same one Mother Nature had called "Apollo" before.

"You did well, Nicholas. What was the other question you had for Gaia?"

"I'm glad you asked. I'm not sure if I should discuss it with her or not."

The god nodded sagely. "Perhaps I can help you with that."

Nick took a deep breath and hoped for the best. "My girlfriend, Brandee, knows about me and Anthony and the bar, but she's cool with it. She promised never to tell a human soul and I believe her completely. I want to marry her, but I don't want Mother Nature worried about Brandee spilling her guts. Bottom line is, I don't want to worry about Gaia sending me or my girlfriend to Timbuktu. A wolf never deserts his mate—willingly."

Apollo smiled and a warm glow seemed to radiate from him. "There's a saying: 'Sometimes it's better to ask for forgiveness later than to ask for permission now.' Or something like that."

"So, you're saying I shouldn't tell her? And if she finds out, I should apologize?"

"Pretty much."

"I'd never apologize for making Brandee my wife. She's already my marked mate. I'd just be giving her the legal benefits."

Apollo shrugged. "It's up to you, but you know how moody the goddesses can be—Gaia in particular."

"Why is that? Do goddesses have a monthly...event?"

Apollo laughed. "No. That's one of the downsides of being a human female."

"Or a werewolf," Nick added.

Apollo set a hand on Nick's shoulder. "Look, I shouldn't tell you this, but Gaia has a reason for all her frustration."

"Really? She hasn't always been like that?"

"Oh, heavens, no." Apollo spoke in a whisper. "Keep this to yourself. *I'm* not even supposed to know, but it doesn't take a genius to figure it out. Gaia is the primordial goddess. She was born of Chaos and she's only had four paramours. She fooled around with Ouranos in the sky, and all the heavenly gods and Titans were born.

Then she fooled around with Pontus in the ocean and all the sea gods came from that union.

"She even tried a tryst in the hell-pit with Tartarus, and the giants were born. Finally, she gave Zeus a whirl on Mount Olympus and guess what?" He pointed over his shoulder with his thumb. "That's how the rest of us showed up. That's when she called it quits. She swore off sex, not knowing what other immortal creatures she might accidentally create. That was a looong time ago."

Nick scratched his head. "So, you're saying she's sexually frustrated?"

Apollo shrugged. "It would seem so. I mean, she'd have no trouble enticing a lover and she's still fertile. It was the aftermath that did her in. Can you imagine giving birth to giants?"

Nick shuddered. "Ouch. Well, that has nothing to do with me, so I think I'll risk it."

"Good luck with that." Apollo slapped him on the back, then wandered off to join a poker game.

A moment later Mother Nature reappeared, brushing off her hands. "There. The situation is all taken care of, thanks to me."

"What happened?"

"Well, first I had to find the right jail, because *someone* forgot to tell me which one our dragon was in."

Nick remained silent despite wanting to point out that she hadn't given him a chance to tell her much of anything.

"Then I appeared in his cell and removed his immortality. He took one look at me and had a heart attack on the spot. I love situations like that."

"Like what?"

"Incidents that take care of themselves. In other words, self-solvers."

Nick had to be sure. "So he's dead?"

"As a doornail."

"What about his men? He had a lot of people in his employ."

"And they're all singing 'Ding Dong, the Dragon's Dead' right now."

She seemed satisfied with the outcome and Nick relaxed a bit. "That's great. Thanks for your help. My client can rest easy now."

She offered him a rare smile. "And I thank you for your help too. I rather like Boston."

It's now or never, I guess. "Goddess, there's one more thing I'd like to discuss with you."

She sagged and rolled her eyes. "Oh, that's right. I forgot you had *two* questions for me. Well, what is it?"

"I want to marry Brandee—"

"And you're asking my permission? How very old-fashioned of you."

"No, not exactly. I realize that you're concerned about humans knowing the ins and outs of the paranormal factions."

"Yes, yes. We both know this. Get to the point."

"I want you to know beyond the shadow of any doubt that Brandee can be trusted. She'll *never* reveal what she knows to anyone. She promised Anthony and kept that promise, even when it would have been tempting to tell me what she knew. But she wants the truth. She's my mate and I need to be honest with her."

"What if you're overheard when you're opening up to her?"

"We won't make that mistake again. Besides, if she moves into my place, the possibility of someone over-hearing us becomes highly unlikely. I can't let anything separate me from my mate."

"Hmmm…" Mother Nature tapped her chin. "Your being overheard *would* be less likely if you two were living together."

"Exactly. I had hoped you'd see it that way."

"Fine. Marry the human as soon as possible."

"I'm glad I have your blessing, but there's one more little thing…"

"Oh, for the love of—All right. What is it?"

"As you know I have a very long life span. I was wondering if there's anything you can do to extend Brandee's life as well. The thought of her mortality shakes me to my core."

Mother Nature reared back and stared at him as if she'd been slapped. "Haven't you heard? You're not supposed to mess with Mother Nature."

He lowered his gaze. "I'm sorry. I just thought… Well, never mind. I appreciate what you did."

"You're welcome, but don't push it. All right? It's time for you to go. Don't take this the wrong way, but I hope I never see you again."

"Understood." To tell the truth, Nick hoped he wouldn't have to see her again either.

Chapter 24

FOR THE NEXT WEEK, NICK AND BRANDEE WORKED around her schedule so they could spend part of every day together. They met at her apartment and Nick usually brought takeout food. Right after the meal, they found their way to his apartment—and his bed. They couldn't get enough of each other. They knew every inch of each other's bodies and then some.

Today, Nick wanted to take her out and show her a good time. He and Brandee strolled slowly through the Museum of Fine Arts' Impressionists exhibit, with his arm around her waist most of the afternoon.

"I'm glad you have this evening off," Nick whispered. "I know just how to spend it."

Brandee gave him a knowing smile. "In bed, I imagine."

"What a good idea. I never would have thought of it."

Brandee laughed. "Like hell you wouldn't have."

Nick gave her a side squeeze. "Actually, I thought I'd take you out to dinner, and the place I have in mind is kind of fancy. Do you have any formal dresses or skirts you can wear?"

"You mean besides my uniform?"

Nick groaned. "Please tell me you have another skirt besides that one. It probably smells like a brewery."

"Yeah, I can come up with some options. What's the special occasion?"

He smiled to himself. "You'll see."

He'd already bought the ring. A two-carat, emerald-cut diamond with a smaller diamond baguette on each side. He liked the gold wedding bands that went with it. Hopefully, she would too, and then he'd have them engraved.

He tried not to be nervous. She might think his proposal was awfully sudden, but he couldn't be more sure.

"I know I can find something to wear. I have a very formfitting dress in blue silk. Would something like that be appropriate?"

"Perfect."

"Now I'm super curious. Can you give me a hint?"

"Well…"

"Come on. Please?" She batted her eyelashes.

He laughed. "When you're being adorable, I can't say no to you." He took a deep breath and hoped she wouldn't guess and ruin the surprise. "I've heard you like the ocean."

"That's true. So it must be a place with an ocean view?"

"You'll see."

She stared at the ceiling. "You're killing me."

"Don't die yet. We have a lot of fun ahead of us." Nick wished she wouldn't die at all. Perhaps if she'd agree to be changed… No. He shouldn't get his hopes up. He genuinely doubted any human would go for that electively. His sister-in-law Roz had flatly refused, but Konrad married her anyway, knowing he'd outlive her—perhaps by another hundred years.

A wolf needs his mate by his side as much as he needs to breathe. Nick figured he'd have to be Konrad's support system when Roz was laid to rest. Now he hoped Konrad would be his. If he didn't get his mind off this morose topic, he'd bring himself down, and it was too special a day to let that happen.

He pointed to a painting by Monet. "Monet's first wife, Camille, was his model for many of his paintings. That's Monet's wife in the Japanese kimono."

"I've seen other paintings of her. I thought she was a brunette," Brandee said.

"She was. He had her wear a blond wig to emphasize her Western heritage. Paris was excited about all things Asian in those times."

"How do you know that? I thought you didn't like art."

"I like you and you like art, so I studied up on it." Nick kissed her red hair.

"Awww."

When Brandee gazed up at him, her eyes took on a soft blue light, reminding him of the sky in one of Monet's paintings.

We'll have some beautiful blue-eyed children some-day. Few werewolves married outside the pack, so he had no idea what to expect regarding reproduction. Hopefully their children would be as long-lived and healthy as wolves but as gentle as their mother.

"What do you say? Are you ready to get out of here? Maybe we can get in a little afternoon delight before dinner."

"Well, since you put it that way." She grinned and his heart leaped.

"We can always come back another day."

"That would be nice. It's a great place for inspiration. Look at the way Monet painted the same subjects at different times of day. It's something I enjoy doing with my photographs, playing with light and shadow like he did."

"So, you're still working on your photography?"

"Of course."

"Good. Can I see some of your work?"

She hesitated. Eventually she said, "Sure. As long as you don't expect them to look like a Monet."

He chuckled. "I don't imagine you can do that with photography."

She gave him a sly smile. "You'd be surprised by what I can do."

"Are we still talking about photography?"

She elbowed him. "Leave it to you to take everything I say in *that* direction."

He laughed. "I can't help it. You inspire me."

~~~

Back at Nick's condo, they kissed their way to the bedroom, stripping off their clothes at the same time. Nick was an incredible lover, and Brandee had never experienced the kind of mind-blowing orgasms she had with him every single time.

They stumbled in, hampered by their twining legs, and Brandee laughed as she almost hit the floor. Nick swooped her up and laid her on his bed. He kissed her again, and she melted into a heated pool of desire.

He gathered her ass in his big hand and pushed her against his erection.

God but she wanted him. With every fiber of her being, she wanted to be possessed. Held the way only Nick could, showing how much he cherished his "mate." She'd gotten used to the word and enjoyed its double meaning.

His hands caressed her excited skin. His breathing was

urgent and he leaned heavily into her, pressing his erection against the apex of her thighs. Brandee's sexual appetite became ferocious, and she whimpered into his mouth.

She restlessly moved against him, trying to appease the ache between her thighs. She longed for him to fill her, and she was wet with need. His warm male skin shivered with her touch. The room was warm and she was burning, so he had to be shaking with lust, not cold. She kneaded the thick muscles that rippled under her hand. Her fingers found his flat male nipples, and she squeezed each one until he gasped for air, then groaned.

"Brandee. I need you."

She laughed. "And the problem with that is..."

"I want to be inside you—now."

She was so swept away, she almost forgot to ask. "Condom?"

He nuzzled her ear and whispered, "Do we have to?"

That startled her for a moment, but she was on the pill and believed him when he said he was healthy.

She pulled his mouth to hers for another kiss. He nipped her lips and she tasted a drop of blood. He lapped at it, and the pain quickly faded. When she touched her mouth, there was no blood to be found.

"Oh, God, I love this woman."

Had she actually heard his thought? He must have been talking to himself and the sound was muffled by the sheets or something.

He cupped her breast and flicked her nipple with his thumb. Her womb clenched as if reaching for him.

He rolled her on top and adjusted so he could capture her hard nipple and suck greedily. She arched back and moaned as a symphony of sensations raced through her body. He lavished the same attention on the other breast, and she thought she'd come any moment. He wasn't even inside her yet!

She couldn't make him wait any longer. Hell, *she* couldn't wait any longer.

She broke the glorious suction just long enough to sit up straight and lower herself onto his erection. They moaned together. He began to move his pelvis up and down, and she rocked forward and back. Dear Lord, the ripples of bliss started as soon as he hit her G-spot.

Don't come right away. Try to hold off for him.

"Or come more than once." It sounded as if his voice had answered her in her head. His lips hadn't moved, so her imagination must have taken over and formed what she thought he'd be thinking. He added a clit rub to their lovemaking and that sent her spiraling.

A few strokes later, all thought deserted her. She came with a crash of sensation, causing her to cry out. She clutched his shoulders as she convulsed against him. The powerful orgasm washed over her in sharp waves, and she couldn't stop her screams of bliss. Tears actually formed in her eyes.

Nick shuddered with his own release and gentled his hold on her as if intentionally trying not to hurt her. She imagined he could if he lost control, but Nick wasn't one to forget his strength.

She collapsed against him and he gathered her into his arms. Gently cradling her against his chest, he murmured something that sounded like, *"That was the most beautiful thing I've ever experienced."* Except it wasn't a murmur. He was panting the whole time. She had heard his muffled thought.

"Nick?" she whispered when she could form words again.

"Yes, sweetheart?"

"This is going to sound crazy, but I think I heard your thought just now."

He let out a startled gasp, and she lifted her head so she could see into his wide eyes.

"I thought I heard yours too. Quick, what was I thinking?"

"I think you said what a beautiful experience you just had. Did you say that out loud?"

He rolled her onto her side and propped himself on his elbow. Instead of answering her question, he grinned and thought, *"I knew it."*

"Knew what?"

He laughed. "That you're my one true mate. I could tell the first time I kissed you. Others may have doubted it, but I never stopped hoping and, deep down, believing."

"Does hearing each other's thoughts mean we're true mates?"

He leaned over and kissed her nose. "It certainly does. Roz and Konrad are able to communicate telepathically I had always hoped we would…"

As if so moved he couldn't speak, he gathered her in his arms once more and tucked her head beneath his chin. "I love you, Brandee. I understand it may take a while to learn how to block our thoughts when we don't want to share them. But right now I couldn't be happier about this."

"Do you mean you're able to hear every bizarre thought that travels through my brain?"

"Not every thought. Just the strong ones. Konrad told me what it was like for him and Roz. I imagine it will be pretty much the same for us."

THEN WE CAN TALK SIMPLY BY THINKING LOUDLY?

"You don't have to shout. Just form the words as if you're speaking to me, intentionally."

"I guess that could come in handy if we're ever kidnapped again."

He laughed. "Yes, it could."

"You heard me!"

"If you were thinking about our ability to communicate, should we ever be kidnapped again, then yes, I did."

"Oh, my mental megaphone."

———

Nick anxiously waited downstairs in the bar for Brandee to get ready for their dinner date. He was so filled with nervous energy, he drummed his fingers on the bar while waiting for his glass of water. He didn't want to have any alcohol until after dinner, and then he'd order a bottle of champagne.

Angie glanced at him as she brought another customer a martini. "I'm getting to you as fast as I can, Nick."

"Huh? No, I'm not impatient with you, Angie. It's something else completely."

She eyed him as she got his water. When she brought it over, she asked, "You're all dressed up tonight. Does it have anything to do with my roommate?"

He smiled. "Yes, but I can't tell you what we're doing. I'm saving it for a surprise—"

At that moment, when the door opened and Brandee walked in, Nick lost the power of speech. She was stunning. Her blue silk dress fit her perfectly. It nipped in at her waist and ended a few inches above the knee.

Her hair was left long and loose. The light captured the shine, reminding him of a beautiful gemstone he'd seen once. He thought they were called carnelians. He'd have to look for some kind of jewelry made with them and buy it for her. Right now, he had a different piece of jewelry in his pocket.

She smiled and strolled over to him. She set her beaded evening bag on the bar and telepathically asked, *"Are we ready to go?"*

He answered her in his mind as well. *Yup. But I'm afraid I'll have to chase off every man who sees you tonight. You look gorgeous.*

They had done it! They had established purposeful mental telepathy with one another. He waited a moment to see if any unwanted thoughts passed between them.

Angie walked over and set a hand on her hip. "Are you two just gonna to stand there grinning at each other all night?"

Nick glanced at her. "No. We're leaving. I'm taking my gorgeous girl somewhere special tonight."

Angie looked her roommate up and down. "I can see that. So where are you going?"

Brandee raised her eyes to him and they sparkled. "Yeah, Nick. Where *are* we going?"

"I guess I can tell you now. You'll find out soon anyway. We're going out on the *Odyssey* for a dinner cruise."

"Oh, Nick. I've always wanted to do that."

"I'll just call a cab." Nick reached for his cell phone.

"Why don't we take my car? The waterfront isn't that far, and I should start it once in a while so it doesn't petrify."

Nick scratched his head. He didn't want to insult her bucket of bolts, but it didn't seem right for the lovely evening he had planned. Maybe he should have hired a horse and carriage.

Oh, hell. Who was he trying to impress? If she wanted to go in her ancient Toyota, what difference did it make?

"You don't want to take my car, do you, Nick?"

Did she hear me? Nah, I was probably just hesitating too long. "No, it's fine. If you need to give it a little exercise, the short trip to the waterfront is probably good for that." *If we break down, it's not that far to walk.*

"Good. Let's go then."

She held out her hand and he enclosed it in his. They waved to Angie and left the bar. Strolling down Charles Street, Nick asked, "Is it still parked on Revere Street?"

"Yup. Same place. I kind of hate to move it and risk losing my spot."

"So, you're saying you haven't moved it in weeks?"

She gave him a sheepish grin. "Not so much."

The wind blew and she shivered. "It's starting to get cold."

"Do you want to go back to your apartment for a coat? The wind off the water is apt to be even colder."

"Actually, I have a wool shawl in the car that would serve just fine."

As they rounded the corner onto Revere Street, he dropped her hand and wrapped an arm around her shoulder. "I'll keep you warm until we get there."

"Thanks, honey."

He grinned. "That's the first time you've used an endearment."

"It is?" Brandee sounded incredulous, but Nick was pretty sure it was true.

"I like it," he said.

"I-I like it when you call me sweetheart too. I'm sorry I never called you anything but your name until now."

He shrugged. "It's no big deal. I think I fell in love with you faster, but I'm glad you're catching up."

"Me too."

They stopped just long enough to share a tender kiss. At last they arrived at her car and she dug the keys out of her bag. In a few moments, they were in, although Nick's knees hit the dashboard and he had to push back the seat. The engine coughed and sputtered a couple times, but eventually it turned over.

Would you like to practice telepathy while we're driving? Nick asked.

"Sure. What do you want to 'talk' about?"

How about your photographs. Taken any good ones lately?

"Oh, yeah. I forgot to show them to you. I guess I got distracted. Are there any other surprises I should expect?"

From telepathy?

"Or from falling in love with a werewolf. I still can't get used to the idea that I'm actually dating a character from horror movies."

Hey, we're sensitive about that, you know.

She glanced over at him and said out loud, "Really? I'm sorry. I didn't mean to—"

Nick laughed. "I'm kidding. Not much bothers me. I'd be more apt to get upset if someone was speaking to you in a derogatory way."

"I like that about you."

The drive to the ship's parking lot was uneventful, thank goodness. Nick was afraid the car would give out in the middle of some busy intersection and their night would be spent getting a towing company to rescue them.

So far, his plan was unfolding pretty much the way he'd imagined it. Maybe better. The unexpected transfer of thoughts he'd worried about hadn't happened. Konrad made it sound as if he and Roz had a hard time learning how to control the telepathy. Brandee hadn't *said* anything he didn't want to hear…yet. And as far as he knew, he hadn't either. *Whew*. It might be hard keeping his proposal a secret otherwise. *Speaking of hard, my cock gets stiff every time I look at my lover*.

Brandee giggled as she was getting out of the car.

Uh-oh. Did she hear me thinking about my hard cock?

"Yes, she did."

Damn. I'll have to watch my thoughts more carefully.

"*Or not. I like knowing that looking at me turns you on.*"

He swept her into a tight embrace and kissed her passionately, right there in the parking lot. They'd had to wait a while before developing telepathic communication, but maybe that was a good thing. When Konrad and Roz said it was hard to control, he expected more slips of the mental tongue. But the other couple had it thrust upon them so quickly, they barely knew each other.

Perhaps because he and Brandee had been able to deepen their relationship first, it wasn't as difficult to filter thoughts the other might not want to hear. Regardless, Nick couldn't be happier to know beyond any doubt he'd found his mate at last.

—◦◦◦—

The cruise around Boston Harbor had been wonderful. The ship's dining room could rival the most elegant restaurant in the city. The fact that they could lean on the railing and watch the city lights float by just added to the experience.

Brandee felt so lucky to have found love at last, and her heart swirled. Just like she did in the arms of her amazingly graceful dance partner.

Nick rose and held his hand out to her again. She happily jumped at the chance to dance with him once more.

As the slow beat began, she asked, "How did you become such a good dancer, Nick—I mean, honey?"

He smiled. "Are you surprised I know how?"

"Not really. Just amazed you're so good at it. Big guys like you aren't usually agile."

"Well, sweetheart, I've stepped on my share of toes, but I had to keep practicing so I could function at the policemen's ball each year."

"Oh, I forgot they had those."

"It's usually a good time. I wish I could have taken you just to show you off."

"That's okay. I'm sure you showed off plenty just by bringing a different girl each year." Had he really been such a player? Brandee knew intellectually that he had, but she'd never have guessed by the way he treated her. He never looked at another woman and never talked about any of his past conquests. She *almost* felt secure. She wondered if she ever would, completely.

She thought she heard him say something.

"What did you say?"

"Huh? Oh, nothing. I was thinking too loud, I guess."

"Are you sure? I thought you were wondering about the time."

Suddenly he stopped dancing. Holding on to her hand, he led her back to their table. Brandee found it amusing that every time they got up, the waiters refolded their napkins. It was as if the napkin fairies had been there when they weren't looking.

He pulled out her chair for her but angled it so she'd face him instead of the table. She thought it a little odd, but maybe he just wanted her to be able to watch the dancers and talk to him at the same time.

To her shock, Nick pulled a small box out of his suit jacket and dropped onto one knee.

"Brandee Hanson. You're the love of my life. I want and need you by my side always. Will you do me the honor of becoming my wife?" He opened the box, revealing the most beautiful diamond ring she'd ever seen.

At first she couldn't speak. All the air had rushed from her lungs. Then, as if on cue, the music stopped and she exclaimed, "What are you, nuts?"

People all around them stopped what they were doing to watch the scene. Nick's smile disappeared. A blush crept up his neck.

"Of course, I'll marry you!" she cried and threw her arms around his neck.

Everyone applauded, but Nick seemed slow to hold her.

Nick, this is so sudden. Are you sure you want to do this—now?

"*Absolutely. I couldn't be more positive, but* you *don't seem sure.*"

I'm sure I love you. I just hadn't thought about marriage yet. Perhaps we should have a long engagement.

"*If it will make you feel better.*"

She leaned back and held out her hand, allowing him

to slip the ring on her finger. It sparkled like sunshine on snow and took her breath away.

Nick rose, angled his chair to face her, and took his seat. She glanced around to be sure people had gone back to minding their own business and they wouldn't be overheard.

"Oh, Nick. It's beautiful, and I *do* want to marry you, but we only started dating in September. It isn't even Halloween yet." She lowered her voice. "By the way, is there anything funky about Halloween for you guys?"

He chuckled but seemed hesitant. "Not for wolves. But there is one more thing I have to tell you. It's not about the paranormal. Just about me. I'll tell you later."

Can't you tell me now?

"I'd rather wait for the right time."

She sighed. *Please? I hate these surprises. Knowing there's another one will drive me crazy.*

He took both her hands in his and smiled. "This news isn't going to upset you. At least I doubt it will, but I had to be sure you'd marry me *for me* before I told you this one last secret."

"Okay. So now that I proved myself, out with it."

He sighed. "All right. Brandee, I'm rich as shit. I only work because I'd be bored stiff if I didn't. I liked police work and I enjoy being a private investigator even more. I don't want to quit, even though I could."

Her jaw dropped. "But you were a cop. How—I'm sorry, but I know cops don't make much money. How did you get rich?"

He stroked her cheek. "I've always been good about managing my finances. I made a couple of smart invest-ments, my brother and I sold our company, and voila.

I'm a millionaire. You don't have to waitress anymore if you don't want to."

"You'd be okay with my concentrating on my photography career full time?"

"Absolutely."

She laughed. "Un-freakin'-believable. It's about time you hit me with some *good* news for a change."

On the way home, Brandee's car began to sputter. *Oh, no.* "Don't give out on me now, Clara," she mumbled.

"Clara?"

"Yeah. I know it's silly, but I name my cars. I should have named this one Christine."

Nick snickered. "Pull over under that streetlamp. I'll take a look at it."

"No, we're almost home. I think she can make it another few blocks."

Brandee continued on, but the long, steep hill and her car had other ideas. The sputter turned into a choking noise and it died.

"Crap. Right in the middle of the street."

"Don't worry, sweetheart." Nick opened his door and hopped out. "Stay there and steer."

He leaned into the open door and pushed with all his might. The car edged forward.

"Jeez, Nick. Don't have a heart attack pushing this junk heap uphill. It's not worth it."

"Don't worry about my heart. I'll be fine."

"Just help me get her off to the side. I think we passed a parking space back a ways. I'll let her roll downhill and maybe you can help guide her into it."

Nick held the car still and looked over its roof. "Yeah. I see it. Let me get behind her in case the brakes give out too."

"Oh, hell no. I don't want to run you over."

"I won't let that happen. I'll just brace myself against the trunk and walk downhill so it doesn't roll too fast." *I'm plenty strong, sweetheart. I could push Clara home if you wanted me to.*

"Are you sure, honey?"

He leaned down and smiled at her. "I'm positive." He took off his suit jacket and tie, and tossed them onto the passenger's seat.

Reluctantly, she agreed and kept her foot on the brake until he jogged around and braced himself against the trunk.

"Okay, sweetheart. Let her go," he called out.

She let up on the brake very slowly. *Please tell me if it's too much and I'll step on the brake right away, all right?*

"I will."

She heard him grunt a couple times as they rolled slowly down the hill. Eventually, the car was even with the truck parked in front of the empty space.

"How are you with parallel parking?" Nick asked telepathically.

I have to parallel park all the time. You can let go and I'll steer her in.

"I'm not letting go, but I might need to move when we get close to the car below."

Brandee wished he'd move onto the sidewalk just in case. She'd rather hit a parked car than pin her lover between the bumpers.

She applied the brakes lightly and steered Clara into

the spot as best she could. If her car were running, she'd go forward a couple feet and straighten out.

She rolled down the window and called out, "I think that's good enough. At least she's out of the way."

When Nick didn't answer, she panicked. "Nick? Are you all right back there?"

"Roll up the window and don't get out."

Why? What's wrong?

Brandee set the emergency brake and turned around. Nick stood on the sidewalk with another guy, and it took a moment before she noticed the gun pointed at Nick's midsection. *Oh, my mugging.*

"Stay where you are, sweetheart. I've got this."

Shit.

The guy moved up to her window and yelled, "Get out of the cah."

She unlocked the door.

"No," Nick shouted. *"Stay there and distract him."*

Distract him? How was she supposed to do that? Stick out one shapely leg at a time and hope he liked what he saw?

Can you transform or shift or whatever you call it? That ought to distract the hell out of him.

"Not in front of a human unless I have a vampire handy to erase his memory. Otherwise, I'd have to kill him. Think of something else."

"Hey, dipshit. We just got engaged and you're ruining our beautiful memories of this night," she said. It wasn't poetry, but it got the job done.

The guy inched closer and said, "Lemme see the ring."

Oops, that I didn't count on.

"Let him see it. It's the distraction I need."

As much as she hated to think the robber might try to grab it off her finger, she trusted Nick's reflexes. She gripped the steering wheel, allowing the man to see the ring on her left hand but making it difficult to take it off her finger.

He took his eyes off Nick to look at the diamond, and before he could say, "Hand over the rock," Nick had grabbed his wrist and twisted it hard.

A horrible grinding and a pop were followed by a male scream. The mugger sank to his knees. Fortunately the gun fell to the ground, and before they could grapple for it, Brandee jumped out of the car and snatched it up. She held the weapon with two shaking hands and pointed it at the mugger.

The guy was breathing hard but managed to laugh and say, "It ain't loaded, so you can drop it, bitch."

"I don't know…" Brandee said. "Maybe I should put it down so I can call the police."

"Keep the gun pointed at him." Nick growled. *"I'm going to let go, and he'll probably run."*

So you want to let him get away?

"For now."

Oookay. Brandee waited until Nick let go, and as predicted, the guy took off. What she didn't expect was that Nick would run after him.

"Crap," she muttered, as she watched the chase. *He just wanted to get the guy away from me.* They disappeared down a side street. She hoped the mugger didn't have another gun or a knife stashed somewhere. *Nick? Come back. He's not worth it.*

Either he was too far away to communicate or too busy with his pursuit—regardless, he didn't answer her.

Brandee got back into her car, locked the door, rolled up the window, and prayed for the best.

—-m—

After he paid the cab driver and walked Brandee to his front door, Nick said, "This was quite a night."

Brandee let out a breath in a whoosh. "You can say that again." She waited until they were inside Nick's stairwell and then whispered, "So, even though you could have sniffed him out as a wolf, you had to let him get away?"

"I couldn't take the chance of anyone seeing me, sweetheart. If someone had been looking out their window or walking around the corner, I'd have exposed our existence, and I'd be in deep shit again."

"What do you mean by 'again'? And shouldn't we go inside instead of talking out here in the hall?"

"It's fine. My neighbor uses a different staircase. Remember that conversation I was having out in the alley with a middle-aged-looking woman?"

"Oh, that time the woman you called 'mother' bitched you out?"

"Exactly." He gently rubbed Brandee's arms. "She wanted to send me to Mount Vesuvius for revealing myself to you. It's absolutely crucial that you keep my secret—that you keep the secret for *all* paranormals. You'll be in danger of a fast trip to Timbuktu if she thinks you revealed our existence to another human."

"Timbuktu? She could do that?"

"She certainly could."

Brandee tipped her head. "So she's paranormal too. Why did you call her 'mother' if she's not your mother?"

He smiled. "Are you sure you want another secret to keep?"

She rolled her eyes. "Why not? Lay it on me."

"That was Mother Nature."

Brandee gasped and her mouth hung open as if her jaw hinge suddenly let go. When she snapped her mouth shut, her teeth clicked. At last she gathered herself and whispered, "I met Mother Nature?"

"You did, and you *don't* want to see her again—at least not in person."

A voice from the top of the stairwell said, "Too late, asshole."

Both of them gazed up the stairs to where a woman in a long white robe stood. Brandee recognized her as the same woman who had been at the bar before, but wearing an eighties vintage outfit. The "mother" who'd confronted him in the alley.

Nick slapped a hand over his eyes. "Oh no. What did I do wrong now?"

Mother Nature descended the stairs until she stood only two steps above them. "This time I'm not here because you did something wrong. I'm here because you did something right."

Nick dropped his hand. "You're kiddin',"

"No, I'm not. And I've been thinking about what you had asked me the last time we met."

"Wait." Nick paused as if recalling the conversation. "You mean when I asked if there was a way you could make Brandee as long-lived as I am?"

Brandee gazed from Nick to the woman and back again. *Is this conversation really happening? In Nick's stairwell?*

"Let's go inside where we can sit down and discuss this further," Mother Nature suggested. Without waiting for them to agree or disagree, she ascended the stairs so gracefully, she appeared to float.

Nick grasped Brandee's hand and followed the white-robed woman upstairs. He dug the door keys out of his pocket, but before he could use them, the door opened of its own accord.

Freaky.

Mother Nature led the parade inside and sat on one of the armchairs. Nick closed the door behind them and sat on the couch next to Brandee. He took her hand and tucked it around his arm at the elbow, then he covered her hand with his.

"Hang on to me, sweetheart. If either of us is sent anywhere, maybe we'll go together."

Focusing on Mother Nature, he said, "I don't know whether I should introduce you two formally or not. I don't want to slip up again."

Mother Nature smiled. "Smart. It's all right since I'm right here, but let me do it." She gazed at Brandee. "I'm Gaia. You may call me Mother Nature or Goddess. I think Gaia is a little informal, but that's my name."

"It's an honor to meet you, Goddess," Brandee said.

Mother Nature raised her eyes toward the ceiling. "At last. Someone who shows me a little respect."

Nick gave Brandee's hand a squeeze and smiled at her.

"Now, as I was saying," Gaia continued. "Ever since the Industrial Revolution, I've been thinking about adding a couple of new muses. With all the inventions and advanced technology, the usual nine really can't handle it all."

Brandee had to clarify for herself what the woman

was talking about. "Do you mean the nine muses, as in the muse of poetry, the muse of dance…like that?"

"Yes, Brandee. Exactly like that. My muses are lesser goddesses who have traditionally been immortal. Each takes care of a different area of the arts and sciences. In a nutshell, there's Clio whose area is history; Urania takes care of astronomy; Melpomene, tragedy; Thalia, comedy; Terpsichore, dance; Calliope, epic poetry; Erato, love poetry; Polyhymnia, songs to the gods; and Euterpe, lyric poetry."

"Wow. There's a lot in the poetry field."

"No kidding, and poetry has really fallen out of fashion, so they're kind of useless." Mother Nature rose and paced with her hands clasped behind her back. "I tried reassigning them to things like steam-powered engines and other inventions as they came along, but now with high-tech advances, they're having a hard time handling it all. I often catch them grumbling about the good old days."

And this affects me, how?

She whirled on Brandee, who immediately shut off her thought. *Nick, can she hear what goes on in our heads?*

"I don't know, sweetheart. Maybe we'd better think about kittens and puppies just in case."

Mother Nature smiled, but that didn't comfort Brandee.

"So, you see, dear, I could use your help. I understand you have a background in photography."

"Oh." Brandee sat up straight. "Yes, Goddess, I do."

"Great. I want you to be my muse of still and motion photography."

"Digital or traditional?"

Mother Nature raised one eyebrow. "All of it. I'm going to give you some limited powers, and you'd better be prepared to use them."

"Gaia, wait," Nick interjected. "I need to ask a question."

She let out a deep sigh. "Yes, Nick. I'll extend her life span."

"Awesome!"

"Wait." Brandee rose. "I'm not sure I want to be immortal. I-I don't want to outlive Nick any more than he wants to outlive me."

Mother Nature crossed her arms, and Nick rose quickly. He clasped Brandee in a protective embrace.

"She has abandonment issues," he said defensively.

"Hmmm…" Gaia began pacing again. When she stopped, she faced them squarely. "I'll grant you limited immortality."

What the heck does that entail?

"I'll let you live as long as your husband, and when he passes into pure energy, you will too." She waved a dismissive hand. "By that time, there's sure to be some kind of *newer* technology, and I'll need another young one to pick up the slack, so it'll all work out."

Nick tipped up Brandee's chin so she could see his eyes. They danced with excitement. "How about it, sweetheart? I don't think we could ask for anything more."

She had to mull this over. "It sounds like a big responsibility. To tell you the truth, all I wanted was a little gallery where I could showcase my own work and that of other up-and-coming photographers."

Mother Nature shrugged. "You can have that. You'll need a base of operations anyway."

Brandee's heart leaped. Her own gallery. Nick. A long and fruitful life. What more could she possibly want?

"Is there some kind of on-the-job training that comes with this muse gig?"

"Of course. Hold on a minute." Mother Nature turned her back and called out, "Erato, Come!"

A beautiful younger woman appeared out of nowhere. She was wearing jeans and a clingy red sweater over an impressive rack.

"You called, Gaia?"

"Yes, I did. I want you to take this young lady under your wing. Teach her how to be a muse. She'll be taking care of everything in the area of technical photography, all still and moving images."

"Everything on film?"

"And digital images, too," Gaia added.

Erato slapped a hand over her heart. "Thank you, Goddess. *Finally*. We can use the extra help keeping those idiot war correspondents alive."

"I knew you'd be pleased."

Brandee held up her index finger. "Just one thing…"

Mother Nature's eyes narrowed.

"Nick and I just got engaged." She bravely forged on and hoped for the best. "I don't want to leave him and go traipsing all over the world."

Erato clapped. "Oh, fab. I love a good love story." She spoke behind her hand, as if hiding her words from Mother Nature. "I'm the muse of erotic poetry. I can teach you some things for your wedding night."

Nick laughed. "I think we've got that area covered, but thanks for offering."

Gaia smiled at Brandee. "You won't have to *traipse* anywhere anymore. Simply think about where you want to go and snap your fingers."

Brandee's eyes widened. "You mean I have supernatural powers now?"

"Try it and see."

"Can Nick come with me?"

Mother Nature shrugged. "That's up to you. Simply think about the two of you in a new place. Just be sure no one sees you as you come and go."

"How do I do that?"

"I'll teach you," Erato said.

Brandee faced Nick and held both of his hands. "How do you feel about this, honey? Do you want me to take the job?"

"It's your decision, sweetheart. I'll support you no matter what you decide."

Gaia nodded. "You're a good man, Nicholas Wolfensen. I always knew you'd be an asset if you could just keep your paranormal trap shut."

"An asset? Do you have a job for me too?"

"Not at the moment, but if I ever need a private investigator, I'll know where to find one."

"You can count on my help anytime, Goddess. And thank you."

"For?"

"For making Brandee's and my dreams come true."

"Oh, that." She waved away the compliment as if it were nothing. "Come, Erato. Let's give your new sister and her fiancé some privacy."

Mother Nature vanished.

Erato took a step closer. "I'll check in with you tomorrow, Brandee, muse of film and digital images."

"Wow. That's a mouthful of a title," Nick said.

"When should I find my gallery? And how will I pay for it? Oh, my promotion. I have so many questions!"

Erato took her free hand and patted it. "We'll work

it all out tomorrow. Meanwhile, get a good night's rest and practice for your honeymoon."

"Aren't those things kind of mutually exclusive?"

Erato smiled. "I'll give you some stamina tips."

"Thank you." Before Brandee could say another word, Erato winked and was gone.

Nick enveloped Brandee in a huge hug. "This turned out to be an even more memorable evening than I thought possible."

"No kidding. It sounds like we won't have to worry about airfare when it comes to our honeymoon, and I guess we could have our pick of places to go."

"Are you still thinking about a long engagement?"

Brandee tipped her head and tapped her lower lip. "Not so much. Let me talk to Erato tomorrow. I have the feeling she'll have some pre-wedding advice."

Nick lifted her off the floor with a whoop and lowered her just enough to kiss her. "I love you, Brandee Wolfensen."

Brandee threw her arms around his neck. "And I love you, Nick Hanson. That's another thing we can work out tomorrow," she said, and they both laughed.

"Good, because right now my mind is on other things." He scooped her up into his arms, and she held onto his neck as he carried her up the stairs to their bedroom.

Epilogue

THE BELL HANGING ABOVE THE GALLERY DOOR tinkled, and Brandee looked up to see Nick walking through it. She ran around the cash register and leaped into his arms. He caught her so easily she might as well have been a basketball. The image reminded her of what her stomach would look like in eight months. She couldn't wait to tell him.

"Hi, sweetheart."

"Hey, lover."

They shared a quick kiss.

As Nick set her on her feet, he asked, "Can you get away for lunch?"

"I'd love to, but I probably shouldn't. I had to put the 'Back in Five Minutes' sign in the window twice this morning."

"Are your muse duties really keeping you that busy?"

"Yeah, but I got a few awesome shots while saving some fool trying to video his hike on Mount Everest. You should have seen him, hanging on to his tent pole and waving in the wind like a flag."

Nick laughed. "I can't wait to see the pics. Did you use digital or thirty-five millimeter film this time?"

Brandee strolled to her desk and pulled out the chair next to it, inviting Nick to sit down with her. "I used the thirty-five, but in the future, I think I'll go exclusively digital. We're going to need the small bedroom."

Nick raised his brows. "Oh? Are we having guests?"

She flashed him a sly smile. "Sort of. He or she will be staying for about eighteen years."

Nick's mouth opened, but in a rare moment of speechlessness, no words came out. At last he cleared his throat and asked, "Are you telling me what I think you're telling me?"

She grinned and nodded.

He shot to his feet and grabbed her around the waist. Lifting her high over his head, he looked up at her and cried, "Oh, my, hallelujah!" Then, as if suddenly remembering her "delicate condition," he lowered her gently until her feet touched the floor and enveloped her in a tender hug.

Brandee snuggled against his chest. "I know you wanted children, but do you mind that it happened so soon?"

"I don't mind a bit. That's why I told you to throw away your birth control pills."

"And you don't care if our kids aren't wolves like you?"

"Hell, no. I'm glad they won't be. Thank goodness your muse buddies were able to answer that question for us." He stroked her long hair over her back. "Why don't I go get lunch and bring it here? I don't want you skipping meals."

"I'll get it," she said.

"If you're planning on pickles and ice cream, I'd rather get my own."

Brandee set a hand on her hip and gave him a look that she hoped would tell him where he could stick his pickle. "I'll be right back."

In the blink of an eye, or more accurately the snap of a finger, she was home. In record time, she had made a giant sandwich for Nick and a much smaller one for herself. She put them on the bamboo tray Kurt gave them as a wedding present and snapped her fingers, taking her back to the gallery. Nick was looking at his watch.

"So, how long was I gone?"

"Three and a half."

"What? There's no way I took three and a half whole minutes."

Nick shook his head. "Not minutes. Seconds."

"Seriously?"

"You should probably try to slow down a bit. You don't want to give the baby whiplash."

"Oh, my wonderful husband, I hope you're not going to treat me like I'm some kind of fragile vase. I'm semi-immortal now, like you."

"But is the baby?"

"I asked Erato and she said she's not sure. This is kind of a whole new situation. She suggested I see the midwife the muses go to. I think her name is Hestia."

Nick picked up his sandwich. "I'll never get used to all those Greek names. How do you keep them straight?"

Brandee handed him a napkin. "It helps to meet them and put names to faces. I've only met a few and most of them are muses."

"The only one I met besides Gaia was Apollo," Nick said.

"You're lucky. He sounds like one of the nice ones. I understand some gods are downright selfish or cranky."

"And the gods think the goddesses are the cranky ones."

She chuckled. "They sound pretty human, don't they?"

"Shhh...don't let them catch you saying that."

"Do you think they'd send us to Outer Mongolia?"

"As long as we go together, it's okay if they do."

Read on for an excerpt from

How to Date a Dragon

Coming soon from Ashlyn Chase
and Sourcebooks Casablanca

"I'M NEVER ATTENDING A DESTINATION WEDDING AGAIN."

Bliss Russo dragged her garment bag and carry-on up the ramp to her Boston apartment building. Her purse had fallen off her shoulder ten minutes ago and dangled from her wrist. She needed the other hand to hold her cell phone to her ear so she could bitch to her friend Claudia.

"Oh, poor you. Someone made you go to Hawaii." Claudia chuckled. "The bastards."

"Seriously...do you know how long the flight is? Or I should say flights. First there's the leg from Boston to L.A., then L.A. to Honolulu, and finally Honolulu to Maui. Two days later, I go from Maui to Honolulu. Then Honolulu to L.A. Then L.A. to Boston. Plus I had to follow Hawaiian wedding tradition—at least what the bride's parents assured us was the tradition—and party all night. I haven't slept for days."

"You're exaggerating."

"No, I'm not. Unless you count the five-minute nap I took at LAX. I was so exhausted, I woke up on the chair next to me when the guy I had apparently fallen asleep on got up and left."

"Sorry. Okay, you're right. It was a lousy, miserable thing to make you do. So where are you now?"

"Almost home. In fact, I'll probably lose you in the elevator. Give me a few days to sleep and I'll call you back."

"Call by Thursday if you can, and let me know if you want to go out Saturday night."

Bliss jostled the door open, and one of the residents held it while she maneuvered her luggage through. "I shouldn't. I worked a little harder and got a few days ahead so I could go to this damn wedding in the first place, but I really can't afford to take any more time off. The competition will crush me."

"That's what you get for landing in the finals of your dream reality show. What is it? America's Next Great Greeting Card Designer?"

"It's not called America's Next…oh, forget it. I'm at the elevator now and I'm too tired to care. I'll call you."

"Okay, sugar. Sweet dreams."

"Thanks." Bliss hung up and dropped her phone into the bowels of her purse. She yanked and stuffed her luggage into the tiny elevator, which she rode to the second floor. Eventually, she dragged everything to her door, rattled the key in her lock, and brought it all into her bedroom. Passing out on top of her bed fully dressed seemed like the only good idea she was capable of having, so she donned a sleep mask, did a face-plant, and stayed that way.

Hours later—or maybe days—Bliss awoke to a deafening blare. Still disoriented, she had no idea what the hell the noise was or, for that matter, if it was night or day.

She tore off the sleep mask and still couldn't tell what was going on. But what was that smell?

Oh. My. God. Smoke! That ear-piercing noise is the friggin' fire alarm.

Bliss tried to remember what to do. *Oh yeah, crouch down low and get the fuck out of Dodge.* Thank the good Lord she lived on the second floor, because she couldn't use the stupid elevator.

Bliss remembered just in time to put her hand to the door before opening it. It didn't feel as though there were an inferno on the other side. Staying low, she opened the door. The smoke was so thick she could barely see. She held her breath and charged toward the end of the hall.

Suddenly, her head hit something firm and she fell backward. "Oomph." The sharp intake of breath resulted in a coughing fit.

Looking up to see what she had hit, she realized she had just head-butted a firefighter's ass.

He swiveled and mumbled through his mask. "Really? I'm here to save you, and you spank me?"

Despite her earlier panic, Bliss felt a whole lot safer and started to giggle. *Oh no. My computer!* "Wait, I have to go back…"

"No. You need to get out of here, now." The firefighter lifted her like she weighed nothing— an amazing feat in itself—then carried her the wrong way down the rest of the hallway, through the fire door, and down the stairs.

"Wait!" She grasped him around the neck and tried to see his face through watering eyes.

His mask, helmet, and shield covered almost his whole head, but she caught a glimpse of gold eyes and a shock of hair, wheat-colored with yellow streaks, angled across his forehead. She thought it odd that the city would let firefighters dye their hair like rock musicians.

As soon as they'd made it to the street, she could see better and noticed his eyes were actually green and almond shaped. She must have imagined the gold color. He set her down near the waiting ambulance and pulled off his mask.

What a hottie! But I don't have time for that now. She staggered slightly as she tried to head back toward the door.

He grabbed her arm to steady her. "Hey," he shouted to one of the paramedics. "Give her some oxygen."

"No, I'm fine. I don't need any medical attention." *Thanks to the gorgeous hunk with the weird hair.*

"Please...let them check you out."

"I'd rather let *you* check me out." She covered her mouth and grinned. "Sorry. It must be the smoke inhalation.

He laughed. "Seriously? First you grab my ass, and now you're hitting on me?"

"I didn't 'grab your ass.' For your information, I ran face-first into your...behind."

"Oh. Well, pardon me for being in the way."

His smile almost stopped her heart—or was it the lack of oxygen? Regardless, she *had to* rip herself away from him and get her computer out of the building before it melted. No matter how hard she pulled, he didn't budge.

"You need to go back in there for my computer. Apartment twenty-five, halfway down the hall."

He took off his gloves. "Look, I'm sorry, miss, but if I went back in there now, my chief would have my hide."

"But my whole life is on that computer. I'm in the finale of a huge TV competition."

He didn't seem impressed, so she tried again.

"It's my greeting card business and all my newest designs are there. This show would pay for a whole ad campaign and give me fifty grand if I win." Realizing she sounded like a babbling idiot, she pressed on. "I've worked so hard to make it this far. If I lose my work, I'll never catch up. I'll wind up presenting a half-assed portfolio, and not only can I forget about winning, but it could ruin me!"

―――――

Drake couldn't believe what he was hearing. His weakness might be beautiful brunettes, but did she honestly expect him to risk his life for an object that could be replaced? Could she not see smoke pouring out of the building? Sure, he could probably manage it, being fireproof and all, but after the chewing out he got the last time...

"Don't you keep a backup file online?"

"No. I don't trust the Internet," she said with the saddest expression in her beautiful brown eyes. "There are too many hackers out there, and this greeting card competition is outrageously competitive. Pleeeease!"

All this hoopla for a place of paper that reads, "Roses are Red. Violets are blue?" The brunette didn't appear to be insane, no matter how stupid this reality show sounded. There were crazier things on TV.

His chief had already warned Drake about risking his neck and told him to knock off taking stupid chances. He'd lucked out the last time. The mayor, a big dog lover, heard that Drake had gone back into a two-alarm

blaze to rescue a greyhound. Then Mr. Mayor made
the chief disregard any thought of suspending Drake
by giving him a medal. But that sort of luck wouldn't
hold, especially if this insubordination was about an
inanimate object.

Drake reached out and physically turned the woman
around so she could see the inferno behind her. The feel
of her soft, warm skin sent an unexpected jolt of aware-
ness through him.

Her hands flew to cover her mouth, and the same sad,
desperate sound all fire victims made as they witnessed
the destruction and loss of something precious eked out.
The tears forming in her eyes did him in.

If he weren't fireproof, running back into that building would toast him like a marshmallow, but being a
dragon, he knew he could do it.

"Ah, hell." Before anyone could stop him, he dashed
in the side entrance. He could always say he thought he
heard a call for help.

"Stop. Oh, crap," was what he really heard.
Apparently the brunette had changed her mind, but he
was committed now.

Second floor, halfway down the hall, he repeated to
himself until he found it. She had left her door open.
Fortunate for him, not so much for her apartment.
Smoke and flames were everywhere. He felt the familiar tingle just under his skin that signaled an impending
shift. *Fan-fucking-tastic*. Skin became scales. Fingers
became claws. His neck elongated, and out popped his
tail, creating an unsightly bulge in the back of his loose
coveralls. His wings were cramped and folded up under
his jacket, but it couldn't be helped.

His sight was greatly improved in his alternate form, and he spotted the Mac on her glass tabletop. The flames hadn't reached it yet, so he did his best to grab it with his eagle-like talons and carry it against his chest.

Lumbering down the hall, he wondered where, and if, he'd be able to shift back before anyone saw him. *Maybe it's cooler in the basement—but what if I get trapped down there?*

Instead of heading down another level, he opened the emergency door just enough to toss the laptop onto the grass outside. The outside air was so much cooler that he thought he might be able to shift back right there.

Concentrating on his human form, he inhaled the fresh air and sensed his head and body shrinking and compacting. He glanced down and saw his human hands again. His back felt enormously better without squished wings digging into it.

Ah...I made it undetected.

Or had he? The brunette was standing a few feet away, wide-eyed and open mouthed—hugging her computer.

———— ᨒ ————

"What the..."

The handsome firefighter, who had appeared like some kind of dinosaur in the smoke only a moment earlier, stepped out of the building and stretched as if trying to work a kink out of his spine. He whipped off his mask and stared at her.

Bliss scrubbed her eye socket with the heel of her hand. *My eyes must have been playing tricks on me.* There was no other possible explanation. Between her jet-lagged brain and smoke-filled vision, her mind's eye had concocted a reptilian form that was really her hero firefighter.

Oh, fuck it. "Thank you!" *He deserves a reward.* She rushed up to him and cupped the back of his head, dragging him down until she mashed her lips to his in the mother of all adoring kisses. He wrapped his arms around her back and pulled her against him, returning her kiss. She fit his body as if they'd been made for each other. The fire he'd just rescued her from had nothing on the heat in his kiss.

Unfortunately for both of them, the chief came striding around the corner along with the paramedics. The paramedics led her away while her hottie fireman received the dressing-down of a lifetime, complete with explicit and crude language.

"Please don't be mad at him," Bliss called over her shoulder. "It's my fault. I asked him to go back in." But it was too late. A paramedic slapped an oxygen mask over her face as she heard the chief sputter the words "suspended" and "get the hell out of my sight" to her hot hero. She tried to wrestle off the damn mask, but by the time she did, he was gone.

Upon their return to the fire station, the guys whistled at a curvaceous blond waiting for them with a camera. Drake vaguely remembered the chief saying something about their posing for a calendar.

"Terrific," he muttered.

The chief spotted her and groaned. Then he pointed at Drake. "He goes first."

As they hung up their jackets, the chief strode to his office.

"Drake, buddy," Benjamin said, "I'd hang around and watch, but I gotta shower." He slapped Drake on the back and jogged up the stairs with the rest of them.

Drake glanced down at his filthy hands as the blond sashayed over to him.

"Hey there, handsome," she said.

"Look, I hate to make you wait, but I should shower before you take any pictures. We just…"

She finger-walked her way up his chest. "Oh, I know. You were out fighting fires and saving people. I think that's sexy as hell. Don't change a thing. Except, take your shirt off."

Drake stifled a groan. He was tired and about to be suspended. This was the last thing he wanted to do right now.

Figuring he was in enough trouble for defying the chief's orders, he whipped off his white undershirt, faced the blond female photographer as if she were a firing squad, and asked, "How do you want me?"

She chuckled and raised one eyebrow.

"Uh… What should I be doing?" he asked.

From the look in her eyes and the way she licked her lips, the answer was X-rated. Maybe they shouldn't have sent a woman to shoot the annual firefighters' calendar. At this rate it would be December before she finished taking the pictures.

"I don't want to be rude, but I really don't feel like doing this right now." When she didn't respond, he waved a hand in front of her eyes. "Hello," he said to break through the woman's vacant stare.

"Your hair…I've never seen yellow streaks like that. They're like primary colors."

"Yeah, it's unusual, and before you ask, it's natural. My whole family has them." *It would be so much easier if I could just come out and say it's how dragons know each other by clan.* But, of course, he could not. Dragons were governed by the same rule every paranormal faction had to live by—namely not to reveal their existence to humans. To do so would cause widespread panic, witch hunts, and they'd probably wind up as government lab rats.

Strange Neighbors

by Ashlyn Chase

He's looking for peace, quiet, and a little romance...

There's never a dull moment when hunky all-star pitcher and shapeshifter Jason Falco invests in an old Boston brownstone apartment building full of supernatural creatures. But when Merry MacKenzie moves into the ground floor apartment, the playboy pitcher decides he might just be done playing the field...

A girl just wants to have fun...

Sexy Jason seems like the perfect fling, but newly independent nurse Merry's not sure she's ready to trust him with her heart...especially when the tabloids start trumpeting his playboy lifestyle.

Then pandemonium breaks loose and Merry and Jason will never get it together without a little help from the vampire who lives in the basement and the werewolf from upstairs...

"The good-natured fun never stops. Chase brings on plenty of laughs along with steamy sex scenes." —*Publishers Weekly*

For more Ashlyn Chase, visit:

www.sourcebooks.com

The Werewolf Upstairs

by Ashlyn Chase

———ᨆ———

Petty crime never looked so good…

Alpha werewolf Konrad Wolfensen sees it as his duty to protect the citizens of Boston, even if it means breaking into their businesses just to prove their security systems don't work. But when his unsolicited services land him in trouble with the law, he'll have to turn to his sexy new neighbor for help.

She should know better…

Attorney Roz Wells is bored. She used to have such a knack for attracting the weird and unexpected, but ever since she took a job as a Boston public defender, the quirky quotient in her life has taken a serious hit. Until her sexy werewolf neighbor starts coming around…

———ᨆ———

"Original and full of laughs, steamy sex, and madcap mayhem." —*Night Owl Romance*

"Beyond funny, extremely sexy, and jam-packed full of eccentric character-driven chaotic fun from cover to cover." —*Bitten by Books*

For more Ashlyn Chase, visit:

www.sourcebooks.com

The Vampire Next Door

by Ashlyn Chase

—⁓—

Room for Rent: Normal need not apply

This old Boston brownstone is not known for quiet living… first the shapeshifter meets his nurse, then the werewolf falls for his sassy lawyer, but now the vampire is looking for love with a witch who's afraid of the dark…and you thought your neighbors had issues!

Undead Sly is content playing vigilante vampire, keeping the neighborhood safe from human criminals, until Morgaine moves in upstairs. Suddenly he finds himself weak with desire, which isn't a good place for a vampire to be. And Morgaine isn't exactly without her own issues—will the two of them be able to get past their deepest fears before their changes at "normal" slips away…

—⁓—

Praise for The Werewolf Upstairs:

"Witty and wonderful…the entertaining plot, humor, sizzling sensual scenes, and romance make this story unforgettable." —*Romance Junkies*

"Original and full of laughs, steamy sex, and madcap mayhem." —*Night Owl Romance*

For more Ashlyn Chase books, visit:

www.sourcebooks.com

Acknowledgments

As always, my thanks go to my critique partner, the unflappable, talented Mia Marlowe. She laughs in all the right places and gasps when I take things one step too far.

A huge thank you to my fantastic, brilliant agent, Nicole Resciniti. I'm so lucky to have found her. This petite Jersey girl not only loves my work, but can and will wrestle anyone to the mat for me.

More thanks to Leah Hultenschmidt, my editor, and Aubrey Poole, her assistant. Their feedback and suggestions were spot on, and I'm grateful they were delivered in a kind, constructive way.

And a special thank you to my husband, Mr. Amazing. Without him, I'd be working in an understaffed medical facility, terrified that I might accidentally kill someone. Now I kill characters on purpose and have fun doing it. Muahahaha...

About the Author

Ashlyn Chase describes herself as an Almond Joy bar. A little nutty, a little flaky, but basically sweet, wanting only to give her readers a scrumptious, satisfying reading experience.

She holds a degree in behavioral sciences, worked as a psychiatric RN for several years, and spent a few more years working for the American Red Cross. She credits her sense of humor to her former careers since comedy helped preserve whatever was left of her sanity. She is a multi-published, award-winning author of humorous erotic and paranormal romances, and is represented by the Seymour Agency.

She lives in beautiful New Hampshire with her true-life hot, hero husband (who looks like Hugh Jackman if you squint). They're owned by a spoiled brat cat.

Where there's fire, there's Ash.
Check out my news, contest, videos, and reviews:
www.ashlynchase.com
Join my facebook fan page: www.facebook.com/pages/Ashlyn-Chase/101303673285353
Chat with me: groups.yahoo.com/group/ashlynsnew bestfriends
Tweet with me: @GoddessAsh: twitter.com/#!/GoddessAsh
Ask me to sign your Kindle ebook: www.Kindlegraph.com